KIND & SENSIBLE

KIND & SENSIBLE

Dr John Firth

The
Book
Guild

First published in Great Britain in 2025 by
The Book Guild Ltd
Unit E2 Airfield Business Park,
Harrison Road, Market Harborough,
Leicestershire. LE16 7UL
Tel: 0116 2792299
www.bookguild.co.uk
Email: info@bookguild.co.uk
X: @bookguild

Typeset in 11pt Minion Pro

Printed and bound by CPI Group (UK) Ltd, Croydon, CR0 4YY

ISBN 978 1835741 085

British Library Cataloguing in Publication Data.
A catalogue record for this book is available from the British Library.

MIX
Paper | Supporting
responsible forestry
FSC
www.fsc.org
FSC® C013604

To those I've learned from

ONE

THE WALL

There are two ways to see the world. One is by doing a lot of travelling; the other is by sitting on the low wall outside the front of King's College, Cambridge, and doing so was one of Dr Old's Saturday morning routines. He preferred this: no fears of missing flights, no crowded airports where you feel you cannot breathe, no being expected to eat rubbery food off plastic trays with brittle implements unfit for purpose, no being unsure whether it is morning or evening, no being disorientated because of all the above. If you sit on the wall for long enough, the whole world walks by. Under challenge Dr Old would agree that it's not perfect: the stone can cut into your tail end after a while; on proper inspection the grass is not unblemished, which is gratifying to those of us who try to keep a lawn; some of the students walking by are noisily overconfident with such high estimation of themselves that I think one can be forgiven for hoping that something unpleasant will happen to them to take them down a peg or two. Purely for their own benefit, of course.

Dr Old had had some interesting discussions sitting on King's Parade. Cambridge is a good place to sit around on walls. In most towns or cities it would be assumed that you were unemployed or living somewhere dire, such that you just had to get out. You would certainly be avoided by nearly everyone who walked past, and some would be frightened of you. In Cambridge, however, it might be that you are brilliant, albeit possibly awkward in engaging in normal human conversation. Such prospect is harmless, however, and does not alarm.

It was there that she found Dr Old. She was very polite.

'May I sit here?' she asked.

'Yes,' he replied, adding, 'please do,' because that's the sort of thing he was brought up to say and couldn't stop saying even if he wanted to, and of course it will have been her upbringing that made her ask for his permission. I'm not sure who owns the wall or the rights to sit on it.

She was tall and slim, wearing an olive-coloured alpaca jacket, close-fitting light brown corduroy trousers and ankle-length dark brown boots that someone being critical would say were in need of a polish. She sat very upright and poised, probably a result of a lot of pilates or yoga or perhaps both. Dr Old knew his mother would have approved: she had often told him off for slumping at the table, which she regarded as a crime. In her mid-forties he guessed, with minimal make-up, although enough to enhance rather angular features. Her voice was relaxed and with no hint of shrillness. Dr Old had always felt both attracted to and intimidated by women like this, which is why he remembered the occasion, although nothing more was said and after a few minutes she left.

Dr Old carried on reading his book for a while, then got a text message from one of his daughters with a picture of a grandchild on a swing in her local park, grinning suitably. Eight teeth now, he noticed, and replied demonstrating his ability to count. I do hope that there is no adverse long-term consequence of excessive image capture in early childhood. By the age of one most children nowadays have had more pictures taken of them than I have in my entire lifetime. Perhaps an opportunity for someone to define a new psychiatric disorder.

Dr Old checked the news and sports headlines. Nothing much had happened since breakfast time. A minister had made a statement to justify a recent change in the government's approach to a problem. A strident opposition spokeswoman had trumpeted that this was another U-turn. Those reporting and commenting on the matter were as usual taking issue with both the minister and spokeswoman. No one made the point that the problem had been around for ever and wasn't easily soluble, and the notion that it was a mature approach to try one thing and then – if it wasn't working very well – decide that you were going to try another, seemed foreign to everyone involved. He wandered home for lunch carrying his shopping.

A week later he was in his usual place. The sun had warmed the stone, making it particularly rewarding to sit on. He'd read for a bit but his mind was drifting and he was finding it difficult to concentrate. A close friend had a habit of saying "penny for your thoughts", to which he often replied that he wasn't thinking of anything, which she found difficult to believe. But honestly, his mind often seemed to be vacant, and he regarded this as a strength as those he knew who never admitted to having vacant minds seemed to be prone to anxiety. Anyway, she appeared again, sitting next to him. I expect she'd asked him if she could, but he hadn't heard her.

'Would you like a latte?' she said, offering one. 'The woman in the coffee shop said you often got a takeout at this time on a Saturday morning.'

After the thanks and reply of "you're welcome" that you would imagine, their conversation began.

'I'm sure you're wondering why I've tracked you down,' she said. 'I wanted to talk with you about the case with the Medical Regulator,' and when Dr Old didn't reply immediately went on, 'I wrote to you about it.'

Dr Old had received a letter a few weeks previously, but after getting the gist of what it was about had not finished it and put it in the rubbish, thinking it unlikely that anything would follow. It had been a couple of years since anyone had got in touch. The experience had confirmed his pre-existing prejudice that it was best to avoid discussions of difficult things in public fora or with people you didn't know very well and could trust to maintain confidentiality, even if you thought the issues important and had carefully considered and moderate views. For a year or so after the hearing the occasional journalist would ask for an interview or comment, and one or two lunatics were interested until, in the absence of any response, they presumably moved their unwelcome attentions elsewhere. Never complain, never explain.

Who was she? Dr Old wasn't confident that he knew what a journalist looked like, but she didn't seem to fit the bill. She certainly didn't have the appearance or manner of someone holding fixed and wild views impermeable to reason. White middle-aged women are generally under-represented within fanatical groups.

'I'm Jonathan Barber's daughter,' she said, 'and I want to understand what happened.'

'Ah,' he said, or something similarly eloquent, 'it's a while since I heard that name.'

TWO

THE BARBERS

'Is that you, Margaret?'

'Yes, Dad, yes, it's me.'

Margaret closed the door, took off her coat and hung it up in the lobby, went through the kitchen into the lounge, but her father wasn't there and so she backtracked through the kitchen into the conservatory. Her father was sitting in one of the ancient chairs, wicker bleached and cracked by the sunlight, cushion faded and a limp memory of what it once was. She must get round to replacing it.

'Would you like a cup of tea?' she said. 'Or do you want to wait until after lunch?'

'No, now would be good. I was sluggish getting up this morning and it's not that long ago that I had breakfast.' The cereal bowl and spoon on the table suggested this was so, with cereal eaten but still the dampness of milk not yet evaporated to dryness.

For most of his working life Jonathan Barber had been a very lively man who never seemed to slow down.

At work and at home he had always appeared to be on the move, even when sitting, and his speech was always rapid, its volume rising and falling to give emphasis where most speakers would have felt that none was required. He'd been a blizzard of ideas, often not easy to follow, but his conversation had never been dull. Even though most people – family and hospital colleagues alike – had found that he was best in small doses, very few were not genuinely impressed by his passionate interest in and knowledge of medicine and all things intellectual, also by a moral approach that drove him to do what he thought was the right thing in all circumstances.

A large man, but seemingly larger on account of his energy, Dr Barber had been a notable figure in the hospital, typically wearing a checked cotton shirt rolled up to the elbows, flannel trousers and brogues that had undergone multiple resolings. At the beginning of his medical career this had been his uniform for both outpatient and inpatient practice, supplemented by gowns, aprons, gloves and masks when required, but like everyone else he had been instructed some years ago to change into surgical scrubs before going onto some of the inpatient wards, which he never managed to be comfortable in. The displayed whiteness of his neck, not revealed to light for many years excepting in his bathroom and bedroom, seemed to proclaim, "I'm new here". Nothing could have been further from the truth, but it made him feel like an imposter. Whilst he understood the reasons for mandating handwashing, being one of few native English-speaking doctors who had read Semmelweis' writings from the obstetric clinic in Vienna in their original language, it rankled with him that there was no strong evidence that his daily laundered shirt was more of an infective risk to patients than a scrub top, which he often had to take from the floor of the changing room where the pile had collapsed from the shelves. His correspondence with the hospital's medical director on the matter had been met with a terse reply and hardened his feeling that the system was not intelligent or susceptible to reason.

Now he was retired, his health was failing, and he frequently used the term "sluggish" to describe his state. In his prime it would have been difficult to think of anyone for whom the adjective was less appropriate, but he was as he was, and Margaret was trying to get to know him after many years when they had not communicated at all.

Margaret could not remember ever having had what she would regard as a real conversation with her father when she was growing up. As far as she could recall he had always been at work. Pleasantries were exchanged at mealtimes, for which he had often been late, much to the suppressed irritation of his wife who wanted these to be "family time". Family holidays had been infrequent but had emphasised the fact that they had little in common. He seemed to be interested only in what she then regarded as "brainy things", which weren't her strong suit. The fact that she was keen on and good at sport seemed of no consequence to him, and she could still remember one occasion when she was fourteen or fifteen when she'd made a real effort to interest him in discussion of the importance of analysis and tactics when playing tennis, as opposed to just running around and bashing the ball, when he'd gone silent and done a very good impression of being incredibly bored. She had found this extremely hurtful, gone off to cry, and promised herself that she wouldn't make the same mistake again. In the absence of much time together, or of any common ground between them, it was therefore not a surprise that she made the important decisions of her life in the absence of any advice that he might have given.

Her relationship with her mother, Joan, had also been problematic. She had been a sister on one of the medical wards in the London hospital where her father was a junior doctor. They certainly didn't seem to have very much else in common, and she had a deference to her husband that Margaret was increasingly appalled by as she grew up. He clearly felt entitled to arrive home in the evening as and when he wanted, with an expectation that a meal would appear in perfect coincidence, and after a muted "thankyou" he would head off to his study. Margaret's mother put up with this without complaint, typically responding to her daughter's criticism that they didn't even have any control over when they were allowed to eat with something along the lines of "your father works very hard". Whilst she could understand that her mother was not her father's equal from an intellectual perspective, she honestly found it difficult to tell whether she had any opinions of her own about anything. Whatever the issue, her mother's dominant concern seemed to be what would her husband want or say? She thought this was outrageous and did not reckon the fact that her father was obviously comfortable with this way of living in his favour.

Only children, who for whatever reason don't develop a good relationship with at least one of their parents, aren't able to make the most obvious compensatory move of agreeing with a brother or sister that the reason for this is that their parents are deficient. They typically migrate to an alternative parental figure or figures, and this is what Margaret did. As she moved through the years at school, her tennis partner was a girl called Sue Bennett who came from a large family who lived in a state of permanently noisy but happy chaos. Their kitchen always seemed to be full of people: Sue's parents, brothers and sisters, their friends, neighbours dropping round, not to mention various dogs and cats. Anyone who mucked in was welcome and it didn't take long for Margaret to realise this. She was very happy to offer to make tea or grab a dish cloth and dry things up when she could see that the precarious pile of crockery in the draining basket in the sink was about to topple over, or take the dog out for a walk when needed. As a result of this she came to be regarded as a member of the clan, was invited along on some family holidays, and it was following discussions round the Bennett's large kitchen table that Margaret – receiving from Sue's parents what she felt at the time was the remarkable advice that she should do what she thought she'd enjoy most – decided to apply for a place to study psychology at university.

Her father had not been impressed. He obviously regarded psychology as an unsuitable course to pursue, but it wasn't clear why he thought this or what he would have regarded as preferable. When Sue Bennett's father suggested that it might be because he had a psychological problem, all present – including Margaret – thought this very funny, but long after everyone else had forgotten the casual witty remark, Margaret often found herself ruminating on it, never with satisfactory resolution.

Following university, where some study of psychology was mixed with a lot of sport and socialising, Margaret found her way into one of the global management consultancy firms. She didn't have a good reason for doing this, but the thought of having to return home after finishing her degree didn't bear thinking about, so she recognised that she needed to get a job and several of her more lively and able friends on the course clearly thought that management consultancy was the thing to do.

It was a surprise to her that she was successful with one of her first applications. When quizzed by her friends, who were also surprised, she couldn't explain this at the time, but looking back a year or so later she recognised two things that were probably significant, both relating to events in the bar on the first night of the two-day final selection process. Firstly, drinks had been good, plentiful and free, but Margaret had not overindulged, which she never did for no more principled reason than because it made her feel rotten if she did. When she met up later with the annual intake of interns it was notable that those who had been loudest and most uninhibited in the bar weren't amongst them. Secondly, when in the bar, she had had a brief conversation with a pale and unhealthy looking man who appeared very lonely and out of place. He explained that he was not good at socialising and that his main interest was computer programming. She remembered this the next day when there was a task that required the applicants to pair themselves up to work on a problem involving spreadsheets. Margaret recognised that this was not a strong suit of hers, but she thought she knew a man who was likely to be good with them, immediately headed in his direction, and was delighted to find that he had not yet attracted a mate. Her intuition proved to be correct. She smiled and nodded whilst his fingers moved at flight of the bumble bee speed over the keyboard and answers that seemed to her to be very plausible emerged from a process she regarded as magical. The result of this team output had clearly impressed the assessor who came round to see what they'd done.

For the next twenty years or so Margaret progressed up the consultancy ladder. She found she enjoyed managing teams and proved to be pretty good at doing so. Whereas for many the business of working for a while on one project in one place, and then moving onto another project in another place, led within a few years to them yearning for some form of permanence, Margaret enjoyed the experience of not being tied down. She found the episodic new beginnings – new client to work with, new place of work – to be stimulating. But then events conspired to change things. A long-term relationship ended, leading her to feel insecure and worried for the first time in her adult life, and having had very little contact with her parents for many years she received a letter from her father, something she'd never had before, saying that her mother had ovarian cancer and was receiving treatment.

Margaret wasn't sure how to respond. Of course, she knew instinctively that she should go home to see her mother: that was not a matter for debate, but when and how to phrase her reply? Dropping everything and suddenly pitching up out of the blue would probably be overdramatic and could seem ridiculous: her father hadn't said or implied that her immediate attendance was required. She spent a couple of days considering what to say and after several drafts decided on a few simple words thanking her father for telling her and asking if it would be possible for her to visit in one or two weekends' time, whichever was most convenient. As things transpired the reply she received about ten days later contained the news her mother had died.

THREE

THE FUNERAL AND THE WARDROBE

Excepting where death has occurred at extreme old age or the deceased was suffering from dementia or some chronic condition producing misery that could not be relieved, funerals are sad and sorrowful affairs. Each mourner has their own reason for sadness and sorrow, and whilst these can be classified in general terms, they are felt as intensely particular and personal. Along with the superficial rituals of dress and behaviour, the sombre clothes and the formulaic exchanges with the immediate family of the departed, the finality of the event leads most to take stock. After reflecting on their relationship with the deceased, the circumstances of their last meeting and what they wished they'd said, there's also a deeper pause for thought. Where are they now in their life, and where do they want to go next? For most, such musings last no longer than the journey home and the next intrusion of everyday life; the text asking for a call, the email requiring a reply, the need to buy some milk because the bottle in the fridge is nearly empty. Normal business is resumed and the memory of the funeral, as of most things, becomes sketchy and vague. It was windy in the churchyard; there was a woman wearing shoes that made a lot of noise when she walked. But sometimes a deeper pause leads to reflections that have effect.

Margaret learned things about her father that she did not know and saw a side to him that she had never seen before. In her experience, accrued almost entirely before she went to university, he had always taken her mother for granted. It could not be otherwise than that he would have a warm house to return to when he wanted, and that a meal would be served when he required it. Acknowledgement and thanks were not required. She couldn't remember a single instance when he'd asked his wife for her opinion, excepting on matters such as whether she'd prefer red or white wine on occasions they dined out, and – whilst ordering what she'd requested – he often managed to convey the impression that he thought it was the wrong choice. Such memories had continued to disturb her and were probably one of the main reasons why she had barely kept in touch, in some years even struggling to write a brief note in response to a Christmas card from her mother which typically said, "Your father and I would love to know what you're doing".

When she got to her parents' house a few days before the funeral she found it largely as she remembered it.

In the front garden a flowering plum tree from which fungus-infected branches had regularly dropped off in windy weather had finally perished and been replaced with what she thought might be an ornamental cherry, but she wasn't an expert on such things and it was difficult to tell in early March. The front door was still painted in racing green and the windows on either side of it looked as though they could benefit from some attention to the putty and a fresh coat of paint.

Inside, most of the rooms had been redecorated since she'd last visited, but without change in style. One variation on the theme of white paint may have been replaced by another, and walls that weren't a shade of white were pale yellows or pale blues as they had been before, although it was possible that some of the previously yellow walls were now blue, and vice versa. The kitchen cabinets in a minimalist Quaker style had been repainted and their handles replaced with simple brass fittings that she thought better than their incongruous predecessors. But when she looked towards the back of the kitchen she had a surprise. Instead of a door leading onto a patio and the garden there was an opening leading into a conservatory.

'Your mother wanted one and we got it built about five years ago.'

She must have looked surprised.

'I don't think we'd told you about the conservatory. It's always a shock when things you know change.'

'Yes, it is,' she replied, not explaining that the thing that had taken her unawares was not so much the presence of an extension to the house but her father's statement that it had been built at her mother's request. She couldn't recall anything remotely like that having happened before.

After the funeral and burial, the mourners, cold at the edges from standing around in a breeze that was more winter than springlike, were invited into the church hall for a cup of tea, which was generally appreciated, and sandwiches, which nobody felt like eating but most nibbled at because they were there and they had a sense that they should.

Margaret felt out of place. At first this seemed very strange to her, but as various distant relatives, friends and ex-colleagues of her parents came into the hall, unsure how to address her but murmuring their condolences, the truth dawned on her. She was out of place. Given that she had had very little contact with her mother and father for a long time, it was not surprising that she knew less about them, and certainly less about the last twenty years or so of their lives, than nearly all of those having a warming drink before departing.

A couple of interactions brought this home to her. The first was with an elderly wrinkled woman who looked frail but introduced herself as one of the church wardens and surprised Margaret by talking in a clear and businesslike manner that, if she didn't have the evidence of her eyes, she would have said was the speech of someone much younger. She described her mother, Joan, as having been a great support to many in the church and a bundle of initiative and energy, always stepping in to give out the hymn books or make the coffee or do whatever was required to keep the church's wheels in motion. Even allowing for the use of rose-tinted spectacles, usual when making observations of the recently deceased, this wasn't the Joan that Margaret remembered, but the church warden did not seem the sort of person who would fabricate an account. She was obviously very articulate and clearly capable of finding some kindly and not untruthful words to say even if she thought that her mother had been an idle lump who sat as if stuffed in the pews, moaned a lot, and never lifted a finger to help in any way.

The second discussion brought home to her even more that her memories of her parents, whilst remaining unchallenged as an account of them and their relationship during her childhood and adolescence, weren't a valid description of their more recent years together. Out of the corner of her eye she saw a couple of men talking with her father, then glancing at her whilst talking between themselves before weaving their way in her direction. Clutching their cups of tea, they introduced themselves as having been colleagues of her father in the hospital before he retired.

After passing routine comments about the service, the Indian man with a bald head and a bulbous nose who approved of the choice of hymns, "Guide Me, O Thou Great Redeemer" being one of his favourites, said, 'I hope your father's going to be alright. He depended so much on your mother, you know.'

In truth, she didn't know this and was silent whilst thinking how to reply. His friend, notable for having a rather squeaky voice and moustache that seemed to vibrate when he spoke and she would certainly have found very amusing on another occasion, followed on before she said anything. 'Yes, after the court case and the investigations he wasn't the same man; he lost his confidence.'

Margaret was thoroughly disorientated. What court case? What investigations? She racked her brain whilst desperately hoping that her confusion wasn't obvious. The bald and moustached pair sensed that she didn't want to talk further, thought this very understandable and prepared to make their departures.

'It was a terrible thing,' one of them said, although she could not remember which. 'It really did knock the stuffing out of him.'

'He had been so incisive and clear thinking before,' said the other, 'and not afraid of anybody. But then the system got him in the end, like it always does. Do look after him as well as you can.'

That evening, when finally left on her own after her father retired to bed, Margaret began to mull over the events and conversations of the day. She'd spoken briefly to many people she partially remembered from the past and to quite a few she had no recollection of at all, un-nerved by the perception that they all seemed to know her better than she knew them. She didn't think she had said anything very out of place and thought it probable that her failure to recognise people or locate them correctly in her parents' lives, manifest as slow and formulaic responses to comments or questions, would generously have been attributed to the stresses of the circumstance.

As regards the matter of "the investigations", she couldn't make much headway, beyond recalling that in one of the Christmas notes perhaps four or five years ago her mother had made reference to her father having some difficulties at work. She hadn't thought this notable at the time. After all, in large part the toad work was about dealing with difficulties; that was what you were paid for. However, her mother hadn't otherwise made comments to her about her father's work, except by impressing upon her as a child that what he did was important. That's all she could remember, with the inevitable implication – even when not directly stated – that had made life at home so miserable for her, that what Margaret or her mother might think or want was of much lesser importance than her father's requirements or wishes. The statement that he was having difficulties at work was different and must, she thought, have been important.

The days after the funeral followed a recurring pattern. There was flatness in the air: both Margaret and her father were conscious that this was a transitional pause between one period of life and another. Conversation was kept at a transactional level whilst emotions were raw. Time was occupied doing things that needed to be done, and some things that didn't need to be done but occupied the time. Both were mindful of each other's need to be silent and careful to check before launching in with words, the obvious avoidance of eye contact meaning, "I'm not ready to speak now, perhaps try again in a while".

Margaret's father made a list of organisations who needed to be notified of his wife's death and proceeded to work methodically through it. Occupational pension, old age pension, banks and building societies were written to, also the utilities, although he wasn't convinced this was necessary. Surely the only thing that mattered to the electricity board was that their bill was paid promptly. But sorting out the addresses and typing out the letters gave structure and some sense of purpose to fill the vacuum.

Margaret set about going through her mother's things. Clothes and shoes were placed into piles to take to the Oxfam shop, where Joan had volunteered for many years. The hospital didn't seem to have any mechanism for taking back the commode that had been provided for her at the time of her final discharge home; in fact the woman that she spoke to in the discharge planning team who had provided it seemed irritated at being asked if they would like it back. Perhaps Oxfam would be more accommodating.

In the back of the wardrobe were some ancient coats, including a navy blue one with a fur-trimmed collar that brought a distinct memory of childhood back to her. She'd thought it very elegant and speculated that her mother might once have been a film star, but thankfully hadn't been naïve enough to share this thought with anyone. She smiled at the recollection.

Behind the coats was a cardboard box containing various papers and folders. She sat on the edge of the bed and began to leaf through it. A picture of her mother in nursing uniform, newly qualified and looking suitably proud. A small album of photographs taken on her parents' honeymoon in Italy. Mostly unimpressive snaps of her mother taken at tourist attractions, with a few of her mother and father together, presumably taken by passers-by who offered to take a picture or were prevailed upon to do so. Some mounted pictures of Margaret herself in various school teams – hockey, rounders, tennis – with names written in ornate and faded script. Wherever were her teammates now? Along with these, a thick brown paper envelope containing the badges of sports colours that she had been proud to wear on her games tops. Her mother must have cut these off and saved them when she eventually consigned the shirts to the basket of rags used for dusting the furniture or shining the shoes. And then there was a translucent plastic file, through which she saw "Investigation into the conduct of Dr Jonathon Barber".

Margaret held her breath and looked up immediately to check she hadn't been observed. No, there was no one there. She listened carefully to be sure. Silence, except for the very faint noise of traffic. Her father; where was he? Almost certainly in his study downstairs, writing notes to thank people who had sent their condolences or having a nap, which he did most afternoons. No creaks from the stairs or landing. She remained motionless and disconnected from the world for she didn't know how long, but probably only a matter of seconds, before thoughts started to return and she began to own again arms and legs which had temporarily become someone else's property, or at least not fully hers.

FOUR

CHECKING FOR CAR BOMBS

It was a few evenings later that her father showed an inclination to talk. Margaret had cooked one of her staples for their supper – pasta shells with tuna, tomatoes and capers – which she could do without needing to think at all. Having got the ingredients from the larder and the fridge it all happened automatically. Rather like driving home on a familiar route, where you can arrive without feeling that you've looked at the road or anything else on the way at all and couldn't if quizzed be absolutely confident of the route taken beyond saying, "the way I usually go". However, you've managed to arrive without crashing, so you must have been paying some sort of attention, and similarly you've boiled and strained the pasta without getting scalded. This had been followed by some grapes that looked rather sweeter than they tasted.

Her father had finished the washing-up and was drying his hands on a tea towel. Margaret had made the drinks: a mint tea for herself and a decaf coffee for her father.

'Do you fancy sitting in the conservatory or going into the lounge?' her father asked.

'The lounge. It's a bit cold for me in the evenings in the conservatory,' Margaret replied.

Her father crouched down to switch on the gas fire. After a couple of clicks the pilot flame ignited and within a minute or two the flames were leaping in the grate over the ceramic coals and looking surprisingly realistic.

'Your mother's idea, this,' said her father. 'We almost never used to get round to lighting the old fire, and she always said she could smell smoke when we did, although I never could. But it was a good idea; we sat here for a bit most evenings in the autumn and winter.'

They settled themselves into their chairs, one either side of the hearth. Her father's chair had a small square table next to it, its top a few centimetres from his right elbow, marked with the rings from many drinks and a reading light on it. Joan's chair, where Margaret was sitting, was identical, but the table next to it was circular and illumination provided by a standard lamp behind.

'I think these chairs are nearly perfect,' said her father. 'You can fall asleep in them and not wake up with a dead leg or a dead arm, or almost never.' And after a pause, 'Will you tell me what you've been doing, Margaret?'

'What would you like to know about? Work? Friends?' she replied.

'Let's start with work.' He was sure that this would be the easiest subject on which to start a conversation with his daughter, who he didn't know and now recognised that this was because he'd never tried to get to know her.

His work had been all consuming and having children hadn't been on his agenda at the time of his marriage, but Joan had wanted a child so very badly. He could recall conversations where she had raged at the prospect of them not having a child, also the occasions she had promised him that he wouldn't have to do more than he wanted to in terms of parenting. In this she had been as good as her word. No doubt she had hoped that his attitude would change when confronted with the wonderful reality of a son or daughter, his own flesh and blood. She probably thought it impossible that his feelings could remain unaltered, but they hadn't changed. Babies and infants seemed to him to be the most appalling inventions; incessantly demanding and providing no reward.

'I'm a management consultant,' Margaret began.

'I don't think I really know what they do,' said her father. 'They sometimes used to have them in the hospital, but I was never sure why they came and went. It all seemed very political and the management always kept me away from them, or them away from me; I was never sure which.'

Margaret was very familiar with explaining her role, as are all management consultants. Whatever she had been told by the executives who had recruited her, the first days and weeks in any new job invariably involved meeting lots of people who said they didn't know why she was there or what she had been asked to do. In many cases this would be true, and virtually without exception they'd be on guard and suspicious, with views ranging from the "borrow your watch to tell you the time" brigade at one end of the spectrum to those seeing her – or at least what she represented – as an incarnation of Lord Voldemort or whoever was their most feared devil. Very understandable if they were concerned that she might recommend that their post or their department should be done away with.

On comfortable ground she talked over how her skill, and that of her team, was in analysing processes, whether these were concerned with the manufacture or selling of mobile phones, or the utilisation of operating theatres or outpatient clinics in a hospital. They would then talk with staff in the company or hospital to work out how things might be done more efficiently and explore the blockers to this, and how these might be overcome. She would then advise the executives who had hired her of their options, with the risks and benefits of each, and they would need to decide what to do. She fully recognised that in many instances nothing at all was changed following her input, but she didn't think it necessary to mention this point, elaborate on the host of reasons, or go into the many and various circumstances that led businesses or hospitals to bring in management consultants or be required to do so.

As they talked and Margaret explained what she did, who she had worked for and where, she was amazed at how little her father seemed to understand of her world, or the difficulties and challenges of trying to manage such complex organisations as the large hospitals in which he'd spent his entire working life.

'I never saw the point of management in the hospital,'

he said with disarming frankness. 'What I wanted to do was to look after my patients.'

'On your own?' asked Margaret.

'Of course not,' replied her father. 'Along with the nurses, physiotherapists and others on the ward. And my secretary who managed my post and my outpatient clinic. But it became more difficult over the years.'

'Why?'

'It all became fragmented and more complicated. When I started there was a physiotherapist attached to my firm, and an occupational therapist and a discharge planner. I knew their names, and whether they were sensible. We spoke about the patients nearly every day. They told me how they were doing and what they thought about them.'

'And what happened to change things?'

'They were taken away from me, from the firm. We didn't have our own physiotherapist or occupational therapist or discharge planner. There was a pool of them in the hospital. You never knew when one was going to turn up on the ward, and it was rarely the same person for more than a few days in a row. They didn't know the patients, excepting for what had been written in the handover notes, and I didn't know whether I could rely on anything they said. I did try to stop it happening, but got nowhere.'

'How did you try to stop it?'

'I wrote to the medical director.'

'And what did he do?'

'He told me that the decision had been made within

the Division of Medicine and I should speak with the divisional director.'

'And what did they do?'

'She told me that it had been necessary as part of the division's cost improvement plan; that a paper had been presented to the divisional board where the matter had been discussed; that I and all other medical consultants had been sent the paper and invited to comment, which I hadn't done.'

'Did you ever read the papers and send comments?'

'No.'

'Why not?'

'To tell the truth, I didn't understand them well enough to feel able to say anything. They were about money, not about medicine. I learned a few of the names, but not much more. Table after table of actual versus planned activity, monthly and year to date. Column after column of income versus expenditure, with corrections for pass through payments and accounting adjustments or some such gobbledegook. Jumping from payment by activity to block contracts and back, seemingly at random. It all seemed so pointless.'

'But someone had to manage the money, didn't they?'

'Yes, I suppose they did. It's certainly all they seemed to care about. Every year there'd be a call for cost improvement plans, and every year they'd cut back on things. One fewer secretary for the department so the doctors had to open their own post. That sort of thing. When a doctor raised an objection to something, I can't remember a single occasion on which they were listened to.'

'Did you ever suggest something?'

'Yes, I did, and all hell broke loose. Asif, the bald man who spoke to you after the funeral, told me there'd be trouble, and he was right.'

'What was it you said?'

'I said we should do away with most of the multidisciplinary team meetings.'

'Why did you suggest that? I thought MDT working was how things should be done.'

'The theory sounds good, but the practice is very different; slow, inefficient and often making poor decisions.'

'Talk me through that – why slow? Why inefficient? Why poor decisions?'

'Well, they never happened more than once a week, so if the meeting of a particular oncology MDT is on a Wednesday and the patient makes the mistake of being admitted on a Thursday, then even if it is blindingly obvious they have misfortune to have that sort of cancer they are stuck in hospital for six days before their case can be considered. It is as if everyone has been paralysed. Nobody can make any decisions and it isn't really possible to send someone home with a message they'd inevitably understand as, "we think it's pretty well certain that you've got cancer, and this is so important to us that we're going to send you home and someone will give you a phone call in a week or so's time to explain what the options are". They need to be seen by a doctor who's going to look after them and go home with a clear plan.

'I made some notes at about five consecutive oncology MDT meetings. All sorts of people were there. Several types of oncologist, surgeons, radiologists, pathologists, nurse specialists, various treatment coordinators and some people I didn't recognise. Some of them never spoke and most didn't contribute anything of any significance at all. Why were they all necessary?

'And in terms of the decisions. These are based on a potted history: always simplified and sometimes inaccurate. It's rare for someone who actually knows the patient properly to be present, and even if there is, there isn't time to discuss things adequately, so it's not surprising that the decisions are sometimes poor.'

'What happened when you said all this?'

'I put it in an email to the divisional director who'd asked for cost improvement plans and she circulated it to the divisional management board. Malcolm – the man with the moustache who you met along with Asif at the funeral – was at the meeting where it was discussed. He told me that I'd better check under my car for bombs before I drove home that evening, and later he told me that some of the nurses who attend the MDTs had written to the chief nurse complaining that I didn't value their contributions.'

It was getting late and time for bed. Margaret got up, collected the mugs and took them to the kitchen and put them into the dishwasher whilst her father turned off the fire, which gave some terminal splutters before going out. The ice had been broken and further conversations would follow.

FIVE

DIPLOMATIC IMMUNITY

Margaret had now been off work for two weeks and didn't know whether she wanted to return, or in truth, would be able to do so. She certainly wasn't in a state of mind where she felt she could step back into it as if she was returning from a fortnight's holiday. She didn't have a plan for dealing with the many things now pressing on her and found this very disturbing. At work she had been very proud a year ago when someone had written in her annual 360 feedback, "Margaret is a go-to person. She always has a plan or can make a plan". This praise now mocked her: "Margaret always has a plan or can make a plan – but not for herself". Although aware enough not to be openly disparaging of people who didn't have plans or couldn't make plans, she privately thought that they were weak, and yet here she was, weak and uncertain.

Whilst very good at rapidly assessing other people and situations and working out how best to engage with them, Margaret wasn't an innately reflective person. She'd never given much thought to her approach to things or needed to give it any. Everything happened naturally and was automatic; at least it didn't depend on any cogitation, and it seemed to work. That is, work until now.

For a few disturbing days Margaret was very worried. Perhaps this is how depression began or what it was like. An overwhelming feeling that you didn't know what to do, coupled with a perception that you had no energy to do anything anyway, and a pervasive fear that this would never change. An email from her boss, Peter, helped to move things on. "How are you doing?" he asked. "It would be good to catch up."

What would she say to him? She didn't know and initially felt panicky, but over a couple of days managed to work out an approach. What would she do if a member of her team came to her and said they were muddled and weren't sure whether they wanted to continue in the job, or give it up and do something different, but didn't know what that something different would be? Her approach would fundamentally depend on whether she thought they were a good member of the team. Did they have enough credit at the bank? Was she prepared to have the hassle of making short-term fixes to retain the prospect of them returning, grateful for the help she'd given them? Although not in good spirits, Margaret wasn't so low that she was unable to recognise that her account must have a fair amount of credit in it and she replied, subsequently setting up a Zoom meeting.

Peter was about the same age as Margaret and she'd known him for a long time. He had joined the consultancy about five years after her. In common with most people she hadn't rated him initially. He was physically unimpressive, with an underdeveloped chin, and his speech was quiet and hesitating. His glass-half-empty outlook was notably different from that of most working in the business, and bullish colleagues had christened him Pessimistic Peter, or PP for short. He wasn't a man to give speeches to rally the troops, but he was particularly good at listening, which unknown to those who'd given him the PP moniker is much more than simply a matter of not talking. He was in fact a very shrewd operator and Margaret's view of him changed dramatically after she gave an internal presentation outlining her plan for a pitch for a big contract with a new company. Such presentations were important for many reasons: the firm always wanted new business, and the manager making the presentation was performing in front of their teams, peers and bosses, with some in the audience keen to ask a devastatingly incisive question for the primary purpose of getting noticed. Careers of middle-graders could be made or broken. The presentation had gone well and Margaret had been congratulated on her performance by the partner chairing the meeting.

Peter hadn't spoken at the presentation but called her that evening.

'Have you got time to talk?' he asked, almost apologetically. 'I have some concerns,' and went on to list them. As he spoke, Margaret, even though slightly tipsy from a few celebratory gin and tonics, recognised that he was making some very good points, also that most of those who had listened to her that afternoon would have been delighted to have made any one of them in the public forum. They agreed that the best thing to do would be to ask for a joint meeting with the partner to discuss "new information" before further action was taken.

It was therefore with some confidence that there would be a fair and reasonable discussion that Margaret joined the call with Peter, and as she spoke she found his familiar manner curiously reassuring and comforting. Here was a man who didn't sound as though he always had a plan or would be critical of someone who didn't. After a few appropriate preliminary enquiries about how she and her father were, Peter asked Margaret what she was thinking in terms of returning to work. She felt that she could be honest with him and said she wasn't sure and didn't know.

Very skilfully, without her noticing how he did it or feeling intruded upon, he managed to get into the conversation that he knew that she'd "had to deal with a number of things recently", establish that she was eating and sleeping more or less normally, and somehow gave the impression that it was her idea that she might take a period of unpaid leave, which she had been wondering about. It was agreed that Margaret would think this over and let him know or ask for another conversation if she wanted one, and a few days later – after a few practical contractual details had been sorted with the HR department – it was agreed that she would have three months' unpaid leave and speak with Peter again in two months' time. Margaret was left feeling very relieved:

she had some time to think and no pressure to come up with an immediate answer to a question she hadn't yet formulated clearly.

A couple of evenings later Margaret and her father were settled into their usual post-supper chairs.

'What are you doing about work?' he asked. 'You've been away for quite a while.'

'I know,' she replied. 'I had a chat with my boss earlier this week and have arranged to take a couple of months off.'

'Oh,' he said. 'Does that mean there's something amiss?'

There was a long pause whilst Margaret seemed to concentrate on a slight crack in the glaze of her tea mug. Eventually she spoke.

'I'm not sure,' and after further delay, 'I'm genuinely not sure.'

'Not sure about what?' her father enquired.

'That's the problem, or at least part of the problem,' she replied. 'I just don't feel easy, but I don't really know why.'

'Has anything happened?' he asked, his voice quieter than usual.

'No, nothing that I can obviously put my finger on. I just don't feel that carrying on with what I'm doing is the right thing any longer, but I don't know why I feel like that, and I don't know what I'd do instead.'

'Funny thing, life,' her father observed. 'You can be pottering along with everything in the garden seeming rosy, and then something happens. In medicine you see that. Someone seems perfectly healthy and then, bang, they have a stroke or get a cancer and their world is changed.'

'It must be hard dealing with that all the time,' Margaret replied.

'Well, many doctors don't deal with that sort of thing at all, and for those that do it's not all the time,' her father said. 'It's much less often than people think, and it isn't very difficult. Your business is to be empathetic, but also to remain emotionally detached. Doctors can't give good advice or make good decisions if they've got tears in their eyes.'

Margaret said she understood the point: 'I suppose that's the same as me giving advice to a company that a particular part of their activities isn't competitive and should be run down because it's unlikely that they can make it profitable. Better to cut their losses and get out. We call it restructuring the business. Unfortunate for those who work in that area, but if the company folds completely, then they aren't going to be employing anyone.' She went on, 'But how do doctors deal with the thought that they might get ill, or something bad might happen to them?'

'There isn't a one-size-fits-all answer to that one,' her father replied, 'but I think that most medics, me included, hope that we have some sort of diplomatic immunity. Of course, we know that we don't, but we take care not to think too hard about things because we'd probably become jabbering wrecks if we spent time considering possible sinister causes of every minor symptom that we have, that everybody has.'

It was now his turn to slip into silence, during which he looked thoughtful and seemed to be blowing the surface of his coffee as if it were very hot although it wasn't. 'But then apart from illness, other things can throw you off course,' he said, and took a very slow sip.

Margaret spoke softly. 'Like complaints about you?'

After a further pause he spoke. 'So you know about them?'

'Something,' she said. 'Asif or Malcolm at the funeral, I can't remember which, told me that you'd not been the same after some investigations, and I found something in Mum's wardrobe when I was sorting out her clothes.'

SIX

BLOODY WELL

The next few days were busy for both Jonathan Barber and his daughter. He had an appointment in town to visit the solicitor's office to go through his wife's will, not that there was anything complex about it, and make some consequent minimal alterations to his own. The facade was traditional, with mahogany-coloured ornate woodwork and flowery gold script proclaiming the business's name, like something out of Dickens, but inside there had been a minimalist makeover with angular steel-framed furniture on a grey carpet and a couple of pot plants that he thought were probably too perfect to be alive. He considered going to have a very close look at them and feel of their compost but was deterred by the gaze of the receptionist, whose make-up also fell into the too perfect to be alive category. If there was a warm person behind it, they would have had a devil of a job to escape. She didn't look like a woman to be messed with and so he sat and waited.

The solicitor turned out to be a pleasant man in his mid-thirties wearing an expensive shirt but no tie or jacket. He introduced himself as Michael with an unmistakably northern accent. Jonathan doubted that any of the partners would have been seen in such a state of undress in the first hundred years of the firm's existence, or been known to their clients as anything other than "Mr", and he mused inwardly about when the first partner who spoke anything other than Home Counties English would have been appointed.

He kept these thoughts to himself as Michael explained matters in flat tones, using phrases he'd no doubt employed hundreds of times before, in the same way as Dr Barber had had his stock, honed over many years, from which he'd draw a selection as required when talking to patients or relatives: "Are you someone who likes to know exactly what's going on?"; "I'd like to say something different, but…"; "I am not hiding anything, but…".

'Do you have any questions?' Michael asked, which jolted Jonathan out of his reverie on turns of phrase used by professionals speaking to lay people.

'No, thank you,' he replied, because he couldn't think of any, but also conscious that he was following in the footsteps of countless others replying to countless professionals, even when there were very good questions that they could and should have asked.

He also had to go to get some new spectacles. His two pairs of bifocals had done good service, but he had broken one when he accidentally sat on them in his car about six months previously, and he had been far too busy with his wife's illness to get them replaced at the time. The remaining pair were on their last legs. The nose bridge kept separating from one of the lenses, and although he could push it back into place, the arrangement was becoming more and more precarious and the need for repair increasingly frequent. When he'd left it too long with some previous glasses, his attempts with Super Glue had proved terminal, so he'd booked a slot at the opticians.

An Asian woman checked his visual acuity and fields in a splendidly efficient manner that as always made him reflect on the rough and ready nature of the examination of these things that was part of a doctor's standard neurological examination of a patient. The puffs of air reported that his ocular pressures were normal. The photographs of his ocular fundi on the computer screen looked normal to him and he was pleased when the optometrist confirmed this, saying that they were "very good" with an intonation that seemed to imply he could take some credit, as if – like flossing and brushing his teeth – he'd given the backs of his eyes a thorough polish every evening and this was why they were in such good condition. He declined having a retinal scan for which he'd have to pay extra.

He was then sent out to the waiting area to choose the frames he wanted. His initial impression was of an almost infinite range, but as at previous visits, he rapidly concluded that almost all would look ridiculous on him. A sulky teenage girl was having an argument on the subject of suitable frames with her overweight and sweating mother, who looked as though she'd administer corporal punishment if it weren't for the fact that they were in a public place, whilst someone he took to be her father stood in embarrassed silence staring vaguely at the floor a few feet away.

For a couple of minutes he looked at some tortoiseshell frames similar to those worn by Michael, although he suspected that his would have come from some boutique source and not a high street chain. He tried a pair on, thought he might be able to get used to them, but then headed to the stand of frameless "eyeglasses" and chose those most like the ones that were giving up the ghost. A rather pathologically enthusiastic assistant with spiky hair then conducted the final stages of the procedure and he left the store with a receipt and plan to return the following week to collect two pairs of new glasses, the second – he was told – being "free".

Margaret, meanwhile, had organised to go back to her flat to check that everything was in order. She had left it in something of a fluster about three weeks previously and was pleased to find nothing seriously amiss. It was a bit difficult to open the front door because a pile of post had built up behind it, none of which was significant and the vast bulk both unsolicited and unwanted, but there were no signs of break-ins or water leaks or other feared events. Unpleasant smells emanating from the waste bin and fridge were solved by a couple of trips to the dustbins, a few wipe-downs with kitchen cleaning fluid, and opening the windows.

She then made a brief trip to the local store to get some milk and croissants for the next day's breakfast before taking a shower and sprucing herself up to meet her best friend for drinks and supper. Whatever the circumstances, time spent with Ann always seemed to make her feel better, although it wouldn't do to look anything other than ready for a night out on the town when meeting with this force of nature. If Margaret was feeling a bit low or run-down for any reason, then Ann's account of her latest romantic disaster, the last she'd heard involving a body-building second-hand car salesman who turned out to be a needy hypochondriac, was a sure pick-me-up.

Most gratifyingly the evening proved to be no exception, with Ann warming to her task with the aid of a bottle of Rioja and notably describing her current boss's penchant for talking incessantly about the culture of the organisation, avoiding making any decisions under any circumstances, and looking terrified if forced into a situation where he might have to. Earlier that day she had particularly enjoyed asking him whether his preference for black tea instead of tea with milk was due to the taste, health considerations or was racially symbolic, and delighted when – by her account – he had retreated in confusion to his office, almost spilling the cup as he did so. After this the conversation had degenerated, somehow leading to speculation about whether it would be possible to copyright a version of Wordle that only recognised obscene words and if there were enough of five letters to make this viable.

As the evening drew to a close the conversation over coffees quietened and became more serious, as it often did. Margaret explained her uncertainties and that she was disturbed at realising how she'd drifted away from her parents over many years and now never would have a chance to get to know her mother. She said she knew that her father had been through a bad time but didn't know the details.

'Well,' said Ann with refreshing directness, 'at least you can do something about that – bloody well ask him!'

Fortified with this advice, Margaret mulled over how best to do this as she sat in the taxi going back to her flat and was only jolted from her thoughts when she became conscious of the driver saying, 'We're here,' with an irritation in his voice that suggested it wasn't the first time he'd tried to attract her attention. She got out and paid, pressing the button to give a 12.5 per cent tip rather than her usual 10 per cent out of embarrassment, realised there was an unpleasant drizzle in the air which she'd entirely failed to notice before, and hurried inside.

SEVEN

LEMON FACE

Margaret plucked up the courage to start asking her father about his difficulties at work a couple of days after her evening with Ann. They were sitting in the conservatory after lunch. The weather hadn't been good for the previous week. The combination of wind and rain meant that his paper had got wet on the journey back from the newsagent that he visited every morning, but the damp bits had been systematically dried out over the Aga and he'd now looked it through. Margaret had scanned the websites she frequented each day. The afternoon continued blustery and unpleasant outside so there was no enticement to venture out. This seemed like a suitable opportunity.

'Would now be a good time to talk about things? About what happened at work; about what happened with Mum?' she asked very timidly.

'Yes, as good a time as any,' he said slowly, 'but difficult to know how to begin.'

'Well, perhaps I could start,' Margaret replied. She knew from much professional experience of managing difficult conversations that getting them started wasn't easy, and that it could be hard to get back on track if they began clumsily. She was also aware of the power of being honest and admitting to personal uncertainties and insecurities when trying to encourage open dialogue. "If you keep your cards close to your chest, you can't expect others to show you theirs" was a line she remembered from some course she'd been on or some coaching she'd received, although she couldn't remember who'd dispensed this wisdom, or when or where. Seeing that her father seemed to welcome her continuing, she played some cards.

'I said before that I feel uneasy, not sure what to do workwise, and I don't remember ever feeling like this before. Coming back home for Mum's funeral, speaking to people there, makes me realise that I didn't know her as well as they did and I don't know you as well as they do, and that disturbs me. I can't say why, but it does. I've been thinking about that a lot and in fact it isn't surprising. Looking back on things I don't recall us ever talking about anything in any depth before I left home about twenty-five years ago. All I can remember are a few arguments when Mum asked you to speak to me about things like what time I'd come home from a party, or when I'd stayed at a friend's house overnight without planning it in advance. You always seemed to be working and I'm sure I was an opinionated and headstrong girl. There was no real need for us to talk and so we didn't;

we just went our separate ways. But now I feel I want to connect. I don't know why, but I do.'

'I feel the same way,' her father replied after a pause, 'and I also know about getting into a situation where I didn't know what to do. The circumstances weren't the same as yours, but the worry and the feelings...' He was clearly finding it difficult to go on, but Margaret waited and he did. 'Things became extremely difficult for me at work. I still find it hard to understand how they got into the state that they did. They never should have done. A court case and referral to the Medical Regulator started by some relatives, and a hospital investigation into my conduct leading to a disciplinary hearing. Your mother said it was evil and I think it was.'

It was clear from the pallor of his face and a tremble in his voice that the memories were still dreadful to him, but he continued.

'I was an old-fashioned doctor. I had my patients and I looked after them. I was happy to be called about them any time. I talked with them, examined them, organised investigations when I thought they needed them, treated them when I thought they needed treatment, referred them to colleagues I trusted when I thought they had something I didn't know much about or needed something doing that I couldn't do, and I tried to make sure that they were comfortable when it was clear that they were dying.'

'But isn't that exactly what a doctor should do?' said Margaret.

'Well, I thought so, and I still think so, but I don't think it's possible anymore.'

Margaret looked confused. 'How come?' she asked.

'Everything. Lots of things,' he said. The first words came in a trickle and then the floodgates opened.

'It's all become so impersonal. There are so many doctors. If you wanted an opinion on a patient's heart you had to make a referral to the cardiology team. You'd no idea who was going to pick it up, and half of the time the person who did knew less about the heart than I did and would demand that we organise a hatful of investigations, often without even seeing the patient. Unbelievable! At least I would have said it was, excepting that every specialty moved into operating in much the same way.

'When I trained, investigations were hard to get so you thought carefully about them. I can still remember the first CT scanner arriving in the hospital. To get a scan of a patient's head you had to go in person and make your case to whichever one of two consultant radiologists was on duty. My goodness, they put you through the mill to get one. Everyone joked that getting a scan was more difficult than passing the Membership, the Royal College of Physicians' exam. I'm not saying that was ideal, but in some ways it was better than the situation now where dozens and dozens of unnecessary scans and other sorts of tests are done, and then very few doctors have the common sense and confidence needed to stop further pursuit of minor abnormalities that are irrelevant to what might be wrong with the patient.

'I couldn't stop this sort of thing and it was so, so frustrating. Patients who were clearly dying and who no anaesthetist would put to sleep, even if a surgeon unwise enough to want to operate on their painful and tender bellies could be found, would be sent off for CT scans of their abdomen and pelvis.

'Sometimes I would be on the ward and able to intervene before the porters came to take the patients. I used to invoke King Lear, *he hates him that would upon the rack of this tough world stretch him out longer*, or quote one of my former bosses, a small quiet man who pottered around the Intensive Care Unit wearing elegant shoes, colourful socks, suit trousers and shirt with rolled-up sleeves – this was in the days before scrubs and crocs – and half-moon spectacles. As a young doctor I was repeatedly resuscitating a man whose heart kept stopping. After about forty-five minutes or an hour of this he quietly drew me aside and said very gently, "Jonathan, I think you're doing a marvellous job, but there is a rule… which is that patients should be allowed to die". The Lear quote came up in the disciplinary hearing, along with other phrases that I used to use.'

'That must have been incredibly hard,' observed Margaret.

'Yes, it was – hearing your own words repeated as if they were meant with malice. None of them were. Yes, I'm sure I was irritable at times, and I said some things that it would have been better if I hadn't, but things got totally out of proportion; investigations and hearings focussing on details and refusing to recognise the bigger picture. Talking about leaves and parts of leaves whilst missing trees and woods. It was like a bad dream that went on and on and I couldn't wake up from.'

There was a pause in the flow and Margaret ventured, 'So how did the formal processes start?'

'In a very ordinary way,' her father replied. 'I got a standard email from the Patient Advice and Liaison Service, PALS for short, which is where patients and relatives are directed if they want to make a complaint, and they sent it on to me as the consultant responsible for the patient, an elderly woman who'd died very shortly after admission to the hospital.'

'Was it common to get complaints?' Margaret asked.

'Well, it wasn't uncommon, perhaps once or sometimes twice a year. I always used to offer to speak to anyone who complained but over the years the system moved more and more towards written responses. The PALS office would look at the complaint, work out who needed to inform the response, which doctors, which nurses, which discharge planners, etcetera, etcetera, but this always included the consultant who'd been responsible for the patient. They'd send you a copy of whatever the patient or relative had written and you were expected to send a response to the PALS office, who'd collate everybody's accounts, do some corporate topping and tailing, and then send it off. Usually that was the end of things.'

'But not this time?' Margaret queried.

'No, I'm afraid not. Unfortunately it was just the beginning,' her father replied with a tremor in his voice.

'So what was the case?' Margaret asked.

'Nothing unusual at all. I'd seen dozens if not hundreds similar over the years. An elderly demented woman sent to the Emergency Department from a nursing home, very unwell with abdominal pain.'

'What did the relatives complain about?'

'They said that no one contacted them from the hospital when their mother was admitted. That the hospital didn't provide the care she should have been given, and they asked for copies of her medical records, which they were entitled to have.'

'What did you say in reply?'

'I responded as I always did. I explained what happened. One of the nurses in the Emergency Department tried to contact the next of kin using the phone number in the hospital record, but she couldn't get through. One of the junior doctors, who recognised that the woman was very ill and likely to die, also tried and didn't get an answer. It turned out that we had the wrong number in our records and so of course we apologised for that.'

'And how were you involved?'

'The junior doctor quite rightly called me to ask for advice, so I went and saw her. She was a very frail woman in her late seventies. She'd had diabetes for many years, several heart attacks in the past, gradually become demented over the previous two or three years, and been admitted to a nursing home after a stroke six months or so ago which meant that she couldn't be looked after at home even with a big package of care. She'd become acutely unwell over about twelve hours; not eating or drinking when the staff tried to give her food or water, with pain in her stomach.

'When I saw her she couldn't speak but was obviously in a lot of pain and it was clear that something catastrophic had happened in her abdomen. Her pulse was racing, her blood pressure was very low, and when I felt her tummy she cried out and the muscles went into spasm, which is a protective mechanism that happens if the gut has perforated – gets a hole in it – and bowel contents have leaked out, or something equally devastating has happened.

'If you saw a previously well person in such a state you'd be calling for immediate help from colleagues on the Intensive Care Unit, putting up drips to give fluid, organising urgent blood tests and an emergency CT scan to find out what had gone on, and giving the surgeon on call a ring. But that wouldn't be appropriate in a woman like this, so I explained what I thought had happened to her in my response to PALS and said that my main priority had been to make sure that she was comfortable, which I did by organising for her to be prescribed morphine, and she passed away a few hours later.'

He paused for a moment, obviously living the scenario again and wincing at the memory, and Margaret felt it appropriate to say something.

'That all seems very reasonable to me,' she said quietly. 'Why on earth did it cause so much trouble?'

'You might well ask! Because of the relatives.'

'Why? What did they do?'

'A few weeks later they, or rather a solicitor acting under their instruction, wrote to the hospital's chief executive with complaints and allegations. They said we hadn't made adequate efforts to contact them when their mother had been admitted. They said that I, acting on behalf of the hospital, had behaved in a paternalistic and judgemental manner, denying her the chance of living by deciding not to try to resuscitate her and failing to pursue investigation of the cause of her acute illness, and that I had failed to make proper medical records.'

'And the chief executive?'

'He, or someone in his office, passed the letter onto the medicolegal department and they invited me to a meeting with the hospital's solicitor to discuss how we should respond.'

'And what were they like?'

'I'm not sure what to say,' her father replied after a pause. 'I found them interesting.'

'Interesting? In what way?'

'It was like entering a parallel universe. He was a neat, clean-shaven man in his forties, wearing an expensive suit with collar and tie, rather like surgeons cultivating private practice used to when I was a young consultant. I almost asked him where his buttonhole was, and if he had a card with his private secretary's number on he could give me. She – the head of the hospital's medicolegal department – was similarly well dressed and manicured, and she reeked of having been to an expensive girls' private school. That presence, that way of speaking, never leaves them – if you know what I mean.'

Margaret did and she smiled.

'No one looking like them could possibly work in a hospital, at least not in any part of one that I'd had dealings with before, and as we talked over the relatives' letter it became clear that they didn't think like anyone who'd ever had any involvement in looking after a patient or been in a clinic, ward or hospital Emergency Department.

'I think that for a few minutes I thought that a brief explanation from me was all that they'd require. They'd see the sense of what I said, write it down, and then go off and explain it to the relatives' solicitor, and that would be the end of things. But that was me being naïve.'

Margaret could imagine the legal pair gradually manoeuvring the conversation into their, as her father put it, parallel universe.

'As they talked, it gradually dawned on me that things I regarded as blindingly obvious weren't obvious or accepted in their world. When I said that it was clear that the poor woman was dying, they asked me how I knew that.'

'And what did you say? How can you tell?'

'I explained that although some people who appear well can drop down dead suddenly, this is unusual, and before most people perish, they become drowsy. They don't speak but may mumble, their breathing becomes laboured and often erratic, their hands feel cold, and their blood pressure drops. And at that point you have to decide whether to try to resuscitate them, which means putting in drips to give fluids and asking anaesthetic colleagues to put a tube down their throat to get them on a breathing machine and giving them cardiac massage – pressing up and down on their chest – if their heart stops.

'They asked me if I'd made an active decision not to resuscitate Mrs D, and I said that I had. They asked me why I'd made this decision and I only just restrained myself from saying that doing anything else would have been complete and utter bloody madness, but it would have been. I explained that with the burden of all her pre-existing illnesses – diabetes, heart problems, dementia, stroke – and the certainty that something catastrophic had happened in her abdomen, there was no chance that she could survive or that any treatment could restore her to an acceptable quality of life.'

'Weren't they happy with that?' Margaret asked, feeling confused because what her father was reporting seemed eminently sensible to her.

'No, they wanted explanation and justification of everything I'd said. How did I know that something catastrophic had happened in her abdomen without a scan or test of some sort? I said that when I felt her abdomen it was obviously very painful and the muscles all tensed up, and this is what happens when the bowel perforates or something similarly awful happens.'

'And were they satisfied with that?'

'No, they both, but particularly the woman who was head of medicolegal, looked unhappy. It may have been a misfortune of how age had affected her facial features, sometimes it isn't kind, but she looked as though she was sucking a lemon as she listened to what I said. But I may have been over-interpreting.

'They asked me which bit of the bowel might have perforated and what else it could have been if it wasn't a bowel perforation. I listed a couple of common causes and sites of bowel perforation – appendicitis, pouches on the large bowel, diverticulitis – and a few other things that can have a similar effect – inflammation of the pancreas, pancreatitis; leaking of blood from a swollen main blood vessel in the abdomen, an aortic aneurysm; death of some of the bowel because its blood supply has been cut off, ischaemic bowel. I asked them how many other less common things they'd like me to list. They said they didn't need to know any more causes, but asked whether any of them were treatable and I said not in a woman like Mrs D.

'They asked me whether in retrospect I thought I should have asked for a second consultant opinion, and I said no.

'They asked me whether I ever asked for opinions from other consultants and I said that I often did, almost always because I thought the patient had a problem that required their specialist opinion or treatment, but very occasionally because I wasn't sure what was going on and thought it would be good to get a fresh pair of eyes involved.

'They pressed me on why I hadn't got a fresh pair of eyes to see Mrs D and I found myself repeating that it was obvious that something catastrophic had happened and making the point, which they glossed over completely, that the Emergency Department of the hospital – which often does a very good impression of being a war zone, not helped I might add by the way that some of the emergency doctors practise their medicine – would seize up completely if doctors weren't able to make obvious decisions without asking for second opinions left, right and centre. I suspect I got a bit agitated saying all this because I knocked over a glass of water on the desk and we had to scrabble around to find some paper towels to mop it up.'

Margaret smiled, imagining increased contortions of the lemon face.

EIGHT

DID YOU TELL MUM?

A lull in the conversation led Margaret to realise that she felt thirsty and fancied a cup of tea. Her father welcomed the idea and perhaps subliminally influenced by recent thoughts of lemons they decided on a pot of Earl Grey, which Margaret went off to make. As they settled back into their chairs with hot mugs in their hands, Margaret started the ball rolling again.

'I guess they went on to press you about other things?'

'Yes, everything in minute detail. They picked up on the fact that I'd said that I didn't think that any treatment could have restored Mrs D to an acceptable quality of life. What did I mean by that? I said that I didn't think she could have survived at all, whatever treatment was given, and that trying to resuscitate her would have been prolonging death rather than sustaining life, but they kept coming back to the point that if she had survived, however unlikely that was, what did I mean by saying an acceptable quality of life?'

'And what did you mean by it?' Margaret asked, genuinely interested in the answer.

'I'm pretty sure I waffled. I can't remember precisely what I said at the time, but since then everything that's happened has made me think about it a lot. The capacity of people – patients and their families – to deal with death and dying, and their thoughts about it, have changed greatly since I started out with a stethoscope nearly fifty years ago.'

'What was it like when you were a young doctor?'

'Much more trusting, much more accepting, much more thinking about others.'

'Trusting? Accepting others?'

'Trusting of doctors. If a doctor told a patient's relatives that they were dying, then they were believed. The doctor was trusted. That's less likely now. Not, I think, because doctors are less trustworthy, in fact I think they're probably more trustworthy, but because it's now not the fashion to trust anybody. Most people had seen someone who'd died, usually an elderly relative who'd passed away in a bedroom at home. They knew deep down that death happens – it really does. I think that led to them being better able, not that it was ever an easy thing, to accept that they, or their nearest and dearest, were dying.'

'And thinking about others?'

'Yes, a deep sense that many had that it would be wrong to want to live for long in a state of dependency, where their continuing life would be at the expense of the lives of their children.'

Margaret, although she'd never spent any time

thinking about death and dying, could see immediately that this wasn't how things were now. 'I guess that was all very easy – no, that's not the right word – convenient for the doctors,' she said.

'I guess that it was. If we said that a patient was dying, then that was rarely challenged. If we said that a patient was not going to be able to recover to have an acceptable quality of life, then that was usually taken as fact. And behind it all was the understanding that no one wanted to be a burden.'

'And now?'

'Changed utterly. Doctors score very highly compared to other professions and occupations on surveys about "who do you trust?" but when it comes to the crunch many patients and relatives don't if the doctor's message isn't what they want to hear. The fashion is to challenge all authorities.

'Don't get me wrong. I'm not saying that I think that bovine acceptance is a good thing, but I do think that challenge of the black is white variety makes sensible discussion and sensible decision-making difficult.

'Of course people nowadays understand intellectually that everybody dies, but they've never actually seen it, so it's perhaps not surprising that they find it more difficult to accept. It can't be me, soon. It can't be my nearest and dearest, soon. There must be some mistake, and – because bad things can't just happen – there must be someone to blame. That's a thing that's changed a lot.'

He broke into a smile, which confused Margaret until he went on.

'I remember one of the last patients I ever saw in my clinic. A man in his eighties who'd worked on a farm all his life. Going to the hospital to see a specialist was an important thing. He was wearing his best tweed jacket and trousers, a spotless collarless white cotton shirt and ferociously buffed shoes. When I examined him I noticed that one of his feet was plastic, and I asked him what had happened. He gave a chuckle, told me that most doctors didn't notice it – or I suppose didn't comment on it if they did – and then said, "I was standing in the wrong place". I asked him what he meant and he said that when he was four he was in a field when they were scything the wheat, and he was standing in the wrong place. I have the image in my mind of a picture postcard farming scene on a gloriously hot summer's day, as might have been painted by Constable. I can hear the whispering sound of the blades rhythmically cutting through the stalks; and then a sudden scream; and him being told off for causing trouble!'

'And then being a burden?'

'A phrase that's rarely heard now.'

He lapsed into silence and introspection.

'Was there anything else that they wanted to quiz you about?' Margaret asked.

'Oh, yes. In fact a lot of the trouble came from something that I thought wasn't very important; at least I didn't think it was at the time. I hadn't filled in a form – the advanced care planning form.'

'You said before that they complained you hadn't made proper medical records. Is that what they were referring to?'

'Yes.'

'So what's the form about?'

'It's a form on which it can be recorded what treatments a patient wants to have and what treatments they don't want to have, the most significant bit being whether or not they want someone to try and restart their heart if it stops.'

'Why hadn't you filled it in?'

Her father took a deep breath and was visibly shaking as he replied. 'Because it isn't fit for purpose!' he said, rather louder than he meant to. 'If you're dealing with a woman like Mrs D, who's demented and very ill and to use the jargon "lacks capacity" – meaning she can't make decisions – and you can't get hold of any relatives to talk to, then there isn't a way of completing it that says "I've decided to keep this poor dying woman comfortable because it's clearly the right thing to do".'

Margaret paused for a while before proceeding. 'So what did you do instead?'

'I wrote instructions in her notes. I can remember precisely because they were phrases I'd used many times before and they ended up being quoted in court and in the Medical Regulator's hearing. I put down that "Attempts to resuscitate would be futile. Management should be directed to relieving symptoms and allowing Mrs D to die as comfortably as possible", and that's what happened.'

'I can't see how that would cause a lot of bother,' Margaret observed, feeling genuinely mystified.

'It never had before,' her father said with a wry

expression, 'but everything changes when lawyers and courts and the Medical Regulator get involved.'

'Lawyers and courts and the Medical Regulator?'

'If you run into the wrong patient or the wrong relatives there is nothing to restrain them. You can only hope that you don't. They complain and accuse by every route and means they can think of. It seems to become their sole purpose in life. Letters and emails to everyone you could possibly think of and many that you couldn't, and they all have to do something, even if a straightforward reading of whatever they've been sent makes it pretty well certain that the author is unhinged and what they say is most unlikely to be true, or at least a very skewed perspective on whatever happened. The poor doctor is swept off their feet in a tsunami of investigations and processes that they can't control and can only hope to survive.'

'And that's what happened to you?'

'Yes, that was the start of it. The hospital was taken to court by Mrs D's relatives over the failure to attempt resuscitation and,' he said with a tinge of anger still audible in his voice, 'they referred me to the Medical Regulator. Anyone can refer any doctor to the Medical Regulator any time they want to.'

'Is that a bad thing?'

'No, I don't think it could be otherwise. If a doctor does something wrong to somebody – anybody – then it must be right that they can say so and expect action to be taken. The problem is the response, which is incredibly slow, leaving doctors in limbo for ages, and mainly designed to cover the regulator's back. They're there to protect the public and I suppose they do, but they look after themselves first, and,' he went on with some bitterness, 'the doctor, if they've been put through the wringer and it's been decided that they've done nothing wrong, is just sent a letter saying that the case is dismissed with no action. No action, after months and years of anxiety and misery. No action!'

Margaret stayed silent for a while and then went on. 'One thing would have been bad enough, but it must have been awful with two going on. Did they happen at the same time or one after the other?'

'One after the other. The court case first.'

'And did you get any help to deal with it all?'

'Yes, the woman from medicolegal told me that I should get some professional advice to support me through what she kept calling "the processes".'

Margaret thought that perhaps the person behind the lemon face may not have been quite as sour as she looked.

'I didn't do anything about it at first but a few days later Malcolm came to find me. I don't know who told him, or whether anyone asked him to talk to me. He knew that I sat in my outpatient clinic room at the end of Tuesday afternoons to dictate my letters. The nurses and the reception staff used to leave, always asking me to close the window and turn the lights off when I left. It was nice and quiet.

'Malcolm appeared. He seemed to know what had happened – he always knows about everything that's going on in the hospital – and what was going to happen. He talked very calmly about it, but I knew he was worried because his cheeks were flushed and he was doing the funny thing with his lip that makes his moustache quiver when he's stressed about something. He told me that I had to get professional advice; "that's what you've paid your subscriptions for over the years," he said. I'm very glad they both said this because it was only after I'd spoken to someone who was used to dealing with things of this sort that I began to see that there might be a way through it all.

'I got in touch with my medical defence organisation. I'd joined them when I qualified because everyone seemed to do so and it didn't cost very much at the time. I never thought I'd need their help, but it turned out that I did.

'She was a businesslike young woman called Samantha who I think had some sort of paralegal background before she worked for the medical defence organisation. I'd met many men who wore pinstripe trousers, but I remember she often wore a grey pinstripe skirt that seemed uncomfortably tight, and she had one of those oblong attaché cases with latches that spring back with a ferocious click.

'She explained to me that the regulator would probably decide to wait for the outcome of any court process before they decided what to do, and that's what they did.'

'Did you tell Mum?' Margaret asked.

'No, not right away. Not for a while. I wouldn't have known what to say. I needed to get things in order in my own mind before I could say anything to her.'

NINE

VICTORIA CROSSES

'So what happened in the court case?'

'Deeper into the parallel universe. Common sense out of the window. I found this hard, very hard. Never any question about whether a decision made or action taken was sensible, in the grand scheme of things the right thing to do. All focussed on the detail. If the *Titanic* was slipping beneath the waves it seemed as though the court's main concern would be whether there were adequate policies for aligning or stacking deckchairs in the event of it sinking, and if these had been properly implemented.'

Margaret had read the papers she found in her mother's wardrobe very carefully. The file had contained three bundles of these relating to the investigation in the hospital, the investigation organised by the Medical Regulator, and the court case brought against the hospital.

She wasn't familiar with medical matters or with legal documents, but parts of the court case did seem abstruse and the language difficult to understand, but so far as she could work out from a summary paragraph, the relatives' complaints were that Mrs D's human rights had been breached by the fact that the hospital failed to adequately consult her or her family about the decision not to resuscitate her, failed to notify her of the decision, failed to seek a second opinion, failed to make its Do Not Attempt Cardiopulmonary Resuscitation (DNACPR) policy available to her, and failed to have a policy which was clear and unambiguous.

As she expected, and of course as it was their job to do, the judge had worked through the issues systematically, quoting from Mrs D's patient record and referencing decisions of previous courts. The nuances of some of these eluded her, confirming an impression she'd got from occasional interactions with commercial and corporate lawyers that she'd encountered in the management consultancy world, namely that the law was an intellectual game played by lawyers to determine who was cleverest.

The judge seemed to make an enormous meal out of the failure to consult Mrs D about limitation of her care and the decision not to attempt resuscitation. Several densely worded pages were occupied stating that, had Mrs D had capacity to be involved in decisions about her care, including decisions about limitation of care and resuscitation, then there was no doubt that the law would have required that her views should have been sought.

In his submission to the court the lawyer representing the hospital had quoted national guidelines stating, "when a clinical decision is made that CPR should not be attempted, because it will not be successful, and the patient has not expressed a wish to discuss CPR, it is not necessary or appropriate to initiate discussion with the patient to explore their wishes regarding CPR".

It was unfortunate in the judge's view that no formal test of Mrs D's mental capacity had been made when she arrived in the Emergency Department, there being no evidence of a completed capacity assessment form in her medical records. However, taking into account that her pre-existing dementia was not in dispute and that entries in the medical records included the phrases, "groaning, unable to give any history" and "unable to answer any questions", the judge concluded that she did not have capacity.

There was then a debate between the lawyers as to whether this made the issue of failure to consult her about limitation of care and the decision not to resuscitate her moot. Margaret didn't really know what the word meant, although she'd heard it used in a legal context, and she couldn't understand the fine nuances of the arguments made, but the bottom line seemed to be that the law could not require a doctor to discuss something with a patient that they obviously couldn't understand, but the judge didn't say this in plain English and she felt as though it would probably have been helpful if he had.

The matter of consultation with the family was then considered. The judge noted two entries in the medical notes, one made by a junior doctor and one by a nurse working in the Emergency Department. Both wrote that they had attempted to call the next of kin by phoning the number in the demographics section of Mrs D's medical record: the doctor's note said "no reply" and the nurse's note said "no ringing tone". It subsequently transpired that the number was incorrect, differing in one digit from the right one, which the judge regarded as unfortunate, but he was satisfied that the hospital had made reasonable attempts to contact the next of kin. He went on to note that apologies had been offered for the fact that the phone number had been recorded inaccurately, which was presumed attributable to human error. Further consideration of this was beyond the remit of the court.

If some of this seemed like a meal to Margaret, it was merely the hors d'oeuvre. The next and more substantial course was the matter of a second opinion. The judge noted that Dr Barber, her father, had written "attempts to resuscitate would be futile" in Mrs D's medical notes. In his evidence given to the court he had confirmed this opinion and also stated that, in his view, "no treatment could have restored her to an acceptable quality of life". Much discussion followed.

The lawyer representing the family took great exception to the statement about quality of life. A previous legal case was quoted emphasising the difference between medical issues, such as whether CPR might work, which are matters for clinicians to decide, and questions relating to the welfare of the patient in the widest sense which are essentially for the patient to decide. It was for the patient and not for others to say that a life which the patient would regard as worthwhile is not worth living. She then went on to argue that Dr Barber's statement about quality of life betrayed that he, acting as an agent of the hospital, was guilty of discriminating against Mrs D on the grounds of her disability, defined as "a physical or mental impairment which has a substantial and long-term adverse effect on her ability to carry out normal day-to-day activities". Margaret could understand that severe dementia obviously was a disability but, although she hadn't considered the matter before, felt that it flew in the face of common sense to suggest that this shouldn't influence decisions about treatments that doctors might give to their patient. Indeed, it seemed madness to her that it wouldn't.

After much pontification the judge accepted the defence's argument that maintained focus on the statement that attempts to resuscitate Mrs D would have been futile. He noted that this was what Dr Barber had written in her medical record, where there was no mention of anything to do with quality of life, and he declined to make further comment on any of Dr Barber's oral evidence regarding quality of life of a patient with severe dementia and implications for decisions about treatment beyond saying "the court should be slow to give general guidance".

The judge then moved on to consider the claim that Mrs D's human rights had been breached by the failure of the hospital to provide a second opinion. The family's lawyer sought to press the point that deciding to deny potentially life-saving treatment was surely a decision of such consequence, or potential consequence, that a second opinion should have been obtained. Dr Barber, in his evidence, said that the junior doctor who assessed Mrs D in the Emergency Department shared his view that attempts to resuscitate would have been inappropriate, which this doctor had confirmed in the written account they provided for the court. A senior nurse on duty in the Emergency Department at the time of Mrs D's admission, who had set up an infusion pump of drugs to relieve distress, had also stated that she thought this was the right thing to have done. Margaret in her mind's eye could see her father smiling as he heard the comments from her evidence that the judge chose to quote in his summary of the case, "cruel to do otherwise" being one of them.

The family's lawyer had continued by arguing that a second opinion had not been obtained from an independent medical practitioner, meaning another consultant in the context of admission to the Emergency Department, thereby breaching Mrs D's human rights. The fact that another consultant had not been involved in her care or the decision that resuscitation should not be attempted was not disputed.

The arguments continued with the hospital's lawyer making two main points. Firstly, that the senior nurse who had set up the infusion pump was an independent practitioner. She was a registered member of a professionally regulated medical (nursing) body with a licence to practise, and she had confirmed in her evidence that she thought attempts to resuscitate would have been inappropriate; in fact she had used the word cruel. Secondly, they referred to a judgement in a previous case in which the judge accepted the submission of a hospital's lawyer that there is no obligation to arrange a second opinion in a case "where the patient (a Mr F in this instance) is being advised and treated by a multidisciplinary team all of whom take the view that a DNACPR notice is appropriate".

By this stage of reading the court papers, Margaret was into the swing of things and recognised that no statement, however bland and seemingly uncontroversial, would have been allowed to go unchallenged. She was not disappointed.

The family's lawyer argued that the senior nurse could not be considered to be an independent medical practitioner for the purposes of providing a second opinion on a patient's care. On reading this Margaret couldn't help thinking of one of her friends, Shirley, a nursing sister of substantial size and robustness with a liking for red hair dye, free and forthright with her opinions of doctors that she had worked with, able to drink any of them under the table, and never known to back down in an argument even when obviously wrong. She wondered how the conversation might have developed if she had been told that she wasn't an independent practitioner. Margaret had obviously never seen the lawyer in question, but her mental image was of a person with delicate features, a pale complexion because of much time spent reading legal papers in offices or libraries and thus little exposure to the sun, very fastidious in attention to detail, who perhaps drank a single gin and tonic and a single small glass of Sauvignon Blanc when out for a celebratory evening. If in some future life the two did meet to explore the question of whether Shirley was an independent practitioner, Margaret felt that it would be essential to have a judge present and probably wise to alert the local Emergency Department to the fact that one or more trauma cases may be heading in their direction.

The family's lawyer also sought to argue that the discussion between Dr Barber, the junior doctor and the senior nurse in the Emergency Department could not, with reference to the case of Mr F appealed to by the hospital's lawyer, be regarded as properly constituting a multidisciplinary team. They argued that in Mr F's case the multidisciplinary team had met at a pre-arranged time, had included members other than doctors and nurses, and the output of their discussions had been recorded on a structured form in the medical notes. Margaret could almost feel her father's blood pressure rising to extreme levels as this argument was pursued in court and him having to be restrained from shouting out, not that he was a man who regularly used expletives, "What are you suggesting, that we have an f-ing committee permanently established in the Emergency Department?", or something similar.

The judge accepted the argument put on behalf of the family that the phrase "independent medical practitioner" did mean "a doctor, a person who has been educated, trained and licensed to practise the art and science of medicine", but then took pains to acknowledge that some nurses now undertook roles and had responsibilities that were the preserve of doctors in the past. Margaret thought it unlikely that he would have met Shirley, but it occurred to her that he might know, or even perhaps be married to, a similar nurse, making him chary of making a bald statement that without qualification could be perceived as disparaging of their role.

In relation to what did or didn't constitute a multidisciplinary team, the judge quoted a standard definition that it was "a group of healthcare workers and social care professionals who are experts in different areas with different professional backgrounds, united as a team for the purpose of planning and implementing treatment programmes for complex medical conditions. They work in a coordinated manner with members who are elected to the team depending on the patient's needs and the condition being treated. A multidisciplinary team generally consists of an attending physician, a registered nurse, and other appropriate staff". Based on this, he reasoned, in relation to the assertions of Mrs D's family's lawyer, that there was no requirement for meetings of multidisciplinary teams to be at pre-arranged times; that members other than the attending physician and a registered nurse were only required when appropriate, and he did not see that any others were obviously required in the case of Mrs D; and that there was no requirement for a multidisciplinary team to produce any particular documentation beyond that of practitioners making appropriate clinical notes to explain their interactions with, plans for and care of the patient, as they are generally required to do. Margaret couldn't help but observe that a brief and cursory discussion between any doctor and any nurse might therefore be construed as a multidisciplinary team meeting, but the judge – probably wisely – made no comment about the irreducible minimum requirement.

If Margaret thought that this was the end of the legal meal, she was mistaken. Reading on, she imagined that her father must have felt as though he'd already eaten plenty but was now forced to stomach several large and unwanted helpings of very stodgy pudding. An image of Bruce Bogtrotter came to her mind: the schoolboy in Roald Dahl's fantastic book forced as a punishment to eat a gigantic chocolate cake in public by the evil headmistress, who hopes he will plead for mercy before collapsing into a vomiting heap in front of the entire school.

The family's lawyer next raised concern that the hospital had failed to make its DNACPR policy available to Mrs D and failed to have a policy about its implementation that was clear and unambiguous.

Margaret wondered if the judge might also have been feeling satiated because he dismissed the argument that the policy should have been made available to an extremely ill demented woman very speedily, referring to his earlier statements about consultation with a patient who lacked capacity. From her introduction to courtroom behaviours so far she was sure that, eminently sensible though this was, there must be some legal argument that could be made against it, but perhaps even judges got fatigued by protracted absurd debates to the point where they said something simple and straightforward. She suspected that they might get reprimanded for this later by whoever is responsible for quality assurance of judges' performance, should there be any such person.

The matter of the DNACPR policy and its implementation was not so readily disposed of. The hospital did have a policy, recently redrafted following a previous legal case, and a variety of explanatory leaflets written for patients. After describing CPR these explained that "(y)our doctor will probably ask you if you want to be given all the treatments they think would help you. This is an opportunity to tell your doctor what is most important to you when you are treated in hospital". Further guidance for patients, relatives and staff went on to say "a decision that CPR should not be attempted should only be made after appropriate consultation and consideration of all aspects of the patient's condition. Decisions must be taken in the best interests of the patient, following assessment that should include likely clinical outcome and the patient's known or ascertainable wishes". Following on from this was reference to the form that doctors were expected to complete to record the patient's care wishes and the treatments that should or should not be provided if their condition deteriorated, including or not including CPR in the event that their heart or breathing stopped.

The family's lawyer, perhaps wary of the judge's previous comments, didn't dwell on the fact that there was no record of Mrs D being given opportunity to express her wishes, but made the points that the advanced care planning form had not been completed and therefore, given the presumption that it is in any patient's best interests to stay alive, Mrs D should have been provided with all available treatments.

The absence of a completed form was not disputed. The hospital's lawyer explained that the policy did not say that one had to be completed in all circumstances, or that the absence of a completed form could be taken as meaning that CPR had to be attempted. In his evidence, Dr Barber said, as Margaret had already heard from her father directly, that he had written a clear statement in Mrs D's notes that attempts to resuscitate would be futile and management should be directed to relieving symptoms and allowing Mrs D to die as comfortably as possible, unambiguously indicating that resuscitation was not to be attempted. He had then gone on to comment, as Margaret remembered, that he didn't think that the form was fit for purpose in circumstances such as hers. Margaret could imagine the hospital's lawyer and anyone else attending from the hospital, including perhaps Lemon Face, cringing as her father said this and wanting to put a bag over his head and drag him away, but she could well imagine the tension building in him as the lawyers jousted and the relief he would have got by saying what he thought.

Margaret had a picture in her mind of an elderly man with a slight tremor and tendency to luxuriate in the sound of his own voice, wearing a wig and black silk gown, rather tired after having had to concentrate for several hours and desperately in need of a stiff drink, summoning up the energy to make further judgements. She recognised that this was most unlikely to have been the reality and any video record of the courtroom scene would undoubtedly have disappointed her, but the fantasy amused her.

The judge noted that the hospital's policy did not say that its advanced care planning form had to be completed for all patients in all circumstances, also that it did not say that in the event that a form hadn't been completed the automatic assumption should be that all care, including resuscitation, should be provided. He was able to imagine circumstances where it was not possible to access or complete the form and therefore found the family's lawyer's criticism of the policy in these regards to be unfounded. Perhaps displaying good judgement, or perhaps because the thought of a large whisky was beginning to dominate his thoughts, he made no comment on the detail of the advanced care planning form beyond saying that this was a matter for other authorities to consider.

'I've read the court judgement,' Margaret said, 'so I know what you mean about the deckchairs. But what did it feel like to you?'

'Unreal. It still does,' her father replied. 'I've used the phrase parallel universe before, and I can't think of anything much better. Surreal. Two days of listening to arguments describing something in a foreign language. No, not a foreign language, I could understand the words.'

He paused to gather his thoughts and went on, 'I've never been good at listening to nonsense and letting it go unchallenged, and I know that this is part of what got me into trouble, but I felt like shouting out, "Can we just have a dose of reality here?" or something like that. I'm not sure what would have happened if I did. In the movies the judge would have banged his gavel and a couple of menacing-looking court officers would have appeared and escorted me to the cells.'

'What happened afterwards in the hospital? Did anyone talk to you about it all?' Margaret asked.

'Nothing really. Most people won't have known about it at all. I went back to work as usual.'

'Didn't anyone check in on you to find out if you were OK?'

'Nobody from the hospital management or medicolegal team, if that's what you mean. Mind you, I'm not sure that they could have said anything or done anything that I'd have wanted them to do. Malcolm came round to my office the next day and asked how things went. He laughed when I told him that I'd said what I thought about the advanced care planning form. He said that he and everyone else he knows who actually sees patients of the sorts we see on the medical take thinks the same, just that they're not brave enough or stupid enough to say so. I remember one phrase he used. "Some Victoria Crosses are awarded posthumously", he said, which made me chuckle as well and I felt better afterwards. I've since used the phrase myself.'

Margaret and her father had been talking for a couple of hours. The wind had dropped and the rain had stopped lashing against the windows. The clouds were still low and glowering, but it wasn't so intimidating outside as it had been.

'Thanks for what you've told me,' Margaret said. 'Perhaps we can talk over what happened with the Medical Regulator and the hospital investigation another time. I've been indoors all day and think I need a walk round the block before supper. What do you fancy?'

After hearing her father's request she got up and collected the teapot and mugs and headed for the kitchen whilst he settled back into his chair for a snooze.

'Thanks,' he said as she went out. 'I think it's good to talk things over.' Having put a couple of potatoes into the baking oven, got some bacon out of the freezer to defrost and checked what there was by way of salad things in the fridge, she put on her coat and boots and went out. The misty drizzle on her face was pleasantly refreshing.

TEN

THANK YOU FOR TELLING ME

The next few days didn't present any opportunity for further discussion. Margaret made a further trip back to her flat and had a catch-up with one of her work colleagues, a thoughtful woman called Sarah. She hoped that their conversation might help her work out what she wanted to do, but it didn't. Sarah always gave the impression, at least to Margaret, that – unlike many in the sometimes toxic world of management consultancy – she was quietly comfortable in life, both domestically and at work. She assumed that this was the foundation of her apparent ability to keep all things in proportion and give sensible opinions and advice in a professional context, when interacting with anyone around the water cooler, or when talking to friends.

Margaret had told Sarah that she was taking some time off to take stock of what she wanted to do, so Sarah was no doubt expecting this to come up as a topic during the evening's conversation. However, following on from Margaret manoeuvring discussion in this direction, in fact pretty well straight after she hinted towards it, Sarah's immediate response was, 'That's so brave, I wish I had the nerve to do that!'

Here was a duck that looked calm and unruffled above the surface, but underneath it wasn't a case of the feet paddling like hell but them thrashing about in a dangerously uncoordinated manner; that's if one or both hadn't already dropped off. Sarah, married for about fifteen years and with two children that she'd explained were doing well at private schools, was having a crisis. She felt stuck in a rut, wanted to get out and didn't know how to. She told Margaret that she didn't think her husband found her attractive anymore.

'He doesn't seem interested in me,' she said, 'but other men are,' and went on to confide that a man at work who she found attractive had asked her if she wanted to have an affair. 'Do you think I should?' she asked.

Looking back on the evening Margaret couldn't recall precisely how she replied but doubted that any response she might have made could have been coherent. She remembered an immediate feeling that she had no qualifications of any sort that could justify her playing any role as a relationship counsellor. She'd just split up with a long-term partner and was acutely aware that she'd drifted away from her parents, would never have a chance to get to know her mother, and was in the foothills of trying to establish a relationship with her father. At some point she asked Sarah whether she'd talked to her husband about the way she was feeling, and she knew that at some point she'd observed that sometimes even good relationships can come to an end and it can be better for people to follow different paths. Anyway, she hadn't come away from the evening with any useful thoughts about what she should do and that was a disappointment for her.

Meanwhile, her father was also having a difficult evening. Malcolm and his wife, Annie, had invited him to a concert, and it was the first time he'd ventured out for a purely social event since his wife's funeral. Before Joan had become ill the four of them had often, perhaps two or three times a year, gone out together, often to a concert or a play, sometimes just for supper somewhere. He was beginning to assimilate the fact that Joan wasn't to be found in the house. When she wasn't downstairs as he went round turning off the lights and checking the doors were locked before heading up to bed, he no longer expected to find her in the bedroom; at least most evenings he didn't. When he went downstairs after shaving and showering in the mornings he didn't expect to find her in the kitchen, wrestling with the toaster that always seemed to cause her difficulties; at least most days he didn't.

Now, when it came to going out for the evening, another void hit him. An hour or so before they were due to depart Joan would always be worrying about what she would wear. "Shall I wear my blue dress or the brown one with the leaf pattern on it?" she'd say. Skipping over the fact that he never had a very clear recollection of any of the items of clothing mentioned, he'd not known what to say. On one occasion he had expressed a preference, leading to the immediate response "Don't you like the other one?". Since then, as a matter of course, he would reply with a stock phrase, "whichever you'd feel most comfortable in, my dear". Joan clearly regarded this as unsatisfactory but the conversation would end there and about thirty minutes later she'd appear wearing her dark red dress with black triangles on it, at least very rarely, if ever, one of the dresses he'd been asked to adjudicate between. "That looks very good", he'd say, and they would head off wherever they were going.

He recognised that this interaction was ridiculous, but it had been repeated for over forty years and now it was over. Much of life is formed of such rituals. The repeated conversations of husbands and wives, of partners and friends with each other, of people at work, when each knows what the other is going to say before they've said it. Each conversation unnecessary for that reason, but nonetheless essential. These threads of warp and weft are the base of the fabric on which other things, notable events, are embroidered. Without them, what holds it all together?

Malcolm picked him up in his enormous but ancient BMW with saggy suspension at the appointed time. As expected the front passenger seat was vacant for him to sit in, with Annie sitting in the back as usual. But what to say? Previously Malcolm and he would have started talking together, leaving Annie and Joan alone in their world. He had no idea what they talked about but their conversation never seemed to flag. If they ever had quiet moments they never seemed to coincide with breaks in his discussions with Malcolm. How could a pair plus one converse when two pairs were the natural order of things? He found it hard and it was very clear to him that Malcolm and Annie did too. It was a relief when they reached the multistorey car park and attention was drawn to the practical matters of navigating the barrier and the tighter than seemed necessary turns with higher than seemed necessary curbs, squeezing the behemoth into a parking space ungenerous even for a normal-sized motor, and then trying to climb out of it without ramming the doors into adjacent walls or cars or suffering orthopaedic injury.

As soon as they arrived at the venue, the absence of another ritual became apparent. Joan always wanted a concert programme. He thought that these were ridiculously expensive, contained little useful information, and what's more, neither he nor Joan could read them in the ambient light of a concert hall or theatre unless they took a torch and their reading glasses. With a minor grumble he had always relented and bought her one. Now there was no request and no grumbling, but he found himself getting a programme because he always did. How many of these rituals were there to catch him unawares and give him unpleasant surprises like ice cream hitting a sensitive tooth? Would he ever discover them all, be fully reconciled to the fact that they would never happen again and thereby be protected from the terrible toothache? As he took his seat he didn't think that this was possible.

He had a good ear, enjoyed concerts and knew quite a lot about classical music for someone who didn't sing or play any musical instrument. But this evening his spirits were low and unresponsive, even to one of his favourites. Never before had he failed to be elevated by Vaughan Williams' "The Lark Ascending", but he remained very firmly earthbound as the violin climbed to a pitch that was almost, or perhaps actually, inaudible as the bird rose out of sight. He knew that this was utterly magical, but not this evening. Experiences seemed to have to travel through a deadening filter that made everything flat and joyless. Yes, flat and joyless was a good description.

He was conscious that he was very poor company for Malcolm and Annie that evening. He was so isolated within his own bubble that he had no idea whether or not they'd enjoyed the concert, or recollection of what they might have talked about, and as they drove home he apologised whilst thanking them for suggesting the trip and taking him. Malcolm summed things up well.

'We didn't think it would be easy,' he said in kindly manner, 'but if you'll allow a medical analogy, a patient who's had an illness that's put them in bed for a month has to start to get up. It's very difficult at first, but it does get easier, and the same will happen for you.' Intellectually he understood that this was true, but when he got into the house he sat down in the lounge without taking off his coat, or turning on the light or the fire, and cried in the darkness.

'You've been very subdued since you went out with Malcolm and his wife a few evenings ago,' Margaret observed the following Saturday when they were clearing the kitchen table after an early supper.

'Yes, I've felt that way,' her father replied, continuing to stack the dishwasher as his daughter dried off their wine glasses with a tea towel and put them back in the cupboard.

'It can't have been easy, going out for the first time without Mum,' she said.

'No, it wasn't. All part of the process of getting used to how things now are, I suppose.'

'Yes, I'm sure that's right,' Margaret went on, 'but I guess the old saying is true, you have to get back on the horse.'

Something that could almost have been described as a small smile made a fleeting appearance on her father's face. 'Malcolm said something similar,' he said before his flat affect resumed.

When rooting around in the bottom of the kitchen dresser earlier in the day Margaret had discovered a half-full bottle of pudding wine, which she'd taken a sip of and found to be fine.

'Would you like a taste of pudding wine with your coffee?' Margaret asked. 'I found an opened bottle in the dresser when I was hunting for something this afternoon.'

Her father, who wasn't in his daughter's field of vision at the time, winced as something cold hit the nerve of his delicate tooth. 'Yes, that would be nice,' he said, after a bit of a delay that she didn't notice.

They settled themselves in their usual places by the fire.

'This,' her father said as he held up his glass and looked at the yellow amber liquid clinging to its walls as he slowly swayed it from side to side, 'is one of the few things that your mother enjoyed in her last few weeks.

'The young oncologists were very good; clearly absolutely on top of the latest trials and always talking about which ones Joan might be suitable for. Perhaps we got more of this than usual because they knew who I was and thought I'd expect to be given chapter and verse, but many patients over the years have told me that they got information overload from the oncologists. I know how they felt.

'After a few months it was clear to me that the cancer wasn't responding and mention at clinic visits of second line and third line treatments, which is never a good sign, confirmed my suspicion. Your mother knew too, although she didn't say so until later. It almost seemed as though the young oncologists were the last to recognise what was happening.

'Anyway,' he continued, 'one of the older oncologists drew me aside and said he was sorry, but as he was sure I already knew, things weren't going well and it was probably time to stop thinking about treatments to cure or slow the cancer and time to think about making sure your mother was as comfortable as possible and get what enjoyment she could out of the time she had left. Does she like a glass of sherry? he asked.

'When we got home I asked your mother if she'd like

a taste of sherry with supper. No, she said, but she would like a small glass of pudding wine. So that's what we did. I made sure we always had a bottle open and we had a drink of it together every evening. Her stomach couldn't take much, but she enjoyed having a sip, and she knew that I liked having a glass with her.'

At this point his voice faltered as his eyes filled with tears. 'I just wish it could have ended like that,' he sobbed. Margaret had wanted to ask for details of her mother's death but hadn't felt able to do so, concerned that prying questions would distress her father and harbouring the terrible fear that the reply might be along the lines of, "you would know if you could have been bothered to come".

'What did happen?' she asked very quietly.

He managed to compose himself. 'It was awful,' he said. 'She'd been getting weaker and weaker over a few days, finding it very difficult to get out of bed, hardly eating at all, and I thought she was going to just slip away, but then she got terrible colicky abdominal pains – pain coming in waves that made her roll around and cry out – and started to retch and vomit, not that there was much to come up. I called for the emergency doctor and the person handling the calls said they were very busy but they'd get someone to call me back as soon as they could. After half an hour they hadn't and your mother was in such a terrible state that I called an ambulance. I hoped the doctor would be in touch before it arrived, but they weren't and we went to the hospital.

'The Emergency Department was busy, like it usually is, and she spent about twenty minutes – although it seemed like an eternity – on a trolley in a corridor before we got into a cubicle. I didn't know what to do,' he said, visibly shaking. 'Part of me wanted to prescribe analgaesia and an anti-emetic and get the first nurse I could find to give them, but of course I knew that I couldn't and shouldn't do that, although I'd done it so many times before, including,' he added with bitterness in his voice, 'for Mrs D.

'Part of me wanted to go and find whoever was the senior doctor on for the medical team and ask them to come right away,' he continued, 'but I was frightened of leaving her alone.' He paused, reliving the horror of the situation, but then found the strength to continue. 'I don't know how long it was, probably not very, but after we got moved into the cubicle one of the senior nurses came in to check on the new patient. We recognised each other, and after doing the observations she went off saying that she'd get a doctor. A couple of minutes later a young woman who I didn't know came in and introduced herself very pleasantly as a doctor working in the department. She took an efficient history and then said that she'd organise some blood tests and a CT scan to work out what was going on and put up a drip.' There was a further pause. 'I wanted a big hole to open up in the floor and swallow us both. I've spent years trying to stop people who are dying from being subjected to pointless medical tortures in their final days and moments, and here it was about to happen to my wife.'

'So did you manage to stop it?' Margaret asked.

'Thankfully the nurse had gone and found the senior working on the medical team. He'd had a look at your mother's notes before he came in, so he knew the background. We knew each other, not well but as colleagues who'd shared a few patients very comfortably over the years, and after a brief conversation he advised that no blood tests or scans were needed and that he'd prescribe medicines for comfort. I was incredibly grateful. Your mother died that night in a side room on one of the medical wards. I just wish it could have been at home. It haunts me that her last few hours were spent being bundled into an ambulance, through an Emergency Department and onto a hospital ward, things that no one wants but which happen to so many. It could have been worse. Her final experiences could have been people sticking needles and cannulas into her if I hadn't been there. It shouldn't have been the way it was, it really shouldn't.'

His voice tailed off. Words were not enough. Margaret got up, moved towards him, knelt on the floor and hugged her father. They cried silently together.

'Thank you,' she said eventually, 'for telling me.'

ELEVEN

THREE TIMES A NIGHT

Margaret wasn't sure why, but she felt comforted to have heard the story of her mother's final hours. Not that it altered anything: in whatever way it happened her mother was dead and she'd never see her again, and for some inexplicable reason she felt the fact she hadn't seen her for many years made this worse than if she'd seen her only a day or a week before. Strange thing, the mind.

Over the next few days she kept mulling over why she felt comforted. Perhaps it was the thought that it would be wrong for anyone else, except her father, to know more of the detail; that knowing the detail somehow made her closer to her mother. But as well as being comforted she was also disturbed. As her father had said, it didn't seem right that her mother's final hours were spent the way they were. However good and careful the ambulance men were, it must have been agony, and the thought that – had her father not been present – her mother's final experience in life might have been someone stabbing for a vein was truly horrible. Did other people die like this? She didn't know why, but that thought troubled her a lot and kept returning to her mind.

It was a few evenings later that Margaret and her father were again in the lounge by the fire after supper.

'I was going to tell you about my encounter with the Medical Regulator,' he said. Margaret was pleased and nodded.

'Yes, thanks, I'd like to hear about that.'

'As Samantha – my representative from the medical defence union – had told me they would, they waited for the court case to be finished before they did anything, but then they wrote explaining that they'd received a complaint about me and were gathering information.'

'Gathering information? What did that mean?' Margaret asked.

'Well, I didn't know either. It was one of their awful standard letters that I think they must get Daleks to write. You remember them from *Doctor Who*?' Margaret nodded and he went on, 'Containing sentences that ought to be read in a harsh unmodulated metallic machine voice: "We recognise that this may be very stressful for you". That sort of thing.

'Anyway, Samantha explained that they would be writing to the medical directors of any hospitals I worked at or had worked at in the past to see if they had any concerns about me. Had I been involved in any other complaints? Had I been involved in any serious incidents? If so, how had I dealt with them? What they were trying to find out, she told me, was if I had a track record.'

'And had you?' Margaret asked a bit nervously.

'No, and when I eventually saw how the medical director had responded I thought he was fair. Strictly factual. He said I'd been named in a couple of complaints to the hospital in the previous ten years, but not of a serious nature; that I'd assisted the hospital in responding to them in a timely way; and that they'd been satisfactorily resolved.'

'So did you know exactly what the complaint about you was?' Margaret wondered.

'No, not from their initial letter. A month or so later they wrote again telling me that their case examiner had decided to refer the matter to a hearing and that further details would follow. The Dalek was still dictating their letters. I remember the machine voice giving me a helpline number if I wanted to call and speak to someone, which was the last thing in the world I felt like doing. Talk to some person I didn't know who was paid to say soothing words!' he said in an incredulous voice.

'I imagine you wanted the thing dealt with as quickly as possible,' Margaret suggested.

'What I really wanted was them to say that the whole thing was bloody madness, a terrible mistake, and they weren't going to do anything, but even I wasn't naïve enough to think that likely.

'Samantha was very good. She wrote to them on my behalf asking for clear details of the allegations made, details of the formal process involved, and a timeline for how things were going to be dealt with. They may have sent me this information anyway, but even if her letter had no effect it was good to feel that there was someone on my side. It's a very lonely place being a doctor referred to the Medical Regulator.

'Anyway, when they eventually did write to spell out the concerns, they were much the same as those in the court case.'

Margaret said she found this a bit surprising. 'Wasn't this, what's the proper term, double jeopardy?' she said.

'It certainly felt like that to me, but as Malcolm explained over a glass of whisky and Samantha confirmed, without the assistance of whisky, the court case was about the hospital having to explain and justify its policies and procedures and what happened, unless it wanted to admit fault. I wasn't on trial for any offence although at times it felt like it. The referral to the Medical Regulator was another way for the family to make the points they wanted to make by pursuing me personally.'

In the papers that Margaret had read she'd seen the bald details. The family's case, clearly augmented following her father's appearance as a witness in court, was that his fitness to practise was impaired for several reasons. He made a decision that resuscitation would be futile without seeking a second opinion. His comments about quality of life betrayed an inappropriately judgemental attitude to patients with disabilities. He failed to make proper medical records. His comments about the inadequacy of the advanced care planning form indicated an arrogant disregard of patients' wishes.

'I've seen the list of things they complained about in the papers from Mum's wardrobe,' Margaret said, 'but there wasn't anything about what went on.'

'Do you know how they run their hearings?' her father asked.

'No,' Margaret replied.

'Well, it's a similar arrangement to a criminal court. In essence, the Medical Regulator is the prosecutor, arguing that the doctor's fitness to practise is impaired, and the doctor with their legal support is arguing that it isn't. The court can ask the opinions of expert witnesses to help them make their decisions.'

'That seems pretty reasonable,' Margaret observed after a pause. 'So what happened?'

'Well, in truth, nothing very remarkable in the hearing itself, at least it didn't seem that way to anyone there, but then the balloon went up and there was absolute pandemonium. Complete madness! Took everyone by surprise!'

'Why?' Margaret asked.

'The hearing repeated the arguments heard in the court case, but with the difference that the experts also had their say.'

'Experts. How many experts?'

'Two. A woman who was a professor of medical ethics and a man who was, I'm not sure, perhaps an assistant or deputy medical director in a big hospital. He can't have been the medical director because he seemed to do a lot of what would be called general medicine, at least he spoke as if he did. The sort of stuff I did. The sort of job where you see patients like Mrs D in Emergency Departments. I was pleasantly surprised that they'd got someone who seemed to know what the business was like, who talked as if he'd been there and done it.'

'Don't they always get people who can give good opinions?' Margaret queried, surprised that it seemed necessary to ask.

'I'm afraid the short answer is no,' her father replied with a sigh. 'I think they probably try to, but most doctors who are good at being doctors are very busy doing just that. They don't have the time or inclination to spend hours and hours reviewing patients' notes and writing detailed commentaries on them or attending courts. Of course there are exceptions, but doctors who make a career out of giving medicolegal opinions often don't do much clinical practice themselves, or they're so super-specialist that they've forgotten what's possible in an ordinary hospital, that's if they ever knew. When you read what they write you're left thinking, "Really? That might be possible if given the luxury of limitless time and resources and nothing else to do, but do you think it's reasonable to expect that in the world I or any other normal doctor lives in?".'

Margaret followed on with the obvious next question. 'So what were these experts like?'

'Very different from each other,' her father replied. 'I'd never met a professor of medical ethics before or thought about what such a person would be like – but having seen and heard her I won't forget!'

'She obviously made an impression on you, then,' Margaret observed with a smile.

'She certainly did. She was a young woman,' he began, leading Margaret to smile even more. 'I know, I know,' her father said hurriedly, 'when the police officers start to look younger and all that. Anyway,' he continued, 'she had round features, hair cut in a bob, very angular spectacles, bright red lipstick, and seemed to be extremely anxious when she spoke. At first I thought this was because she was nervous but it persisted as she talked about the advanced care planning form and answered questions, and I noticed she had rather staring eyes and a fine tremor. If she'd been a patient of mine I'd have been checking her thyroid function tests. It turned out that she was one of the members of the committee that produced the advanced care planning form, and what she said confirmed my suspicions.'

'What were you suspicious of?' Margaret asked.

'That it hadn't been developed with input from doctors who were going to have to use it in Emergency Departments where patients like Mrs D were going to pitch up and decisions were going to have to be made. At least, if such doctors had been asked for their opinions, their views had been drowned out by those of lots of others who might have been very knowledgeable about ethical theory but had absolutely zero insight into the practicalities.'

He was clearly on a roll and Margaret didn't comment. In reality, it would have been difficult for her to get a word in edgeways. 'She started by stressing that the form had been developed after consultation with dozens of interested parties, including patient advocates, which she repeated several times, and public consultation. She went on for so long about this that when she started to list organisations who'd been involved, the chair of the panel asked her to summarise the point and move on. She looked rather crestfallen when told to do this but went on to say that the intention of the form was to allow the patient to express their wishes. What did they most value? What were they most afraid of? What were their healthcare priorities? I've no problem at all about any of this, in fact I think it's a good idea, but it just doesn't work in the context of patients arriving in hospital who are confused or demented or too sick to think and talk about anything.'

He paused, leading Margaret to interject. 'You'd better explain that to me.'

'If I asked you now about what treatments you'd want to have if you became unwell I'm sure you could tell me. I think it's unlikely you'd refuse point blank to consider any treatment I might suggest, although I'm pretty sure you'd want to discuss the pros and cons of different options before deciding which to have.

'If I asked you to imagine that you had a stroke, or something else that incapacitated you, and what treatments you'd want to have then, the conversation would be more difficult. You'd find it harder to know what you wanted. Although having a stroke sounds and is very alarming, the effect can vary from fairly minor, a bit of weakness of one side of the face and an arm that lasts for a few days before recovering completely, to absolutely devastating, leaving a patient unable to understand or to speak, with no movement at all of one arm and one leg, no vision to one side of the body, incontinent of bladder and bowels, unable to eat or drink, unable to move in bed, totally dependent, truly awful. We could work through scenarios like this and get a picture of what sorts of treatments you'd want – or not want – to have in different circumstances, including things like breathing machines on Intensive Care Units and resuscitation attempts if your heart stopped. We could document this on the form and use it to guide what treatments you did or didn't get given if you had the misfortune to become very ill in the future.'

'So what happens if a patient just pitches up in the hospital with a very big stroke and they haven't filled in one of these forms in advance and got it recorded in their notes?' Margaret asked.

'That's exactly the problem!' her father replied exasperatedly. 'And they just can't see it.'

'I can't believe that they haven't thought of it,' Margaret replied.

'Well, no, it isn't that they haven't thought of it, it's just they haven't come up with an answer that works well in practice.'

'Go on,' Margaret encouraged.

'They say you should speak to the relatives. Sometimes the patient will have given them formal legal power to make decisions on their behalf, and it's very helpful when they have, assuming of course that you can speak to them. If the patient hasn't done this, and most patients haven't, then it says you need to ask the relatives if the patient has ever expressed views about what their priorities would be if they got very ill, for instance if they had a big stroke.'

'I can see that these might be very difficult conversations to have,' Margaret said thoughtfully, 'so do you think it would be better if you didn't have to speak to the relatives?'

'No, I don't think that. It's true they're often difficult conversations, but sometimes patients have talked these things over with their families. They can tell you what their views would be and that's important; after all, it's the patient we're treating! But most people haven't. And even if they have the relatives often aren't there or can't be contacted at the time a decision needs to be made, as with Mrs D.'

'So what happens then?' Margaret asked.

'If a decision isn't made not to resuscitate, then the default – quite rightly – is that everyone races into action if the patient deteriorates, and if resuscitation is successful the patient lands up on the Intensive Care Unit an hour or so later, with no hope of anything other than a protracted death, and many doctors and nurses lamenting "why did we let this happen again?".'

Margaret followed on, 'So what does the form say you should do if you can't talk to the patient or to the relatives?'

'It doesn't,' her father replied.

'Doesn't?' Margaret asked incredulously.

'That's right. It doesn't.'

'So did that point get made during the hearing?' Margaret asked.

'Yes, it did.'

'And was the medical ethics woman pushed on the point?'

Now it was her father's turn to smile. 'Yes, she was,' he said, 'and the most the chair of the panel could get from her was that this was a very difficult situation. I felt like shouting out that she could come down to my Emergency Department and experience this very difficult situation about three times a night if she wanted to, but you'll be relieved to know that I didn't!'

TWELVE

YOU KNOW IT WHEN YOU SEE IT

'What about the other expert witness, the medical director man? You seemed to have liked him from what you said earlier,' Margaret asked.

'Yes, I did,' her father replied. 'He surprised me.'

'Why?'

'Well, I was feeling very got at,' her father went on, 'which I suspect every doctor referred to a hearing by the Medical Regulator does, and so I assumed that everyone there apart from Samantha and my legal representative would be against me. You know the saying, "just because you're paranoid doesn't mean they're not out to get you". But as Samantha explained to me, the duty of the expert witnesses was to give the panel their expert opinions, not to take one side or the other.'

'So what did he say about the advanced care planning form?'

'Some very reasonable things,' her father replied, 'in a very reasonable manner. He was able to do something I've never been able to manage. Rather than getting irate if someone said something absurd, he could quietly but firmly explain why he had a different view.' And then after a pause he added reflectively, 'If I'd had that skill I may not have got into some of the troubles that I did.'

'And about the form?'

'He said that working through the form was a very useful way of helping determine some patients' wishes and preferences for care in circumstances where you could have a conversation with them to work through the issues. But he said that it was often difficult or impossible to do this properly in the context of hospital Emergency Departments. The many people who were confused or demented didn't have capacity to make complex decisions, and he said he doubted that anyone who was severely unwell, for instance in a lot of pain or struggling with their breathing, could give careful consideration to details about what sort of medical interventions they might or might not want to have in various scenarios, and I particularly warmed to him when he said that conversations about this could make patients even more anxious and frightened than they already were, however well-meaning and careful the doctor was in managing the conversation.'

'I can see why you approved of him!' Margaret said.

'Yes, and he made some other obvious points, including that in his view it wouldn't be wise to require that resuscitation be attempted for every patient who didn't have it documented that this shouldn't be done on an advanced care plan form, simply because there may be circumstances in which it wasn't possible to complete one. For instance, the Emergency Department many have run out of forms, or a patient's electronic medical record may be temporarily inaccessible.'

'So what did the panel decide about you making proper medical records?' Margaret asked.

'They spent a long time saying that they thought the principles underlying the advanced care planning form were good and noting that many authoritative medical bodies encouraged its use, but they acknowledged the expert opinion that this wasn't straightforward in some circumstances and suggested that the relevant medical bodies may wish to consider this. They also accepted the point that in some instances it may be impossible for the form to be completed and that in such cases it was not reasonable to say that resuscitation should always be provided. The doctor, they said, should make clear in the patient's notes the discussions that they had had, the decisions they'd made, and the reasons for them.'

'So they agreed with what you'd done for Mrs D?' Margaret said with some enthusiasm.

'Yes, insofar as they didn't say that my fitness to practise was impaired by virtue of the fact that I hadn't filled the form in, but they did say that whilst my comments in court about the inadequacy of the form, which was widely accepted by medical authorities, did not necessarily mean that I had – to use the family's words – an "arrogant disregard of patients' wishes", they could understand why the family were concerned about my motivation.'

There was a pause in the flow, so Margaret enquired, 'Did they say anything further about that?'

'Yes, they said I should reflect on it at my next appraisal.'

Margaret was mystified. 'And what did you make of that?'

'At the time I thought they were simply pandering to the family to cover their own backsides and was cross that they couldn't just say the concern was dismissed. But thinking about it later, after talking to Samantha and Malcolm, it now seems a reasonable thing for them to have said.'

Margaret was intrigued. 'What did Samantha and Malcolm say to you?'

'Samantha said the Medical Regulator was very keen on doctors reflecting on complaints and showing insight. Malcolm was more down to earth. He said that if you've said something that's led to trouble, it's not a bad idea to think it over and decide whether you'd say things differently next time around in similar circumstances, even if you thought you were right.'

'Sounds like Malcolm's a sensible man!' Margaret observed, thinking this was the sort of thing that her boss, Peter, might have said but also mystified about how pandemonium could have been caused by what she'd heard. 'But I can't see how this would have caused a lot of fuss.'

'No,' her father replied, 'it didn't. It was what was said about futility that set the hounds loose.'

'How come?'

'Well, I didn't see it coming and I'm sure no one else in the hearing did. The Medical Regulator certainly didn't. As I've said before, their number one priority is to make sure their backs are covered, and if anyone's to blame for anything it's certainly not them.'

'So what happened?'

Margaret's father could see he had an attentive audience and settled back in his chair. 'There was much the same toing and froing as there had been in court about the fact that a doctor is not expected to provide futile treatments and cannot be required to do so by a patient or their family, and that it's for the doctor to decide if a treatment would be futile, not the patient or their relatives.

'There was then a lot of discussion about how decisions should be made in difficult circumstances, either when the doctor wasn't sure what to do or when their view was different from that of the patient or their family.

'Everyone agreed that good communication between doctors, patients and families was essential, but then saying anything else would be like arguing against motherhood and apple pie. All were in favour of trying to negotiate care plans that could be agreed by all parties, but then no one in their right mind could object to that. All agreed that getting a second opinion was a proper and helpful thing to do whenever possible.'

Margaret couldn't see where this was going: 'It sounds as though everyone was agreeing about everything,' she said.

'I'm sure they would have if the arguments had stopped there, but the family's lawyer didn't,' her father went on. 'They kept pressing their point about making the decision about futility. They wanted to know, could such a big decision, denying a patient the possibility of life-saving treatment, be made by a single doctor acting alone?'

'What did the expert witnesses have to say about that?' Margaret wondered.

'Not much from the medical ethics woman, although,' he said with a laugh, 'she spent quite a lot of time doing so. She confirmed that the decision about whether a treatment was futile was a medical one and began to go through the issues to be considered in making the judgement, but after she'd been going on about this for what seemed a very long time, the chair of the panel reminded her of the question, which was whether the decision could be made by a single doctor acting alone.'

'And what did she say?'

'She said that when there were difficult ethical decisions to be made it was always a good idea to obtain views from a range of informed parties and try to achieve a consensus.'

Margaret smiled again. 'I'll bet that impressed you!' she said.

'Absolutely!' her father replied. 'But you'll be pleased to know that I managed to restrain myself from saying what I thought.'

Margaret continued, 'And what did the other expert say?'

'His name was David; David Old,' her father replied, 'and he said some very good things. Things I thought were right, and he said them in a much clearer way than I could have done. He said it could be difficult to make decisions about futility because of the danger of self-fulfilling prophecies, meaning that if you decided not to actively treat someone who was extremely ill then it was almost 100 per cent certain that they'd die, how soon depending on the nature of illness they had, but there'd never been a systematic trial that randomised patients who doctors thought should be kept comfortable and allowed to die to receive active treatment and see what happened to them. However, he went on, in any situation where a doctor was considering the possibility that treating a patient would be futile, the thought in their mind should be, "would the only effect of pursuing treatment be to prolong the process of dying, possibly causing distress to the patient along the way?".'

'But what did he say about a single doctor acting alone making the decision?' Margaret asked, wondering if the chair of the panel had had to intervene to get him to address the point.

'He said that they often had to in circumstances like those when Mrs D arrived in the Emergency Department, the alternative being that inappropriate futile treatments would be given to many dying patients.'

'I can see why you approved of him!' Margaret said excitedly. 'But I'll bet the lawyer acting for the family didn't.'

'Indeed not.'

'Were they allowed to cross examine him?' Margaret asked.

'Yes, and he dealt with their questions very well, or at least I thought he did. The lawyer kept trying to press him on how a doctor could be certain that a patient would die, so that they would know that attempts to resuscitate and treat actively would be futile. "Was there anything that could be measured that would indicate this? Perhaps the patient's blood pressure? Or the level of oxygen in their blood? Or something else?"

'No, he said, there's no single thing that tells a doctor that a patient is dying. Yes, if their blood pressure is very low it indicates they're very ill and may die, but some patients with very low blood pressure can be resuscitated and restored to good health. Yes, if the level of oxygen in a patient's blood is very low it means they're very ill and may perish, but some patients with very low oxygen levels can be resuscitated and made better.

'Of course the lawyer was more than capable of pursuing their questions, after all that's their business, but I could see that he was finding it difficult which cheered me up. He continued in his measured and rather ponderous tone, but I could see him becoming a bit red around the collar and starting to sweat a little.'

'So did Dr Old say how a doctor knows that a patient is dying?' Margaret was interested to know the answer.

'Yes, eventually, after responding to lots of leading questions, he said that it involved assessing many things in combination. Knowledge of a patient's medical background and condition was important because it gave an indication of how well they might be able to fight an acute potentially terminal illness. A person who had a chronically bad chest, for instance, would not be as able to cope with a pneumonia as well as someone who had a good chest to start off with.

'It was important to know how a patient's health had been changing over the weeks and months before any acute potentially terminal illness. Someone who had been getting weaker and frailer over this period, perhaps with several recent hospital admissions because they were failing to be able to manage at home, even with care, was not going to have as much strength to deal with an acute illness as someone who was stronger and fitter.

'And it was important to look carefully at the patient with the correct question in mind. "Do they look as though they're dying?" Of course the lawyer didn't understand this and asked him what he meant.'

'And what did he mean?' Margaret asked.

'He didn't quote my favourite phrase when trying to teach medical students and young doctors how to recognise a patient who is dying, "if you're looking for it, you know it when you see it", which I'm sure the lawyer wouldn't have liked. He tried to explain what dying patients typically look like. Grey, listless, exhausted; not responding when spoken to or having things done to them; unable to talk or uninterested in talking, perhaps mumbling, perhaps not able to say anything at all; finding it hard to breathe, or making little effort to breathe; having breathing that oscillates between heavy and quiet; having breathing that makes bubbling sounds which the patient can't get rid of; having cool hands and a pulse that's difficult to feel; having a low blood pressure. He said these were things that doctors who worked with very ill patients got to recognise.'

'And was the lawyer happy with that?' Margaret queried.

'I'm not sure that lawyers in court are ever happy,' her father replied, 'but no, he had more questions. "How could a doctor be sure that a patient in the condition described would inevitably die? Had a trial ever been done where patients that the doctor thought should be allowed to die were treated?" No, Dr Old confirmed, he wasn't aware of any trial that had randomised patients who doctors thought were dying into palliative care versus resuscitation and active treatment. "Given the magnitude of the decision to deny active treatment, did Dr Old think it was reasonable for it to be made by a single doctor without benefit of a second opinion?" Yes, he said, if the doctor was certain, beyond reasonable doubt, that a patient was dying and that attempts to resuscitate and treat would be futile, then he thought it was good medical practice for them to make the decision to palliate and make sure the patient was as comfortable as possible whilst they died. He also added that it would have enormous consequences if it was decided that this was not acceptable: many patients would have protracted deaths; some hospital services would be overwhelmed.'

Margaret could see that this exchange was going to put those hearing the case in a difficult position.

'I imagine that this was very tricky for the panel,' she observed.

'Absolutely!' her father replied, and it was very clear that he'd enjoyed seeing them struggle, which she thought was understandable given his position at the time. 'After listening to the arguments they adjourned to consider them. We were told that we could leave and would be contacted – they had our mobile numbers – when we needed to return.'

THIRTEEN

HELPING WITH ENQUIRIES

'I remember going out to get a breath of air with Samantha and the lawyer from the medical defence organisation who had represented me, a rather rotund man called Roger who I'd only met for an hour the day before the hearing but who I liked and trusted. He told me that he was going to press me with difficult questions, not because he was unpleasant or didn't believe me, but to get a sense of how I was likely to perform as a witness. I thought this was a sensible thing for him to do. There was a park about half a mile from the regulator's building and we went to take a stroll around it. There was a bit of a breeze, certainly not a gale, but when we were about halfway round Samantha stopped talking and I thought she looked rather pale and unwell. I asked her if she was OK and she said that she wasn't. She felt very cold, so we headed for a coffee shop we'd walked past on our way to the park. It was only when we were inside and had got her a hot chocolate that I realised that she was a very thin woman, probably anorexic or ex-anorexic, if you can ever be ex-that awful disease, wearing a thin jacket and a pair of shoes that weren't designed for walking, at least not outside. Roger in his Barbour and me in my quilted jacket sat there, both wearing stoutish shoes and feeling awful that we'd dragged her out into the elements, even though the elements really weren't that bad.

'Samantha's phone sounded to say that she'd received a text. It was the clerk to the hearing saying that the panel were continuing deliberations and we were to return in an hour's time.

'After about forty-five minutes in the warmth Samantha looked a better colour, felt her normal self and was very apologetic, although we explained that she hadn't got anything to apologise for and that it was we who should apologise for dragging her outside when she wasn't wearing suitable clothing. She declined my quilted jacket or Roger's Barbour for the few hundred yards back to the regulator's building but thankfully didn't get too cold again before we went up the worn stone steps, although they were greasy with recent rain and she slipped on them and nearly fell.

'Shortly thereafter we were ushered back into the room being used for the hearing and it was only then that I realised how mundane and shabby it was. A very ordinary sort of committee room containing run-of-the-mill office furniture. Tables with cheap wooden tops and tubular steel legs arranged around a rectangle; similarly legged chairs with padded seats and backrests in need of refurbishment, with a few extra tables and chairs stacked along one wall to be called into duty on other occasions. Noisy plumbing, with the radiators clanking occasionally like a noisy baby unaware of the significance of what was going on.

'I'm sure it says more about me than anything else, but it didn't seem right for weighty decisions about doctors' careers to be made in such a place. I feel the same about churches. I can't believe that God pays much notice to people sitting on plastic chairs to pray. Gravitas and solemnity are required. Oak pews. A panelled room with the panel sitting elevated to make their pronouncements.'

Margaret was beginning to wonder when her father would get to the point and just about to remind him, when eventually he did.

'Anyway, the chair of the panel said that they had heard the arguments about futility and how decisions about futility should be made and found them very difficult. They accepted that doctors could not be expected to provide treatments that were futile, and it would be a bad thing if they did so. They accepted that determining whether a treatment would or would not be futile was a medical decision, not for the patient or their family to decide. But, he went on, the panel understood and had sympathy with two of the arguments made on behalf of Mrs D's family. Firstly, that it was placing an enormous burden on an individual doctor to ask or expect them to make the decision – on their own – about whether treating a particular patient at a particular time would be futile. However, they said they were mindful of circumstances such as those when Mrs D arrived in the Emergency Department, which they recognised as not being uncommon, when in practical terms it would be very difficult and sometimes impossible to obtain a second opinion from another independent medical practitioner. They said that they had looked for guidance in publications of relevant professional bodies and not been able to find anything of practical relevance. Secondly, that making judgements about a patient's quality of life was exceedingly difficult if they lacked capacity. The panel noted discussion about quality of life in the court papers and the opinion expressed by Dr Old that it was proper, in his view which he said reflected standard practice, for doctors to be influenced in their care decisions by whether or not a patient had dementia, and the degree of that dementia, but also the arguments made on behalf of Mrs D's family that doing so constituted discrimination on the grounds of disability.'

'I can see that it would have been tricky for the panel to have come to any conclusion,' Margaret observed.

'Indeed,' her father replied.

'So what did they do?'

'They gave, as Samantha explained to me that they would, their key decisions, with their full determination and reasoning to follow in writing within ten working days. As regards me, they said that they didn't find fault with my conduct or clinical practice and so were closing this element of the case with no further action, which – as I'm sure you can imagine – was an almighty relief! Then they said something that I thought was a bland but reasonable cop-out, and I think – or at least I thought at the time – everyone else in the room did too. They said that they were going to recommend to the regulator that they consider convening a working party or working parties to produce practical guidance for doctors and patients on the determination of futility and relating to broader issues raised by the arguments the panel had heard touching on quality of life, dementia and disability discrimination.'

'I can't see anything very controversial in that,' Margaret said. 'I'd have thought it was pretty standard for a panel to make that sort of recommendation if they heard arguments they couldn't resolve about something they thought was important.'

'Indeed,' her father said again, leading Margaret to remember it was a word he used more often than anyone else she knew and that this had been a particular source of irritation to her as a teenager. She also recalled with some mortification that she used to mimic his use of it to annoy her mother when they argued, and she could feel her cheeks flushing. Her father thankfully didn't notice this and went on, 'Samantha and Roger certainly didn't see trouble coming. We shared a taxi to the station. They both thought that things had gone as well as we could have hoped for. There was a bit of chat about what everyone had planned for the weekend and we agreed that we'd fix a time to meet when the panel had produced its written judgement.'

'So what happened?' Margaret asked.

'The first I knew about anything was when I got a text from Samantha on the Saturday morning asking if I'd seen what was on some of the online news feeds, which of course I hadn't. I didn't know what she was talking about, but she sent me a link to click on. "Doctors' death squad" was the headline!'

'Crikey!'

'I thought the same, or something like that,' her father replied, his voice tailing off before he became silent.

Margaret could see that painful memories were being disturbed and waited before saying anything, but then went on quietly, 'That can't have happened by accident; someone must have planned it.'

'Yes, it took a few days for details to emerge, but it turned out that one of Mrs D's sons was a journalist with a track record of investigating medical matters and writing exposés, the more sensational the better, and he certainly proved he knew how to spin a story and how to get it out.

'It was an education for me. Not an education I had gone looking for or wanted, but it was amazing how within not much more than twenty-four hours it got picked up by all the news outlets – radio, TV, newspapers, and I'm sure even more on websites I never looked at. Looking back, it was very clever how things were done, how something as reasonable and bland as the suggestion of a working party to produce practical guidance for doctors and patients on the determination of futility, which really doesn't sound like something that would make primetime TV news, could be turned into a doctors' death squad. And I'd never have thought the idea that a group should be convened to consider the issues around the appropriateness of medical interventions in patients with dementia could lead to articles suggesting that if you went to your doctor with a problem you might have to take some sort of intelligence test before they decided whether they'd investigate or treat you.'

He paused a while before looking Margaret in the eye and saying, 'We were a bit surprised you didn't get in touch when it happened.'

Margaret felt hollow with a mixture of embarrassment and guilt, mainly guilt. In truth, she hadn't known about it, certainly not that her father had been involved, so it wasn't as if she had been aware that he was having a very hard time and actively chosen not to get in touch. Not that she could have done anything useful beyond offering the animal comfort of being present, if not physically then in spirit. At the time of the hearing, which she knew from the papers she'd found in the wardrobe, she had been out of the country.

'I'm sorry,' she said. 'I didn't know. I was working abroad in Dubai at the time of the hearing and not following the UK news closely. I think I can remember seeing something about it, but I'm honestly not sure if I've imagined this, and if I did I never went past the headlines and didn't know that you were involved.'

Thinking rationally she realised that this was a perfectly satisfactory explanation for her failure to get in touch to offer the support that comes from huddling together as creatures do when it's very cold. A penguin isolated from its colony often perishes in the Antarctic blizzard. People suffering hardship in isolation cope less well than those who are psychologically supported, even if that support is articulated very clumsily or not articulated at all and comes from nothing more than knowing you are not alone, that there is some emotional warmth close to you. A candle in the dark doesn't alter the temperature significantly but makes you feel warmer. This is what families are for, Margaret thought, recognising again how she'd drifted apart from her parents and now lost her mother, who she'd never be able to get close to.

Margaret and her father were both silent with their thoughts. It was getting late, well past the time when they usually turned in for the night, but neither showed any sign of wanting to end the conversation. Margaret was the first to speak.

'I'm sorry,' she said, 'I wish I'd known, but I was so wrapped up in what I was doing, a twelve-month contract in a part of the world I'd never been to before, that I never thought about anything going on in the UK and only checked the news to make sure that there wasn't a war or something like that.' And after a further pause, 'How did things play out?' she asked.

'Very quickly to start off with, but when the dust had settled from the initial flurry there were long-term consequences, or things I'm pretty sure were consequences.'

'Consequences for you?' Margaret asked.

'Yes, other things might not have happened were it not for the court case and the regulator's hearing and the media storm.'

'Did the media target you personally?' Margaret wondered.

'Thankfully not. I wasn't their main target. Mrs D's son had done previous pieces criticising the Medical Regulator, saying they were dysfunctional and not fit for purpose, and he had lots of people lined up who were keen to say that they couldn't be trusted to deal with organising a working party on futility, or a doctors' death squad as he called it. He found out that the chair of the hearing had a minor commercial interest in some palliative care homes and so he went to town on that, implying that the reason the panel recommended that work be done on futility and treatment of patients with dementia was to drum up business. He also had a go at Dr Old who he kept describing as a medical manager, implying that the reason he'd expressed some of the opinions he did was because he wanted to cut costs in the hospital. The fact that Dr Old hadn't said anything of the sort didn't seem to matter.'

Margaret pursued her point. 'And what did they say about you?' she asked again.

'As I said, thankfully not a great deal. Not a good look, Malcolm told me, if they were to attack a poor doctor working hard in difficult circumstances.'

'What happened when you got back to the hospital?' Margaret continued.

'Interesting,' her father began. 'I discovered people that I didn't know existed! First thing on the Monday morning a woman from the press office contacted me. To tell the truth I didn't know that we had one of those and

I certainly didn't know who she was. Anyway, I obviously wasn't making much sense to her over the phone and she very promptly asked me where my office was and appeared about five minutes later. She asked if I knew that reports of the hearing were in the media and I explained that Samantha had told me over the weekend. She asked if anyone else had contacted me to ask for comment and I said that no one had. She advised me that, if anyone did, it would be best for me not to say anything but to direct them to the press office who would release a prepared statement, which I was very happy to agree to.'

'Did anyone else check in with you?' Margaret wondered, thinking her father must have felt very much at sea.

'No, except Malcolm, of course. He appeared as he always did. He was very funny when I told him about the woman from the press office and the prepared statement: "we can confirm that one of our employees has been helping the Medical Regulator with their enquiries" he suggested.'

It was now past midnight and Margaret's father was unable to suppress a yawn. She took the hint: 'Time to turn in,' she said. 'Thanks for telling me; it means a lot to know what's happened.'

'Yes,' he replied, 'it's good to be able to share things, after all…' but then he lost his train of thought or decided against saying what he was about to. 'Time for bed,' he concluded.

FOURTEEN

THE OPPORTUNITY
NEVER AROSE

It was a few evenings later that a chance next arose for further conversation. It had been another miserable grey and drizzly day in which time dragged for them both. Margaret had planned to meet up with a friend for a walk in the afternoon, but they'd rung up an hour or so before saying that they were unwell with a sore throat and a temperature. She was a signed-up member of the "there's no such thing as bad weather, only inappropriate clothes" school of thought, but knew her friend wasn't and mindful of their track record she couldn't suppress the ungenerous thought that this might in truth reflect fear of acquiring a virus rather than actually suffering the effects of one. However, after feeling sulky for an hour or so the upshot was that she and her father found themselves in the lounge after an early supper.

Margaret, once more following her friend Ann's

advice, broached the subject directly: 'You were going to tell me about the disciplinary panel in the hospital. How did that start?'

'Very simply. I was called into the medical director's office and told that there'd been complaints about me from several doctors in the Emergency Department, and from some nurses and operations' managers. He said there was going to be a formal investigation of them.'

'Just like that!' Margaret asked, very surprised.

'Pretty well,' her father replied. 'He was with a woman from the medical staffing department who I'd never talked to before, although I had seen her on the rare occasions I went there. She said I was allowed to carry on working whilst the investigation was going on as long as I didn't interfere with it, or something like that. In all honesty I was so shocked that I'm not sure what they did say, but I do remember the woman saying that I should get some professional advice to support me through the process. Of course I'd heard this before from the medicolegal woman. In fact, whenever I hear the word process I now automatically associate it with a need for professional advice.'

He went quiet for a moment before going on, his voice slightly breaking, 'I made a joke about it to your mother the Christmas before last after I asked her if there was anything she wanted me to get her and she told me that her food processor had broken.'

After a short silence, Margaret prompted him to continue: 'And what did you do then, after they'd told you there was going to be an investigation?'

'I suppose I went back to my office. I didn't know what to think. I felt completely hollow, completely numb. I still do when I think about it, although I think about it less than I used to. I don't know what I did. I can't remember seeing anybody. I must have gone home.'

'So what did happen?'

'As usual the only person who talked to me about things was Malcolm,' her father continued. 'I remember saying to him that he'd get himself a bad name if he kept fraternising with suspected criminals.'

'And what did he say to that?'

'He laughed it off, saying the Devil has all the best tunes, but I don't know what I'd have done if it hadn't been for him and your mother. In many ways being investigated in my own hospital was worse than the court case or the hearing with the Medical Regulator. I could rationalise those as being driven by distressed relatives, but this was criticism from people in a place I'd worked for many years, where many people knew me.'

'Apart from Malcolm, wasn't there any reaction from any of your other colleagues?' Margaret wondered.

'It was a very odd time. The letter I got from the medical director – although I'm sure it was written by the woman from medical staffing and he just signed it – said that, apart from giving my account to the investigator, I shouldn't talk about things with anyone. There wasn't any sort of official announcement.

'I found myself walking down corridors, looking at people and thinking, "Do they know?". Or if someone walked past me without making eye contact, perhaps because they were looking at their phone or simply daydreaming, I'd think "They know about this and they're blanking me". I suppose I should have recognised it at the time, but it was only later that I realised that very few people in the hospital knew anything about what was going on. It's difficult to keep a proper perspective when you're caught up in things and I struggled.'

Margaret could imagine how distressing it would have been for a professionally very assured and confident man like her father, perhaps too assured and too confident, to learn such a thing about himself, which he confirmed as he went on.

'I'd always regarded myself as a steady judge of things and I think other people did too, at least I'd get asked my opinion about difficult cases, so it was very disturbing to feel out of control and unsure what was going on. I had an attack of labyrinthitis once, thankfully not a very bad one, but for about forty-eight hours it was difficult to stand up and walk because something I'd always taken for granted had gone. It took a couple of weeks before my balance was completely back to normal. The hospital investigation and disciplinary hearing were a bit like that, but instead of physical balance it was my emotional balance that was affected, and it went on much longer. In fact, I'm sure it hasn't returned completely to normal even now.'

'Were things triggered by the court case and the hearing with the Medical Regulator?' Margaret speculated.

'I can't imagine that they helped, but the hospital denied it. Whether any of the people who complained about me were aware of them and thought there was a possibility of getting at me when I was down, I don't know,' her father replied. 'I thought about this a lot at the time, but I really don't know.'

Margaret had recently re-read the bundle of papers about the investigation in the hospital. After a letter confirming that there was to be an investigation of Dr Barber's conduct were its terms of reference. She recognised that these must have been crafted with the assistance of the hospital's lawyer if not actually written by them. "Behaviour that was inappropriate, rude and offensive. Giving rise to dysfunctionality. Impacting negatively on individuals. Undermining effective collaborative working. Preventing or inhibiting colleagues from being able to work together in a manner that ensures an efficient and safe service to the hospital's patients. Damaging to the hospital's reputation."

'The MD had clearly been planning things for a while when he spoke with you,' Margaret observed. 'Had he ever talked to you before?'

'No, he hadn't,' her father replied to Margaret's surprise. 'The divisional director woman had spoken with me after the MDT escapade to say that I should be more careful when expressing opinions about nursing and other colleagues, but there hadn't been any other conversations.'

'I don't think that was very good HR practice,' Margaret said.

'Indeed. I assumed that I needed Samantha's help again and got in touch with her. She was, as always, very pleasant but told me the medical defence union didn't deal with disciplinary matters within hospitals and asked if I was a member of a medical trade union. I was – not that I'd previously thought of them in that way. I'd joined when I qualified because members got sent a weekly medical journal. Anyway, following Samantha's directions I phoned them up and in no time at all was speaking with a woman called Rosemary who was assigned to my case. I'm not sure what her background was. She was middle-aged, rather overweight, with what I thought was an odd gypsy-style dress sense, and she carried her papers in what looked like an old shopping bag, but she spoke the same sort of language as Samantha. She talked about proper HR processes and that sort of thing, and she was pleasingly frank – pleasing to me that is – in saying that it wasn't good practice for the hospital to have started a formal process without having made informal attempts to deal with the issues. My legal representative made the point as often as possible during the hearing and the executive director chairing the panel looked uncomfortable and squirmed in his seat every time she said it, so of course she said it as frequently as she could.'

'So who was involved in the process?' Margaret asked.

'Four or five key people. The investigator was one of the consultants in the hospital. A senior – that means older – consultant in the anaesthetic department. I didn't know him, excepting that in the summer he used to wear a checked blazer and drive an ancient Morris

Oxford that brought back memories of a car my father had in the sixties. Our paths never crossed in the hospital, but he had a reputation for being sound and sensible, and he certainly seemed so when he talked with me.

'He asked me what my first reaction was to finding out that my behaviour was going to be investigated. I told him "someone must have been telling lies about Jonathan Barber, for without having done anything wrong he was arrested one fine morning". He recognised the reference straight away. "Ah, should I call you Joseph K?" he asked. The woman from medical staffing who was with him taking notes – not the same one who had been with the medical director when he told me there was going to be an investigation – looked rather mystified, which pleased us both, but by the end of the interviews I thought she was very good, very good indeed.'

'Why did you think that she wouldn't be?' Margaret enquired.

'I don't really know; I just did. I very rarely went to the medical staffing department, but when I did it seemed full of women who clearly spent a lot of time on their appearance. False nails, that sort of thing.'

Margaret suppressed an urge to explain to her father that making an effort to look good didn't mean that less attention was paid to being good at your job; or tell him that she thought that people who looked as though they didn't care about their appearance were probably less likely to bother about other things, including how they performed at work.

'She wasn't loud or noisy,' her father went on, 'but she was good at steering the conversation and making sure that important points were clear. She didn't seem to have an axe to grind. She simply tried to be sure she knew what my answers were to the questions. A bit like when a doctor needs to establish key points of a patient's account of their symptoms.

'She recognised that I wasn't familiar with what was going on. They don't teach you about that sort of thing in medical school, or at least they didn't in my day. She explained it to me in a way that didn't make me feel like an idiot for not knowing it, which was good of her. She also seemed very matter of fact and reasonable in her communications with Rosemary, who attended the meetings with me and told me afterwards that she thought she was good.'

'Meetings?' Margaret asked with a stress on the "s". 'How many were there?'

'Two. The woman from medical staffing explained it nicely. The first was to get my general comments on the items in the Terms of Reference. I was then shown accounts given by other people and asked for my observations on these in the second. The investigation report would then be sent to the medical director who would decide what to do. I didn't understand what the options were to start off with, but it didn't seem likely that he would set up a big investigation if he thought the likely outcome was to do nothing.'

'I'm sure that's right,' Margaret observed. 'So what did you say; did you ask her?'

'Yes, I did,' her father replied. 'She explained the range of possibilities in a matter-of-fact way, ranging from no action to a verbal warning to different sorts of written warnings to dismissal.'

'But as you say,' Margaret interjected, 'it wasn't likely the MD was going to have embarked on a formal investigation if he thought that the outcome was going to be a verbal warning he could probably just have given you anyway.'

'Indeed,' her father replied.

Margaret paused before encouraging him to continue: 'What did you say about the concerns?'

'Not much to begin with,' her father began. 'It was hard to know how to start without knowing exactly what the issues were.

'The anaesthetist asked me about my working relationships with colleagues in the Emergency Department, junior doctors, nurses and operations' managers, and I said I wasn't aware of there being any problems.

'He then asked me what I thought these colleagues would say if he asked them the same questions and I said I didn't know, but no doubt he was going to ask them.'

Margaret couldn't help thinking "Oh dear" but hoped her expression didn't betray this. If it did, it wasn't sufficient to disrupt her father's flow.

'He chuckled a bit and confirmed, yes, he was going to ask them, but he would be interested to know if I thought that they might say they found me difficult to work with.'

Margaret thought that this anaesthetist clearly had skills other than being able to put people to sleep. 'And how did you respond?' she asked.

'I said I didn't know. I said I hoped that people in the ED would say I came promptly to see patients when asked to do so and that I made clear decisions about what should be done with them, which many colleagues don't do.

'I said I hoped junior doctors would say that I wanted to do the best for my patients; that they could always get hold of me if they wanted advice; that I knew quite a lot about medicine; that I was interested in teaching them.'

'And the nurses and managers?' Margaret prompted.

'That they'd say I was available when they wanted advice; that I was polite; that I gave them clear instructions.'

Margaret couldn't help thinking that her father's choice of the word "instruction" was revealing but decided against pursuing this line of thought; after all, she wasn't interviewing him as part of the investigation: 'Was that the end of the conversation?' she asked.

'No, he asked me if I'd ever said anything to anyone that I regretted or would phrase differently if having the conversation again.

'I said I didn't think I'd ever said anything terrible, but also that when thinking about any interaction there are always words or phrases you might change if you were having it again. And he asked me if I had ever spoken to anyone in a manner that could have been perceived as racist.'

'And what did you say to that?' Margaret enquired,

very conscious of the fact that this was difficult territory that got brought up in many complaints about conduct in the workplace.

'I said that I'd never said anything that I thought was racist and would be very upset if anybody said that I had.' Margaret recognised the standard answer, as when pawn to e6 follows pawn to e4.

'The conversation finished shortly after that. The woman from medical staffing said she'd send me her notes of it to check, which she did and they were very accurate. She told me that I'd hear from them in a few weeks' time when they'd spoken to other people, and she asked me not to speak to anyone else about the interview or the investigation.'

'I expect you felt stuck in limbo,' Margaret ventured.

'I certainly did. No one spoke to me about things, excepting of course Malcolm seemed to make a point of bumping into me more often than usual. "Just checking in to see how you're doing" he would say. If others knew about what was going on they didn't talk to me about it, perhaps because they'd been told not to, perhaps because they didn't know what to say, perhaps both.

'Rosemary – I was getting familiar with the methods – wrote to the hospital requesting copies of the relevant policies and procedures. Copies of correspondence to or from the medical director in relation to the investigation. She told me that the hospital might not send everything she was asking for, but it would be helpful to get as much as possible and it put down a marker to say that we were watching them carefully.

'To start off with I wasn't sure if what she was doing was having any effect, but later on it became clear that having advice and representation from someone like her almost certainly made a big difference, which looking back on it still makes me very cross.'

'Why?' Margaret asked.

'I've pondered that and find it difficult to put my finger on it. I think I feel that my behaviour hadn't been unreasonable and so it shouldn't have been necessary to have professional assistance to try to justify it. But it was, and that makes me think that there's something fundamentally wrong with the system, although I don't think I could give you a very good answer if you asked me what should be done instead.'

The bundle of papers in the wardrobe contained the parts of accounts of others that had been shared with her father, along with his responses as captured by the woman from medical staffing in his second interview by the anaesthetist. It was after reading these that the medical director must have decided to refer to a disciplinary hearing.

'So tell me about the hearing,' Margaret encouraged.

'It was held in one of the committee rooms in the management offices. They'd stacked most of the chairs up in a corner, leaving enough for the panel and others attending around the table. It was hot and stuffy because building works going on outside meant that the windows had to be kept closed. I remember they were very mucky, which became more evident as the afternoon progressed and the sun dropped, making me realise that I couldn't remember the last time that I saw a window cleaner in the hospital. They probably don't have them any more as part of the estate services' cost improvement plan. But there was a water cooler in the corner of the room and everyone was provided with a plastic cup and told to help themselves whenever they wanted to. The woman from medical staffing who was recording proceedings had an assistant with her and she kept filling mine up for me.'

'And who was on the panel?' Margaret asked.

'Three people. The chair was one of the executive directors, the chief operating officer, I think. A man in his mid-forties with hair cut so short that he might as well have been bald. I thought he looked like he was auditioning for a role in the US marines, but he asked me to call him Tony.'

'Hadn't you met him before?' Margaret enquired, thinking it odd that her father might not have done so.

'No, I hadn't,' her father answered, continuing because he could see his daughter found this surprising, 'but there's nothing unusual in that. I bet if you went into any hospital in the country and asked all the doctors to name the directors, or pick them out from an identity parade, less than 10 per cent could do so.'

If true, and Margaret had no reason to doubt it, she thought that this said a lot about how hospitals were run.

'But I did google him,' her father went on. 'The hospital's website said he'd trained as an accountant with one of the big city firms and then worked for the national body that oversees hospitals with – I remember this bit – "a focus on supporting organisations to ensure financial sustainability" before he worked for us, so I assume he was the hospital's chief of cost improvement plans and responsible for the lack of window cleaning.

'Anyway, he didn't seem very comfortable chairing the panel and I didn't know why he was doing it as it didn't seem part of his day job. Rosemary explained that the chair had to be one of the directors, so I guess it was Buggins' turn.'

'Who were the others?' Margaret asked.

'A woman who was a consultant ENT surgeon and director of the surgical division. I'd shared a few patients with her over the years.'

'How had you got on with her?' Margaret enquired.

'Fine. Not much in the way of conversation. Very transactional. But she had a good reputation as a surgeon. I had her down as someone I'd ask to do an operation, but I preferred one of her colleagues if I wanted an opinion.'

Margaret interrupted. 'What? I don't understand; what's the difference?'

'All the difference in the world,' her father replied. 'Actually doing an operation is the easy bit. I know that the public think surgery is difficult and that surgeons have near miraculous powers, and if someone is about to cut you open it's helpful to believe this, but – as one of my oldest and best surgical colleagues was fond of saying in a mimicked Scottish accent – "most operations require less manual dexterity than knitting an Aran sweater". The difficult bit is deciding who to operate on and sometimes which operation to do; after that it's a matter of cutting and stitching, sometimes with a lot of fancy kit. What's the quote, "don't believe your own publicity"? Or something like that. Surgeons who buy into the public's perception of their abilities are best avoided.'

'Sorry,' Margaret said, conscious of the fact she'd diverted from the main topic, 'I interrupted. Who else was there?'

'Someone from another hospital,' her father replied. 'There had to be an external member on the panel and he was the medical director of another hospital in the region. Around fifty years old and rather portly, with shirt buttons obviously under a lot of strain around his waist. In the days when he'd been a doctor he'd been a chest physician.'

'I thought all medical directors were doctors,' Margaret observed.

'Yes, I think they are. What I meant was a doctor practising clinically. After I looked him up I had a chat with one of my friends who worked in the same hospital. He said that he'd stopped doing anything clinical as soon as he became MD, which is always a very bad sign.'

'Why's that?' Margaret asked.

'For lots of reasons,' her father replied. 'Most importantly because it means that they can't like the business of being a clinical doctor enough to want to continue doing it. Spend all their time in meetings planning what they're going to tell doctors in their hospital to do, getting further and further away from the actual business and not thinking there's any problem with doing so.'

Margaret couldn't restrain an observation. 'I hope you didn't say that to him!'

Her father smiled. 'No, fortunately or unfortunately the opportunity never arose.'

FIFTEEN

BAT CLOSE TO PAD

Margaret went on, after checking that her father was happy to continue, 'I saw the terms of reference in the papers in the wardrobe but nothing after that. What actually happened in the hearing?'

'I forget the precise order of things,' her father said, 'but the case against me was put to the panel by a lawyer appointed by the hospital and I was represented by a lawyer organised by my medical union, who worked along with Rosemary. The anaesthetist who'd done the investigation was there to provide explanation of anything in his report that the panel wanted clarified. I remember feeling sorry for him: he looked as uncomfortable as I felt and he wasn't the one in the dock! I'm sure he regretted having succumbed to having his arm twisted and agreeing to be the investigator.'

'Were witnesses called?' Margaret wondered.

'Only two,' her father replied. 'The man who was the Emergency Department's service lead and one of the operations' managers.'

Margaret was surprised. 'Hadn't other people been interviewed?'

'Yes, quite a few, but they weren't willing to give evidence in person, and I learned from Rosemary and Julia – she was the lawyer representing me – that they couldn't be made to.'

'Surely that weakens anything that they might have said to the investigator?'

'That was a point that Julia made very strongly. She was a remarkably short woman, despite high heels, but with a very waspish manner and she gave the impression that she was going to sting the US marine in an unpleasant place every time she said it.'

'What did the hospital's lawyer say?'

'He was on the defensive,' her father continued, 'explaining that many of those who'd given accounts to the investigator were vulnerable and it was either inappropriate for the hospital to ask them to attend or they declined to do so. Julia was wonderfully scornful of that and gave the impression, but didn't say directly, that the panel should therefore regard them as inherently unreliable and take anything they might have said with a large pinch of salt. I was a bit surprised how hard she pressed this, not that political correctness is my strong point as I'm sure you realise, and I asked her about it afterwards. She told me that most chief operating officers are straight-talking people who are naturally suspicious of anyone who isn't willing or able to give an account of themselves and she thought it would be helpful to get him to think we were talking his language.'

Margaret waited for a pause and then continued, 'So what did the ED lead have to say?'

'Lots!' her father said in a manner that clearly indicated his profound dislike of the man. 'He had a long list of grumbles about me, saying that I didn't follow agreed protocols for managing patients, that I undermined collaborative and efficient working, that I spoke inappropriately and offensively to junior staff who then came to him to complain about me.'

Margaret stated the obvious. 'I get the impression you didn't like him!' she said.

'He's an appalling man. Young, can't be much older than forty,' her father began. Margaret bit her tongue, wondering if the condemnatory diatribe that was undoubtedly coming was going to say that someone of about her age couldn't have reached maturity by any sensible reckoning. 'And he thinks he knows it all. He regards himself as so advanced that he no longer actually needs to see patients. He sits in his office all day, maintaining oversight of the Emergency Department as he calls it, and everything has to be dealt with according to a protocol. It's madness, utter madness. I used to see patients and talk to them and examine them, and I'd often find after about five or ten minutes that they didn't need a lot of tests doing, perhaps one or two simple ones, and I'd give them some advice or treatment and send them home or – if they were unwell and needed to be in hospital – admit them to a ward. He couldn't stand that; somebody who'd see a patient, make a clear decision and be happy to take responsibility for doing so. He wanted everything done like painting by numbers.'

Margaret was confused. 'Painting by numbers?'

'Yes,' her father went on. 'You know what I mean? I think your mother bought a kit for you one year. The picture – I can't remember what it was – is divided into shapes, each marked with a number that corresponds to a particular colour. You paint each shape and the picture appears.'

She did know what a painting by numbers kit was, had a hazy recollection of having had one, and found herself sidetracked into racking her brains for a memory of the picture. Perhaps it was a horse. She had gone through a horsey phase in her early teens. However, before it was necessary for her to explain to her father that she was confused about the analogy, not about the kits, he explained himself.

'What I mean is this,' he said, 'if a patient arrived in the ED complaining of chest pain, instead of talking to them about it in a bit of detail and examining them in a relevant and thoughtful way before deciding what tests – if any – to do, he wanted everyone managed by the chest pain protocol. Everyone would have to have a battery of tests. An ECG, which is an electrical recording of the heart; blood tests to look for damage to the heart muscle or problems with clots of blood in the lungs; very often a CT scan to look for clots of blood in the lungs and sometimes a CT scan to check that there wasn't a split in the aorta, the main blood vessel coming out of the heart. Often all completely unnecessary and leading to all sorts of anxieties for the patient and an industry of further nonsense.'

'What sort of things?' Margaret enquired.

'I'll give you a common example,' her father began. 'A patient has chest pain of a sort that, if you took the trouble to listen to them, you'd realise was being caused by indigestion, reflux of acid from their stomach into their gullet, but the ECG shows a minor electrical abnormality, which is a common finding. The fact that this is obviously completely irrelevant to the fact that they've got indigestion isn't considered, because what the patient has is chest pain, which can be caused by heart problems. So the patient isn't sent home with advice about how to try to avoid getting reflux and some medicine to help it, they're told that further cardiac investigations are needed and a referral will be made to the cardiac service. The patient and their relatives often assume, and certainly do if they're anxious types, that there's some terrible heart problem and don't want to leave the hospital until they've been seen by the cardiologist. The on-call cardiologist, if there is one, is usually a junior doctor who understandably wants to play it safe, so the patient is admitted and further tests are organised. Apart from the fact that the patient and their relatives have been terrified for no good reason, is it any surprise that the ED and hospital are always full?'

Margaret had no difficulty in imagining why her father and the appalling young man, who she felt sure was trying to do his best to run the ED, weren't on each other's Christmas card lists: 'Did he give examples of this sort of thing to the hearing?' she asked.

'Yes, several,' her father replied with a weariness in his voice. 'I can't remember them all, but I do remember the case of the man with reflux and arthritis. There was quite a lot of discussion about how I'd spoken to the junior doctors after seeing him.

'He was a pleasant man in his seventies with bad arthritis and back pain that he'd had for years. I saw him on a morning ward round. He'd been brought to the ED the previous day because he had chest and back pain. They'd decided that he needed to be admitted and the bed managers, the people who organise where patients go in the hospital, had put him on my ward. The arrangement is that the consultant physician working on each medical ward sees all the new patients who've arrived there first thing in the morning.

'The junior doctor on duty on the ward presented the case to me. He hadn't seen the man, but from the notes he told me that he'd been admitted with chest and back pain, his ECG showed non-specific abnormalities, his blood test for heart muscle damage was normal, his blood test for blood clots was slightly elevated, but a CT scan for blood clots in the lungs was clear and a CT scan looking for a split in his aorta didn't show one.

'Before we went to see the patient I remember asking the junior doctors, there were two of them, if they thought that all these tests had been necessary. They told me that it was the protocol in the Emergency Department to do them.

'We went to the patient and I asked him what had happened. He told me that because of his arthritis he didn't normally leave his house much, but he could potter round inside using a frame to walk with. Because there was a special family event his son had collected him in his car to take him out for lunch. He said that his back had started to play up badly as soon as he'd got into the car, but they'd managed to get to the restaurant and after a lot of difficulty he'd made it from the car park into the building with support from his son. It was hot and stuffy inside and he'd felt unwell, but he didn't want to spoil things for everyone and so he'd tried to join in with the meal. After a few mouthfuls he felt sick and his heartburn started to play up. He felt faint and he remembered his son telling him that he looked pale and someone else saying that they'd called an ambulance. When they arrived he said that he told the paramedics that he thought he'd be fine if he was left alone for a bit, but they brought him to the hospital.

'When he got to the hospital his back was more painful from being jolted around in the ambulance and he heard the paramedic tell the nurse in the ED who was receiving him that he had chest and back pain, and that triggered all the blood tests and scans he had done. No one asked him what had actually happened, and all the unnecessary tests could have been avoided if they had.

'I don't blame the paramedics who can't spend a lot of time waiting around in a restaurant with a patient and must decide pretty quickly whether they can leave them there or need to take them to the nearest Emergency Department, and they have to be safe rather than sorry. But I do blame... no, blame's the wrong word... am massively frustrated by… no, perhaps I do blame, those who reduce medicine to a level where saying chest pain, back pain or any other symptom leads to lots of automatic investigations before anyone's talked properly with the patient and thought about what might be going on.

'So, after explaining to the man what I thought had caused his chest and back pain – which he said he agreed with – and that I was pleased to say that all the tests that had been done hadn't shown anything terrible and he could go home, I told the junior doctors, privately – not in the patient's hearing – one of my stories to make a point about unnecessary investigations.'

Margaret had been waiting for her father to say what he had said to the junior doctors that led to discussion at the hearing and the moment had come.

'I said I thought that doctors in the hospital should be able to organise two sorts of investigation. The first sort the hospital would pay for; the cost of the second sort would be deducted from their salary at the end of the month,' he said with a chuckle.

Margaret could imagine the juniors being reduced to a bewildered silence. 'How did they respond?' she asked.

'I don't remember them saying anything. Most don't, although I've had some responses over the years. A few earnest types have thought I was serious and asked if this really happened. Some have obviously taken the point, and I remember a particularly good trainee saying to me a few weeks later, after I'd congratulated them on managing a case well overnight, that before ordering a CT scan at three in the morning that was absolutely necessary they'd done a mental check along the lines of, "if I order this scan, will Dr Barber bill me for it?".

'So they reported this to the man in charge of the Emergency Department?' Margaret suggested.

'Yes, and he completely failed to see the point I'd been trying to make, or at least did a very good impression of failing to see it. He said it was typical of my attitude and showed lack of respect for colleagues and undermined effective collaborative working or some such nonsense, and he gave another example that had been reported to him when I asked a junior doctor if the relatives had been scanned.'

'Did you ever say that?' Margaret asked with some surprise.

'Yes; I sometimes used to say that to try to make the same point about unnecessary over-investigation, and I know it doesn't sound good – like lots of things don't – when taken out of context and printed in the papers of a disciplinary hearing, but as I tried to explain, I didn't say these things out of malice or with any intention to disrespect colleagues. I was trying to teach junior doctors how to become good doctors, or what I think are good doctors, and they – like everyone else – remember things that are memorable. And he also said I had behaved in a racist manner.'

Margaret had been waiting for this. 'What was his evidence for that?' she asked.

'He said that a black junior doctor had complained to him about me. She'd told him that I'd implied she was lazy and this was a racial stereotype.'

'And had you?' Margaret interjected.

'I hadn't told her she was lazy in so many words, but I had implied it is the truthful answer, and that's what I said in the hearing. The patients coming into the ED with acute medical problems, which happens twenty-four/seven, are dealt with by a day team and a night team. I was on the rota of medical consultants who were responsible for them, which meant that first thing in the morning or early in the evening you'd review all the patients who'd come in on your watch. Whenever possible I'd ask the junior doctor who'd seen each patient to tell me about them, which is the best way for them to learn. Most were keen to do so, but sometimes you'd meet a doctor who didn't volunteer any patients to present and I used to ask them who they'd seen. Sometimes they'd seen quite a few who'd all been discharged home, or there was some other reason why we didn't need to go to see them, like their care had been taken over by one of the specialties. But sometimes I'd find – as on this occasion – that a doctor who'd done a ten-hour shift had only seen two patients. This wasn't common, but when it did happen they would usually be embarrassed.'

Margaret had had more than a fair bit of experience of the many reasons why people struggle to deliver the expected output at work and the difficulties and pitfalls of "performance management" as it's known in the jargon. She suspected that her father wouldn't have been a sophisticated operator in this territory and the recollection flashed through her mind of an episode at a training day she'd been on many years ago, shortly after she first took on a role that required her to manage a team. A particularly direct colleague of hers – universally known as the elephant because of his size, ponderous stiff-legged gait, penchant for baggy light grey suits, and an ability to say what everyone else was thinking – had asked the very earnest woman running the workshop, which had been soporific until his interjection, "Under what circumstances is it proper to administer a good bollocking and what is the best way of doing so?". She recalled feeling sorry for the woman but couldn't remember her response, beyond that it had been inadequate, and contrived to bring herself back into the moment by asking her father, 'So did you say anything else to the black doctor who'd only seen two patients?'

'No, not that I can recall,' he replied.

Margaret followed up with the obvious next question. 'Did she give evidence to the investigation?'

'No, she didn't. Apparently she was asked if she would but declined. The ED service lead reported that she told him she felt embarrassed and humiliated and she thought that Dr Barber was a racist.'

This rang true to Margaret, who recognised that creating a scenario of public embarrassment and humiliation wasn't a good approach to someone that might be struggling for a wide variety of reasons. 'I guess she probably did feel that way,' she suggested before going on with expectations of a fairly rudimentary reply. 'What were you hoping to achieve?'

'In all honesty I don't think I was thinking a great deal. I suppose I hoped that the interaction would prompt her to pull her socks up and do a bit more work next time she was doing a shift in the Emergency Department. I remember one of the other juniors looking rather pleased at her being called out, no doubt irritated by the fact she hadn't been pulling her weight whilst they were slaving away.'

Margaret was of course very familiar with the irritation of having a passenger in her team but knew, not least from observations of the effects of the behaviour of the elephant and involvement at various times in dealing with the fall-out from it, that an approach beginning with a private conversation along the lines of "you didn't manage to see many patients today, was there a reason for this?" would have been better. However, to explore this possibility would have been a digression and so she proceeded with, 'I can understand her feeling embarrassed and humiliated, but how did they argue that it was racist?'

'A good question. Julia was on to it right away. She asked me if I'd ever had a similar interaction with a doctor who wasn't from an ethnic minority, and of course she knew that I had. She asked me to give an account of the details and I told her about an almost identical episode about six months previously where the idle doctor... sorry, the doctor who appeared to have done remarkably little work... couldn't have been more English: a white, blond, dishevelled Old Etonian; all manner and with very little if any substance. She lapped this up, asked if I could remember who was present and asked me to go through all the details I could recall.'

Margaret was keen to find out more. 'What did the panel say about this?' she asked.

'They weren't very impressed,' her father replied before going on to clarify what he meant. 'With the accusation of racism that is, particularly with Julia – whilst acknowledging that it perhaps wasn't an ideal approach to managing poor performance – emphasising that I had recently behaved in exactly the same way towards a white male junior doctor in similar circumstances.'

Margaret could imagine that the US marine and the director of the surgical division on the panel would certainly have taken a dim view of any doctor who only saw two patients in a ten-hour shift and not easily accept any plea of mitigation. 'Did they ask you any direct questions about it?' she asked.

'Yes. The chief operating man was very direct. He asked me if I was a racist and I said I wasn't. I said I treated everyone the same.'

Margaret wasn't at all surprised to hear of this exchange. She thought it vanishingly unlikely that her father had ever thought about or had any training on unconscious bias, and probable that the chief operating officer had ticked the box before promptly forgetting about its contents if indeed he'd made any attempt to consider or remember them. 'Did anyone else on the panel ask you about it?' she enquired.

'The medical director from another hospital did. In fact, he gave something of a speech about the importance of having an inclusive culture where diversity was valued.' Her father smiled to himself before going on. 'I could see this irritating the others on the panel who I think held the view, although they didn't say this – I suppose they couldn't in the circumstances – that they weren't keen on any sort of diversity that led to a doctor seeing only two patients during a ten-hour shift. Anyway, when he'd finished his speech he asked me what I thought the black junior doctor had felt when I gave the impression – with others present – that she'd been slacking, even if I didn't say this to her directly, and whether I could understand why she might have felt this was due to me being racially biased.'

'What did you say to that?' Margaret prompted.

'I said, and I'm repeating myself here, that I imagined she would have felt embarrassed and I hoped it would motivate her to see a few more patients the next time she was working a shift in the ED.'

'And about being racially biased?'

'I said that I hadn't behaved in the way I had because she was black, or for that matter because she was a woman, and pointed to the example Julia had already mentioned as evidence of this.'

'Did he leave it there?'

'No, he kept talking around the point and asking me if I thought I made any assumptions, perhaps unconscious assumptions, when working with black people or those from other ethnic minorities, or with women as opposed to men. I found it hard to follow what he was on about. In the end I landed up quoting Martin Luther King.'

Margaret cringed inwardly. Her father had a wonderful memory for quotes and an unfortunate tendency to come over as very pompous when delivering them.

'His most famous speech. It's absolutely wonderful. "I have a dream" – he said – "that my four little children will one day live in a nation where they will not be judged by the colour of their skin but by the content of their character". I said I tried to judge everyone by the content of their character.'

'Was that the end of the discussion?', Margaret asked.

'The medical director man went on a bit more and I continued to struggle to understand what he was driving at. Eventually I asked him if he thought there were any circumstances when I could ask a junior doctor to do something and expect them to do it, and if these changed depending on the colour of the doctor, or whether they were a man or a woman.'

Margaret recognised that it was unwise for the subject of a disciplinary hearing to argue aggressively with any of the panel members and feared where this altercation might have led. 'Anyway,' her father went on, relieving her of her anxiety, 'I think the chief operating officer had had enough of the discussion; at least he asked his colleague if he had any further questions in a manner that clearly implied he shouldn't.

'Malcolm was incredibly wicked when we talked about it afterwards. He told me again that I had a gift for saying things that many people thought but judged it best to remain silent. He said that most consultants and senior managers were very wary of saying anything that might be perceived as critical to anyone with a protected characteristic because of the high chance they'd be denounced as racist, sexist or some other sort of abhorrent-ist. Accusations which it's very hard to refute.'

Margaret had failed to see any wickedness thus far, but her father continued with a chuckle that he couldn't suppress. "Did you watch the Olympic 100-metre final last week?" Malcolm asked me. "I did", he said, "and you know I felt excluded. Not a single middle-aged white man in the line-up, in fact not a single white man." Her mind temporarily ran riot with arguments that might follow from this observation. Did white men not have opportunities to learn to run quickly? Did white men lack role models to aspire to? She quickly suppressed these inappropriate thoughts but couldn't shake off an image of Malcolm, a bit overweight and slightly arthritic, rising creakily from his blocks, cheeks and moustache rippling with the effort, pulling up with a yelp a second or so later and having to be helped from the track clutching his lumbar spine. For an instant she thought it was just as well that he hadn't been in front of the disciplinary panel instead of her father, although she realised after that fleeting moment that he would have kept his wickedness well under wraps, "bat close to pad, soft hands" being advice he commonly offered.

SIXTEEN

INVIGORATED BY HAVING A PLAN

Margaret was surprised that matters had got as far as a formal disciplinary hearing. It was very clear that her father would have had a well-justified reputation for being difficult amongst many in the hospital's management and operational teams, but a disciplinary hearing? Surely this should have been a last resort, only used if informal attempts to address aspects of his behaviour that were deemed inappropriate had failed to improve the situation. Given the obvious friction in the Emergency Department, had any effort been made to arrange for mediation between him and the "appalling young man" trying to run it? She wasn't naïve enough to think that her father would have been a keen participant in any such endeavour, or that it would have had much chance of a good outcome, indeed he may have flatly refused to have anything to do with it, but it was something that should have been tried.

'I'm left wondering,' Margaret said, 'how this got as far as a formal hearing. Weren't there any discussions with you about how you did things in the Emergency Department, how you spoke to the junior doctors? Wasn't there ever a suggestion that you should sit down with the man trying to run the ED to talk things over, perhaps with a mediator?'

'No,' her father replied. 'When I'd discussed the court case and my referral to the Medical Regulator with the medical director he'd told me that I needed to be careful in how I spoke to people, but nothing more than that. Julia went to town on the issue. It was the closest I've come to having an out-of-body experience, listening to a speech for the defence in a courtroom drama. "It was nothing short of outrageous", she said, "that her client was subject to a formal disciplinary process. Here was a doctor without any previous disciplinary record whose sole aim was to provide the best care for the patients he was looking after and whose only crime, if crime it was, was to dare to make independent clinical decisions in patients' best interests, leading to him being labelled by some as difficult and a problem. Had anyone sought to sit down with Dr Barber to discuss and address management's concerns informally? Where were the minutes and summary notes of any such meetings?" She knew full well, of course, that there weren't any. Given the friction in the Emergency Department and in particular with the ED's service lead, had any attempt been made to provide supported mediation?'

'I'm sure this put the management side on the defensive!' Margaret observed, stating the obvious.

'Indeed!' her father replied. 'They argued that my behaviours were deeply ingrained and persistent, and that the attitudes I consistently displayed in my conversations with medical, nursing, administrative, operational and management colleagues, including failure to follow agreed clinical and operational protocols when asked to do so, meant that I wouldn't engage in a meaningful way with any such efforts.'

'Would you have?' Margaret couldn't resist asking.

'Possibly not,' her father replied, scoring points for both insight and honesty, 'but as Julia said to me, that's irrelevant, they should have made the attempt before embarking on a formal disciplinary process to argue that relationships had irretrievably broken down.'

A cloud then came over his face. He became silent, looked disturbed and peered into the middle distance, not focussing on anything. He gave the impression of wanting to start to speak, but words didn't come. He swallowed. Margaret could tell that he was struggling to get out something important. 'What happened?' she said, very gently and quietly.

After a while he replied. 'It was very difficult. Very difficult,' he said. 'The court case, the Medical Regulator, the disciplinary hearing. One after the other. I couldn't sleep properly. I began to get anxious and stressed. I'd never been an anxious person, but I found myself checking and rechecking all sorts of things. The times of my clinics hadn't changed since I'd started as a consultant, but one Monday I got worried that I'd forgotten to go – although I'd never done a clinic on a Monday – and went along. The nurse in charge was very kind and made a joke of the fact that I'd got the wrong day. "Too keen, Dr Barber," she said, but I bet she thought I was losing my marbles. I sometimes felt my pulse racing and my body shaking, things I've seen dozens of times in patients having panic attacks.'

He fell silent again. Margaret tried to find some words, but there was no need because he began to speak before she said anything. 'I think Rosemary spotted things first, and the woman from the medical staffing department. I'm not sure exactly who said what to whom, but what happened is the hearing got adjourned, I got referred to the occupational health service, and – I learned later – there were discussions between Julia, Rosemary and the hospital's legal and management teams.'

'Oh, Dad!' Margaret sighed, feeling incredibly guilty that she hadn't known this, hadn't been there to offer support – or as much support as a daughter who didn't really know her father could offer – in what must have been the blackest of black times. 'Oh, Dad!' she repeated, 'I'm so sorry,' then continuing after a pause, 'What happened? What did Mum do?'

'Mum was fantastic,' he said. 'The man in the occupational health service said I was suffering from what he called an acute stress reaction – I'm sure in the old days it would have been called a mental breakdown – and he signed me off work and referred me for a psychiatric assessment. They offered me some medication to help me sleep, which I said I didn't want, and sessions with a counsellor. She was a nice woman with a rather husky voice, but she didn't have anything to say that I didn't know and wasn't trying to do already, which was reassuring, and after a couple of sessions we agreed that I'd get back in touch with her if I wanted to, which I never did.

'Mum took over,' he went on, 'and she was wonderful. She didn't press me to talk when I didn't want to, but of course eventually I told her everything, and she did things like going out and buying a paper every day, which she never did during the week when I was working and she was alone at home. For the first week or so I had no interest in anything and didn't look at it, but then one day I found myself picking it up and reading something, and a short while later noticing that it was a lovely day and accepting her suggestion that we go out for a walk. The colours began to return to the garden and the sky and I started to feel better.

'I saw the occupational health man after two weeks and again after four, when he asked me if I felt able to engage again with the disciplinary hearing, saying that he thought it would be best to do so if possible because, whatever the outcome, which wasn't going to be changed by delay, living with continuing uncertainty wasn't going to be helpful.

'I got in touch with Rosemary and then met with her and Julia. They told me about what they called their "without prejudice" discussions. They said the panel were critical of the hospital's failure to try to deal with the concerns raised about me by informal means before resorting to a disciplinary process, but they did accept the hospital's argument that at times my behaviour fell short of the organisation's values in terms of respecting colleagues and working collaboratively. They found me not guilty of racism but thought my approach to junior doctors who failed to meet my expectations was inappropriate and could precipitate allegations of bullying, and that my comments about management plans I disagreed with could lead consultant colleagues to justifiably claim that I was not treating them with respect.

'In terms of a sanction, the panel didn't think it proven that my relationships with colleagues had irretrievably broken down, which would have led to dismissal, and they were minded to give me a written warning along with a requirement to engage with coaching on respecting colleagues and working collaboratively.'

Although clearly better than dismissal, Margaret could imagine what a devastating blow it would have been for her father to hear this. Nearly forty years of work culminating in a formal admonishment and compulsory remedial activity. 'And so what happened?' she asked in a whisper.

'We came to an agreement – a settlement they called it. I hadn't been thinking much about retiring and hadn't developed any clear plans, but I knew it was looming. I was only about six months or so away from being entitled to my full pension and I was given the option of remaining on the payroll but staying off work until then. The disciplinary process would be terminated without conclusion if I agreed to this, which I did. Your mother told me it was the best thing to do, and although it felt very bitter – very bitter indeed – she was right.'

There was a natural pause. Margaret and her father were quiet, mulling things over. Margaret spoke first. 'So that was the end of things in the hospital?'

'Yes,' her father replied. 'Over the next week I cleared my office, not that there was much that I wanted to keep. Most things landed up in yellow plastic bags for disposal. I brought home a pot plant, the one that's on my desk in the study; a few stethoscopes, including the first one I'd ever had as a medical student which I'd had to replace because the mechanism became so loose that when I twisted the bit at the end – it's got two sides for listening to different sounds – it kept falling to bits; and a few books in which I'd written chapters.'

He fell silent, looking old and sad, sitting hunched, head bowed, with his hands in his lap. Margaret felt tears welling. 'I'm sorry. I'm so sorry,' she said, trying but failing not to sob audibly and acutely aware that words could not do justice to the situation, at least none she could find.

'Amazing,' he said hoarsely, 'the summary of forty years.' After a while he continued, slowly at first but then gathering pace. 'Malcolm and Asif came and spoke to me. Best out of it, they said. Over the next month or so I got a few letters and cards and they meant a lot. A couple of young consultants wrote to say how I'd helped them when they were trainees and was one of the main reasons why they'd decided to pursue the careers they had. The sister in charge of the outpatient department sent a card saying I'd been a wonderful colleague with old-fashioned values, always starting my clinics on time and courteous with the patients, her and her staff, even on occasions when things didn't run smoothly. A handful of patients who somehow learned that I was leaving sent cards or notes thanking me for looking after them and wishing me well in my retirement.'

Margaret found it impossible to get to sleep that night. She was deeply troubled by what had happened to her father. Although she had experienced him as cold and unapproachable before she left home, she had never had any doubt about his motivation to do the best he could for his patients and he had been incredibly hard-working. The accounts he'd given of his experiences revealed that these things hadn't changed. Yes, he might have been – no, he certainly was – an irritant to those who wanted everything done in a particular way; painting by numbers he'd called it; and there were clearly problems with his methods for trying to call out junior doctors' poor performance or make points about others' patient management plans that he disapproved of; but was there no place for a very experienced hard-working doctor who was determined to do the best for his patients, displaying commendable old-fashioned values as the nurse from outpatients had put it? Could the hospital's management system not cope with such an individual?

Her thoughts about this were muddled, but beyond those concerning the way her father had been treated by the hospital, she was also confused and worried about what he had told her in connection with the court case and his appearance before the Medical Regulator. Was it the case that patients and their relatives could demand pretty well anything and pursue the hospital through the courts and the doctor through the Medical Regulator if they failed to do what they wanted? This seemed to be her father's account. Given this, was it the case that most doctors felt obliged to continue offering investigations and treatments beyond the point at which, left to their own best judgement, they would think it right to stop? Her father clearly thought this to be the case and, the thing which was most terrible to her, it seemed as though her mother would have suffered unnecessary terminal pain and distress had he not been there. Media accounts of medical matters, when not displaying outrage at some failing, were always trumpeting a breakthrough of one sort or another, but her father had said nothing about any of these. His account was a lamentation of things gone wrong. She knew she wanted to get to know him and, if she could better understand the things that had happened to him, this would surely help.

These varied but connected questions kept her awake, rather as when a school of fish approaches the surface of the water and one breaks it and then another and then another, so there is no peace. Along with these questions came others relating to her own position, as if there were two types of fish in the shoal. What did she want to do with her job, with her life? She realised that there was no obvious logic to this, but she felt in some way that if she could come to an understanding of the one sort of issues it might help her with the second.

Eventually she must have got off to sleep because she woke at the unusually late time for her of nine thirty, and as she lay dozing she decided what she'd do. Her father had been impressed by one of the Medical Regulator's expert witnesses. She'd dig out the papers, find his name and track him down. Perhaps he'd be willing to talk with her. The worst that could happen is he'd refuse to do so.

Invigorated by having a plan, she got up, washed and dressed speedily, and as she was having breakfast set to work on Google, trying without complete success to avoid dropping muesli onto the laptop keyboard. Within a few minutes she knew where Dr Old worked and what he looked like, and by virtue of him having a role in a neighbourhood association in Cambridge that had a website she knew within a few hundred metres where he lived. It was fortunate that this was not much more than an hour's drive from where her father lived, or for that matter from her flat in London.

SEVENTEEN

SCRATCH THE SURFACE

The latte-assisted conversation on the wall outside King's had been interesting. Dr Old had felt very sorry for Jonathan Barber at the time. It seemed to him that he'd had the misfortune of being in the wrong place at the wrong time, although an emotionally more intelligent person would probably have spotted various warning signs and proceeded with more caution than he did. His daughter wasn't a mad woman and she wasn't a journalist in search of a quote to spice up an article. In fact she had some stimulating thoughts and questions about things that had rumbled around in his mind for a long time, without the rumbling leading to anything. It's not an everyday occurrence that someone genuinely wants to talk with you and hear your views on important issues. It's flattering to be asked and hard to resist flattery, particularly when offered by someone attractive.

Dr Old had agreed to meet. Margaret had got a list of things she wanted to discuss and he couldn't resist pulling her leg by asking if she'd put them onto a Gantt chart, beloved of many management consultants, to which she tossed back her head and gave a throaty laugh. 'No,' she said, 'but I can do if you like! Always important to keep things on track and on time and to avoid mission creep.'

She didn't know Cambridge and was happy to go with his suggestion that they arrange to have supper one evening in a restaurant that he liked, mid-priced with a slightly rustic feel, calculatedly unshowy. The sort of place where you could be equally comfortable drinking a pint of beer or having a gin and tonic, serving decent gastropub food and with a short but interesting list of wines supplied by a local man who'd turned what was his passion into a decent business. When Dr Old had started work in Cambridge many years previously one of the hepatologists told him that his shop next to a local petrol station – a small, prefabricated building looking the worse for wear – was where he got his wine. Given his colleague's specialist knowledge in this area he'd followed his recommendation and been a customer ever since.

Dr Old turned up a couple of minutes early for their seven o'clock reservation expecting to be on his own for a while with a chance to settle down, look over the menu and get his thoughts in order, but Margaret had arrived before him. She was seated at a table against the wall in front of a small sash window that looked out from the first-floor dining room over the cobbled street below. She was wearing a dark blue T-shirt with a Peruvian-type pattern on it, a light blue cardigan and tailored linen trousers. The brown boots he remembered from before were again in evidence. He hadn't previously noticed her hair, but this was mid-brown, straight and worn as a ponytail.

'Hello, good evening,' she said as he approached. 'I didn't want to be late and found I got here early so I've been making myself at home.' Aside from her phone there was a bottle of fizzy water on the table.

'Is that what you drink at home?' he asked.

'Sometimes,' she replied. 'Important not to get into the hard stuff too early in the evening, especially when driving.'

Dr Old sipped a gin and tonic and Margaret stuck to her fizzy water whilst they looked over the menu, began their starters and made general chit chat. She explained that she worked as a management consultant and was a bit surprised that he knew something of the business, having assumed that he wouldn't on the basis of exchanges she'd had with her father. Her firm didn't, to use the argot, have a presence in the healthcare sector, but some did and he'd been the beneficiary or victim of various interactions over the years, almost entirely dependent on whether or not the hospital's chief executive was trusted by senior people at national level. If they did, the hospital was left alone. If they didn't, or they wanted to get rid of him or her for any reason, then their standard technique was to arrange for the "independent" hospital regulator to declare the hospital to be deficient in some way and then impose a regime of "turnaround teams" and management consultants until the situation became intolerable and the chief executive stepped down, with plentiful dishonest thanks for their wonderful service and an undisclosed but no doubt significant pay-off.

It's at nodal points, when we feel as though we are at a crossroads and unsure of our direction, that we tend to be at our most honest, and she went on to explain what had brought her home after so many years away. It was no surprise, she said, that she was disturbed by her mother's death, but she was deeply troubled by what she'd learned of her father's experience and some of the things he'd said about the way her mother had died and might have died. She was frank in saying she'd found him cold and unapproachable when she was a child but nevertheless felt deep down in her bones that what had happened to him was wrong, and some of the things he'd said about why they'd happened concerned her very deeply and she wanted to understand. The deep-rooted urge to find explanations for life's misfortunes surfacing in her as it sometimes does in us all.

They settled on a bottle of Australian Chardonnay, which Dr Old generously agreed to drink more than his fair share of, and into their main courses, pork belly for him and fish of the day for her. 'How did you get involved with the case that went to the Medical Regulator?' she asked.

Dr Old explained that he hadn't applied for the job, but that from time to time other hospitals or the Medical Regulator would ask him to help by giving advice and sometimes he'd do so. Mostly it was other hospitals who would typically be wrestling with a disciplinary matter concerning a doctor and everyone in the place was conflicted in one way or another such that there was little or no chance that any decision or action taken internally – however sensible it might be – would be accepted as fair and reasonable.

Margaret asked, and it made him smile, if he'd had any training for this. 'Why do you smile?' she said, trying to suppress a hint of irritation. 'My father sometimes smiles when I ask him similar questions, and I don't understand why.'

'It's because it's a very logical and sensible question and indicates that you've never worked with doctors,' he replied, before realising that this was rather abrupt and continuing, 'Sorry, that was a bit brusque.' She reassured him that she hadn't taken any offence and he went on to expand.

'Medical training is focussed on learning the scientific background to medicine,' he explained, 'with some courses giving more attention to this than others, and on the business of how doctors deal with individual patients. How they talk to them, usually called taking the history; how they examine them physically; what tests and investigations to do; how to use information from these different sources to work out the diagnosis; how to treat whatever it is that the patient's got; and in modern medical courses – not when he trained – how to speak to them when the situation is uncertain or difficult; how to break bad news; that sort of thing.

'There's almost nothing in the courses,' he continued, 'about how you run a hospital, or how to deal with colleagues that behave badly, or what to do with a team that isn't working well together, and the little that there might be is completely swamped by the main agenda. This isn't helped by the fact that the people who do the small amount of teaching on what's usually called "professionalism" tend to be highly principled and well-meaning but totally lacking in street cred. They very rarely have jobs where they're seen actually trying to run services or deal with thorny problems. This stands out a mile and most medical students are very bright and perceptive and generally conclude that it must all be airy-fairy nonsense which isn't examined and can't be of much importance.

'When you've qualified as a doctor and move on to training in a specialty in hospital it's more of the same, with pretty well all the emphasis on how you treat the patient in front of you. That, after all, is the essence of what medicine's about: a doctor working out what's wrong with a patient and trying to help them. The skills that are most prized by doctors are being good clinically, at talking skilfully with patients, at making diagnoses and deciding on treatments; at being good technically when doing operations or performing procedures. Being good at research, the engine that drives new discoveries and treatments, is also highly valued.'

'But what about managing the hospital and managing the doctors?' Margaret intervened. 'Surely that's important.'

'Yes it is,' Dr Old agreed, 'and it's not straightforward for some very basic reasons,' which they went on to talk around in a rambling manner after he'd finished his pork, mashed potato and red cabbage, which had got rather cold because he'd been talking too much and giving it inadequate attention.

'The first thing to say,' he continued after they'd ordered desserts, 'is that there's a disconnect, a chasm, between what the doctor wants to do and is trained to do, which is give the best care they can to the patient in front of them, and what those running hospitals generally want to do, which is provide the best care they can for the population they serve. This isn't a problem when both can be achieved, when there's enough capacity in the system, but this state of nirvana – if it ever existed in the past – will never be achieved again.'

Margaret asked if he was being unduly pessimistic and he said he didn't think so, elaborating that the combination of increasing public expectations and medical developments that advanced the possibilities for treatment, always at increased cost, meant that he couldn't imagine funding ever matching demand in the future. He didn't delve into the further nuance that, even if the money was available, it's a different matter having sufficient numbers of trained people to do the jobs required. He also didn't get into discussing the fact that more medicine often didn't mean better medicine and expensive deaths tended to be prolonged and miserable for all concerned, most crucially for the patient, but they came to that on another occasion.

The next thing, he went on to say after checking that he wasn't boring her rigid – she was kind enough to suggest not – was that 'Good doctors are always difficult to manage. No, challenging is a better word,' and he went on to argue that it was worrying if a doctor or group of doctors weren't challenging to manage because it probably meant they weren't good doctors. 'Most people,' he said, 'including most doctors, are surprised when I say this,' and so was Margaret. 'Doctors aren't trained to follow rules,' he continued, 'and the last person you should ask if you want someone to follow a protocol diligently is a doctor. Doctors need to be able to make decisions, give advice and do things or decide not to do things when there's uncertainty, sometimes lots of uncertainty.

'If a patient is very ill, say they're gasping for breath and looking as though they're about to stop breathing, there's a lot of possible causes for this and talking to the patient – not that people who are trying to perish are great conversationalists – and examining them often aren't enough to be sure what the problem is. Investigations are required; electrical recordings of the heart, blood tests and scans are organised. But if the doctor were to take the view, "I don't know what's wrong here; let's get some investigations done to try and work out what the diagnosis is; when I've seen the results I can start some treatment" then they might as well not bother: they could simply wait for the post-mortem report. They need to get on with giving oxygen and helping the breathing and making their best guess about what the problem is and starting treatment for it whilst they wait for the investigations. They need to keep reassessing how the patient is responding to the treatments they're giving, and as the results of investigations come back they may need to change tack, more than once on some occasions.

'Much less dramatically but much more frequently, it's not at all uncommon for doctors to see patients with extensive lists of symptoms relating to all parts of their bodies. In such cases it is very rare for there to be a single cause that can be diagnosed and treated. Usually there's a complex interplay between what the patient is prone to regard as acceptable medical diagnoses and their mind. I've spent many hours over many years trying to explain that it's not helpful to look at things in a way that regards symptoms driven by some clearly identified physical problem as real and those which can't obviously be attributed to a physical problem as not, and it's better to recognise that the body affects the mind and the mind affects the body, so we need to consider both together. Some patients remain steadfastly unconvinced despite my best endeavours and in such cases I must confess to sometimes finding it hard to remain empathetic as their list of intolerable symptoms grows towards double figures and beyond. I find myself wondering if they think I will be disappointed if they cannot produce another one, and in rare instances I feel like the white fluffy seal in one of the old Greenpeace campaigns against the fur trade, clubbed and bleeding into the ice.

'I digress!' he continued. 'The relevant point here is that every one of the patient's many symptoms could act as a stimulus for investigations to be organised, but if this were done then it's doubtful whether some patients would ever have time to go home, such would be the number of them. A good doctor needs to be able to decide not to do things; not to organise CT scans of the brain whenever someone says they have a headache, not to organise telescope tests of the bowel whenever someone says they have some abdominal discomfort. Could this go wrong? Could something be missed? Yes, of course it could, but if they are alert to warning signs, to red flags as they're often called, then the chances of missing something significant are very small. But make no mistake, the doctor is personally responsible for their actions or inactions and this can put them into a lonely place.

'What all this means,' Dr Old went on, 'is that good doctors who see patients spend their time making decisions as individuals, continually weighing the information they have and deciding, do I do this or do I do that? They'll follow a protocol or a pathway if it seems the right thing to do for the patient in front of them, but not infrequently there'll be something about the particular case that makes them think, no, this time I'm going to advise something a bit different. This ability is crucial to practising good medicine at a patient level but at odds with the ways that healthcare systems are managed in any place with higher aims than just providing as much intervention as possible to those who can pay for it. Given this, it isn't any surprise – in fact it's inevitable – that good doctors will question any changes to protocols or pathways or ways of working that those in management roles seek to implement, and they'll resist them if they're not personally convinced of their good sense. A few will do so openly but the usual tactic is passive resistance, with senior – that means older – doctors almost universally expert in this. You've no hope of managing doctors if you don't recognise what drives them and simply see them as difficult, and by my reckoning any doctors who are readily compliant with management instructions almost certainly aren't good doctors.'

There was a chance that by this time Margaret would have fallen asleep and buried her head in her sorbet, but Dr Old had glanced at her occasionally to check that she hadn't and evidence that she'd managed to stay awake came when she observed, 'I think I'm beginning to understand how my father got into difficulties. In any workforce, in any group of people, there's always a range of how people behave and I guess he was at one end of the spectrum.'

'Yes,' Dr Old replied, 'I think that's almost certainly right. I only met him during the business with the Medical Regulator and he came over as extremely dedicated to his work and extremely principled, but a man who marched to the beat of his own drum and wasn't bothered about the tune that anyone else might be playing, if you know what I mean.' She nodded to indicate that she did. 'He obviously prided himself on his ability to think clearly and make decisions,' he went on, 'and I didn't get the impression he'd be backward in expressing his opinions about anything that went on in his hospital that he didn't approve of, unlike the passive resistors.'

'I presume you're not a passive resistor?' she asked, knowing of course that he wasn't.

'No,' he replied, 'but not in your father's camp either. I'm stuck somewhere in the middle ground. I'm definitely a clinical doctor of the type I think your father would recognise. I see patients and think it's my job to advise them the best I can, whatever a pathway or protocol might say, but I also see that it's necessary to manage the system because – despite laudable intentions – chaos and insolvency would follow if every doctor was able to do whatever they wanted for their patients, or every patient could demand what they wanted from every doctor.'

He paused to take a mouthful of sticky toffee pudding.

'What's it like being in the middle ground?' she asked.

'The honest answer is mixed,' he replied after some delay. 'Sometimes uncomfortable – trying to steer the path can require leaving many people, sometimes everyone it seems, frustrated and angry and not thanking you for it. Being in the middle can sometimes make you feel very alone and uncertain.'

Margaret's shoulders sagged and she suddenly seemed distant. She was thinking about something and for a moment looked as though she was about to say what it was, but she didn't.

'Does that make sense?,' he asked.

After a moment Margaret woke from her reverie. 'Sorry,' she said, and in a quiet voice after some further delay, 'yes, it makes perfect sense; I know what you mean. Sometimes a fair plan leaves everyone feeling equally unhappy.' There was some story here which she wasn't ready to share.

Moving to ground she felt comfortable on she continued, 'I imagine the Medical Regulator asked you to help them because they thought you'd give a balanced opinion, which is another way of saying you occupied the middle ground.'

'That's a generous suggestion,' he replied, 'and it may be right.' His mind gradually filled with thoughts of things that had happened after the hearing. It was his turn to become silent and introspective and hers to bring him back to the here and now.

'You said you sometimes help the Medical Regulator or other hospitals with problems,' she asked with emphasis on the sometimes. 'How do you decide who to help, and why did you get involved in my father's case?'

'A mixture of things,' he replied. 'There are the banal practicalities of how much work needs to be done and what's the timescale; there's the matter of who's asking – some people you don't say no to, or only if you've got a very good excuse; and whether whatever it is seems interesting and important. It's easy to say no to the Medical Regulator but flattering to be asked by them, and your father's case didn't involve a massive amount of work. The documentation wasn't very extensive, it didn't require wading through multiple lever-arch files mindful of the possibility of legal representatives saying things like "Can I bring your attention to the email on page 412 of file four?" and the Medical Regulator doesn't work quickly so you can find time in your diary if you want to. But most importantly for me I thought it would be interesting. The case involved very fundamental issues about treatment of patients and the role of the doctor in making decisions about their care. I thought it would be a useful stimulus for getting my own thoughts in order and good to be part of a discussion that might have important implications.'

'And looking back on it now, are you pleased you got involved?' Margaret asked.

'A good question,' he replied, 'and I'm not sure, at least I think I'd probably give you a different answer if you asked me on different days. It was certainly interesting and it was certainly important, but for a few months afterwards it caused me more worry and sleepless nights than I'd ever had before and thankfully haven't had since. Did your father tell you what happened?'

'He said it caught everyone by surprise. Stories about doctors' death squads in the media. He didn't give a lot of detail, or I can't recall it if he did, but I remember him saying he thought he got off pretty lightly and it was the chair of the panel they mainly targeted, and that you came in for some criticism.'

'I think that's a pretty fair summary,' Dr Old responded after a sip of coffee. 'I didn't have any inkling that anything was going to happen. The panel decided they were going to recommend to the regulator that they consider setting up a couple of working parties to produce guidance for doctors about how they should make decisions about managing very ill and demented patients who arrive in Emergency Departments in increasing numbers. I left the hearing thinking this was a sensible thing for them to suggest and wondering if I'd be asked to contribute.

'If I remember rightly the hearing was on a Friday. I'm not sure what I was doing over the weekend, but it was only on the Monday morning that I realised there was trouble. One of my colleagues sent me a text with a link to an article on a BBC news webpage along with a cartoon of someone sticking their head above a parapet, and I was just digesting this when I got a call from the person at the Medical Regulator's who'd got me involved with the case. He sounded very flustered and asked if anyone had been in touch with me, and had I spoken to the police.'

'The police?' Margaret asked, very surprised.

'Yes; apparently people on social media had threatened the chair of the panel; said they knew where he lived and were going to burn down his house and harm his family.'

'Oh, how awful. Did anyone threaten you in that sort of way?'

'No, thankfully not,' he said, 'but it does happen to doctors sometimes and there's no good way of dealing with it.'

At that moment discussion was curtailed. Some of the ceiling lights in the restaurant were switched on and on glancing around they found that they and a group of four men sitting at a table on the opposite side of the room were the only customers left. All looked startled by the brightness. Picking up on the subtle hint, they settled the bill, put on their coats, and headed outside.

Dr Old said he'd escort Margaret back to her car, which she initially said wasn't necessary, but dispute was rapidly resolved when it became apparent that, although she knew where she'd parked it, she wasn't sure of the best way of getting there.

'Thanks for meeting with me and talking,' she said as they walked, 'although we've only managed to scratch the surface of everything that happened.'

He thought the same but wasn't sure how he felt about it or what to say and remained silent.

'Would you be happy to talk some more?' she said as they reached her car. He nodded. 'Good, and thanks again,' she said as she opened the door and got in. 'I'll send you an email to fix something up.'

EIGHTEEN

RINGING IN HER EARS

Margaret switched the heater on and fiddled with the dial to get the air jets directed towards the windscreen to clear it of condensation, which she tried to speed up by wiping it with an old tea towel kept in the driver's door pocket for the purpose. Within a minute or so visibility was good enough to proceed and she twiddled the dial again to get the jets directed at her face, hoping this would reduce the chances of her dozing off on the journey home. She had to concentrate on following the satnav for a few minutes until she got onto the motorway but could then complete the rest on autopilot. There was one junction where the road layout was odd and concentration was required to make sure that you landed up heading west and not east, but aside from this the driving was easy – there wasn't a lot of traffic on the road – and she had much to think about.

She had been worried that conversation might be difficult and had prepared, if it was, to have as quick a supper as decently possible before making a getaway. But it hadn't been like that. Dr Old would obviously have deliberated over what he might be getting himself into, having supper with this woman who'd appeared out of the blue after tracking him down, but she found him easy to talk to and he'd seemed to be open and honest in what he said. Although he'd gone on a lot about some things, he had checked in with her as he did so to find out if she wanted him to continue, and she liked that. It meant he wasn't a bore, who gives no consideration to their audience beyond the fact that they have one, and he did seem keen to discuss the things she wanted to talk about. There could be other reasons why a man would agree to a woman's suggestion that they spend an evening together, but although aware of and subscribing to the well-known aphorism that the truth is never pure and rarely simple, his explanation of the reason why he got involved with the Medical Regulator's hearing was reassuringly consistent with him having a genuine interest in the subjects that had become important to her because they were relevant to what had happened to her parents.

As she turned the car into the drive she wasn't sure whether she would contact Dr Old again, or what she'd suggest if she did. She thought she probably would but hadn't made any firm commitment beyond saying that she'd send him an email and he certainly couldn't expect this immediately.

The following afternoon Margaret was checking through her emails and there was one from Shirley. A few days after her discussion with Peter, when it was agreed that she'd take three months' unpaid leave, she'd written to several of her friends saying that she was taking some time off work and asking if they'd like to meet up. Most had replied promptly, noting that her wording was different from her usual "I've got a gap between projects and have some free time in the next few weeks" and asking if she was okay. Shirley wasn't good at returning phone calls or responding rapidly to texts or emails so her failure to do so on this occasion hadn't surprised Margaret at all, and neither did her suggestion that they might meet up for supper the evening after next because – to the frustration of many – she never seemed to plan anything more than a week ahead. Her explanation for the short notice on this occasion was that she'd "just discovered" that her husband was out at some work event, which Margaret was sure he would have informed her about many weeks ago and noted on the kitchen wall calendar in his clear, bold hand, which he did routinely to evidence things in anticipation of her regular accusations that he hadn't told her anything. However, Margaret was free and it suited her to meet up with a friend who she was sure would be able and willing to provide her perspective on things they'd never discussed before.

Margaret and Shirley had known each other for about twenty years, first meeting at an open-air lido when by chance they had booked into the same time slot. Shirley had forgotten her compulsory swimming hat and Margaret lent her one, leading to a post-swim coffee and chat where they instantly bonded over both finding a particular man who swam there regularly to be extremely irritating. They agreed that they couldn't put their fingers on why or justify their opinion to someone who didn't share it, but he definitely was.

Shirley had just completed her nursing training and was working as a staff nurse in the Emergency Department of one of the big London hospitals, whilst Margaret was a year or two into her management consultancy job. In the early stages of their friendship Margaret had made a mistake in suggesting that they might go to a concert which she knew Shirley would like, failing to recognise that she couldn't really afford to buy a ticket. After much embarrassment on both sides Shirley had accepted a ticket as a birthday present and they'd both enjoyed the event, although not as much as if payment for the tickets hadn't been a problem. Ever since then, Margaret had been careful not to make very definite suggestions as to what they might do when they went out together, and in line with this asked Shirley to decide where they should eat. She chose a pizza restaurant not far from where she lived and less than a mile from Margaret's flat, and to Margaret's amazement she received a "ping" on her phone the next morning to say that a booking had been made and she was expected there at 19.15 the following evening.

Margaret arrived in good time after walking from her flat through the London streets, full of people going somewhere but not so crowded that it was difficult to move at her natural pace. She found herself smiling as she recognised that she enjoyed the noise, the lights and the bustle, which she realised she'd missed in the few weeks she'd been staying with her father. She was definitely a townie and not a country girl.

Shirley arrived breathless and apologetic a few minutes late. They'd been short of staff, as usual she said, and she'd been delayed getting away. As she took off her coat and hung it over the back of her chair, declining the waitress's suggestion that she take it away to the cloakroom, Margaret congratulated her on her new hairstyle, cut short with a lateral parting, natural wave and dyed a reddish brown, which she thought a definite improvement on some previous vivid iterations. 'More appropriate for my new position,' Shirley explained, clearly very pleased to be able to say that she'd recently been promoted and was now a matron in the Emergency Department.

Drinks were ordered without requiring much deliberation or discussion, a bottle of Prosecco and a jug of tap water, and Margaret said with a grin that she was impressed that Shirley – who had no liking or aptitude for technology – had made an online booking for the evening. Shirley wasn't the type to take praise when it wasn't her due and instead of remaining silent informed her that her son had made the booking. 'At breakfast I was looking at my phone trying to find the number of the restaurant so I could give them a call,' she said, 'and my son told me this was ridiculous – one of his favourite words – took it off me and about a minute of rapid poking later told me the booking had been made and you'd been sent a notification. He's in the sixth form,' she went on, 'doing maths and computer science. He doesn't say much, and when he does I can hardly understand a word, but the teachers tell us he's pretty clever and Eric says he's like the IT people at work, hard to chat with but obviously good at talking to computers, and he says they're very well paid.'

As they began their pizzas they caught up with each other's news. Margaret explained that she'd gone home, which Shirley knew she hadn't done for many years, because her mother had died and that she was trying to get to know her father. 'That's a surprise,' Shirley said in a very matter-of-fact way. 'I thought you didn't like him.'

'That's true, I didn't,' Margaret replied, 'but some things I heard at the funeral made me think. The way people talked about him and Mum wasn't the way I remembered them, and I learned that he'd got into trouble in the hospital and felt bad.'

'Why?' Shirley asked, puzzled that Margaret should feel bad about something that can't have had anything to do with her.

'I don't know, just bad,' she responded. 'Bad that I didn't know my mother was ill until it was too late; bad that I didn't know my father was in difficulties; and I thought of you when I found out about some of the problems.'

It was a good job that Shirley didn't have a full mouth at this moment. 'Me!' she said with some surprise.

'Yes,' Margaret continued. 'It was something that happened in the Emergency Department that triggered things off.'

Shirley was intrigued, slowed the demolition of her pizza, and asked, 'Why, what happened?'

Margaret recounted the story of Mrs D arriving in the Emergency Department, the next of kin's phone number being wrongly recorded, the state she was in, what her father had done, and what had happened afterwards following the family's complaints. 'What do you make of that?' Margaret asked, genuinely interested in what Shirley would have to say.

'The first thing,' Shirley said after a delay that wasn't typical of her, 'is that your dad sounds like the sort of doctor I'd like to work with, and I feel sorry for him.' Margaret, who really hadn't known what she was going to say, was nonetheless surprised and intrigued. In their meetings over many years she couldn't think of more than one or two occasions where Shirley had praised a doctor, and none where she'd expressed any sympathy for one.

Encouraged and led by Margaret's prompting, Shirley went on to explain that the scenario of an old, frail, demented patient arriving in the Emergency Department with a severe acute illness and without it being possible to contact the relatives happened every day, often more than once. 'They shouldn't be sent into hospital at all,' she said. 'They should be kept comfortable and allowed to die at home, or in the care home or nursing home, wherever they are.'

'So why are they sent in?' Margaret asked.

'Because it's the easiest thing to do,' Shirley explained. 'Unless a plan's been made for what's going to happen when someone's dying, it's very difficult to make it up on the hoof, and even if a plan has been made it's no good if there isn't the nursing and medical support. Much easier to call an ambulance and ship the patient to the nearest hospital. Much easier for relatives not to see their mum or dad dying, which is usually an unpleasant business. Much easier for staff in care homes or nursing homes, particularly if the relatives have been critical of the care they've been providing, to get the patient off their premises. Much easier for the doctor who's called out, who just about never knows the patient and has lots of other calls to attend, to phone for an ambulance. So they land up in the Emergency Department.

'What happens when they arrive depends on who sees them. If there's a sensible doctor – someone like your father – they decide to keep them comfortable and let them die, but,' Shirley went on with a voice that was either angry or resigned or disdainful, Margaret couldn't decide which, 'there aren't very many sensible doctors around nowadays. The young ones – poor lambs – are just about all frightened to make any decisions. They organise blood tests and X-rays and drips and antibiotics and generally faff around, and it doesn't make a blind bit of difference except in prolonging the inevitable. Absolute bloody madness, if you'll pardon my French, but they feel they'll be criticised if they don't try to do something.'

'And do they get criticised?' Margaret asked very logically.

'Yes, we all get criticised all the time,' Shirley replied. 'Of course they don't call it that, but there's an industry of people who inspect and criticise hospitals, so I suppose it isn't a surprise that the managers in the hospital have an industry of people who investigate and criticise those of us who are trying to look after the patients. It means they can look tough when the inspectors visit.'

Margaret didn't think this sounded very functional. 'If they don't call it criticism, what do they call it?' she asked.

'They've invented a whole new language since I trained as a nurse,' Shirley replied with a snort of derision. 'There's a whole lot of crap about a no-blame culture, and then all sorts of investigations and reviews of what they call "patient safety incidents" and "preventable patient harm" and ways of grading the amount of harm and people you have to write reports for, and as soon as I've learned the way the process works and what forms to fill in they change them all, and it's all so bloody pointless.'

Margaret could understand the frustration of having to deal with processes and forms that kept changing but couldn't see why it wasn't a good idea to try to learn if something had gone wrong. 'Why's it pointless?' she asked.

'Because the answer's almost always the same,' Shirley replied. 'The reason the old woman got out of bed and fell and bust her hip was because there weren't enough staff on the ward to stop her. The reason the old man got a pressure ulcer on his backside was that there weren't enough staff to nurse him properly, and the nurses on the ward don't take responsibility in the way they used to.'

The suggestion that nurses didn't take responsibility concerned Margaret, but Shirley continued without being prompted. 'When I started off in nursing...' she said, following with a self-deprecating '... goodness I'm sounding old... when I started off in nursing,' she repeated, 'the ward sister would take responsibility for everything that happened on her ward. If one of her patients developed a pressure ulcer she'd take it personally, she'd be ashamed that it happened. Now it doesn't work like that. The nurse in charge isn't out on the ward supervising the care of the patients, they're in the office trying to sort out the rota, writing responses to incidents and complaints, and writing things to explain to the chief nurse why it wouldn't be safe to cut the number of nurses that their ward has any further. If it looks as though one of the patients might be developing pressure damage to their skin the response is that the team calls the tissue viability nurse, who will come and write some advice in the notes tomorrow. What's needed,' she concluded with some passion, 'is a good nurse in charge who is out on the ward, with enough nurses and healthcare assistants to give the care that's needed, and everyone taking pride in doing a good job.'

She stopped for a moment. Margaret hadn't heard her speak about her work in such a way before and was thinking what to say next, but she didn't have chance to do so before Shirley continued. 'It used to be,' she said, 'that the ward sister was the top of the tree. They were in charge of their ward and everything that happened on it. If any of the nurses were a minute late for duty, or their uniform wasn't neat and tidy, or their hair wasn't pinned up properly, well, they probably wouldn't make the same mistake again. When I started, some of the old ward sisters wouldn't allow a doctor to see a patient without asking for permission, and none would let a doctor who had seen a patient leave the ward without speaking to them. It's not like that nowadays and much the worse for it.'

There was now a pause. Shirley looked thoughtful, which again was something foreign to Margaret's experience of her. 'What made it change?' she asked.

'Lots of things,' Shirley replied, 'not just one. More hassle from above. More hassle from below. More hassle from patients and relatives. Invention of much easier nursing jobs that are better paid.'

Margaret knew, as does everyone, that there's more hassle in life generally than there used to be, but the invention of easier jobs that were better paid triggered automatic thoughts of perverse incentives in whatever part of her brain management consultancy resided: 'What jobs?' she asked.

'All sorts,' Shirley replied. 'Specialist nurses, practice development nurses, nurse consultants. Don't get me wrong. I'm not saying they don't do useful things, but the jobs are a heck of a lot easier than being in charge of a ward and a lot less important in terms of trying to run the hospital.'

Margaret was curious: 'So why,' she asked, 'are they paid more than being a ward sister?'

'Because,' Shirley said angrily, 'being a ward sister isn't an academic thing and the people who run nursing are obsessed with everyone having a personal development plan and studying for a Masters. Much less kudos and pay for just being good at the most important job in the hospital.'

The storm seemed to have blown itself out. 'Wow!' said Margaret. 'I've known you for a very long time and I've never heard you speak like that before.'

'Sorry,' Shirley replied, 'I didn't mean to bore you,' the flush rising in her cheeks.

'No, I haven't been bored,' Margaret hastened to reassure her. 'It's been interesting, very interesting; it helps me make more sense of some of the things my father's told me.'

After the storm came the calm. Shirley, feeling that she'd got carried away, busied herself with topping up the chunky blue glasses with water and drinking hers before starting to attend to some Prosecco. A burst of laughter drew her attention to the table of three men and three women immediately behind Margaret. She'd been conscious of them speaking loudly and generally seeming to be having a good time, but someone had obviously just said or done something very funny and a large man wearing a patterned purple shirt was rocking to and fro on his chair and howling to the point where he was finding it difficult to breathe. She thought the woman sitting opposite him may be a nurse who worked in the medical admissions' ward but it was difficult to be sure. Nurses on a night out often bear little resemblance to the version seen at work, but if the Afro-style hair was restrained and the green eyeshadow and dangly earrings removed, then it probably was her. Shirley hoped she hadn't heard her going on about the ills of the hospital and the ills of nursing, but it was vanishingly unlikely that she could have done.

Margaret sipped her water in a contemplative fashion. Virtually everything Shirley had said resonated with things she'd heard from her father. She knew it would take her some time to organise her thoughts, but her immediate response was a powerful feeling that both thought the prevailing culture and system were increasingly at odds with common sense – or at least what they both perceived as common sense – in the way that people who were nearing the ends of their lives were looked after, also that broader changes in the way medicine and nursing were practised were taking things in a wrong direction.

Margaret's musings were interrupted by Shirley topping up her wine glass, admonishing her for not drinking her fair share, and changing the topic: 'You said in your email that you were taking some time off from work; what's that about?' she asked. Margaret explained she wasn't sure, but that after many years in her job she didn't know if she wanted to continue doing the same old same old and had taken some unpaid leave to decide.

If she had been hoping for a sympathetic ear, she was disappointed. For Shirley – as for most people who work hard for a living – the notion of being in the position of not requiring next month's salary was in the realms of fantasy, rather like walking into your bedroom every evening and finding that the room had been aired, the sheets and pillowcases freshly laundered and changed, and the pillows plumped up by unseen hands. She felt that having time off to worry about whether you wanted to continue in your job was a luxury that somehow couldn't have been earned honestly, and if the conversation had been about some third party would undoubtedly have said words to this effect. 'What would you do instead?' she asked.

Margaret repeated that she hadn't got any definite ideas but explained that the sort of skills she had were necessary in running any large organisation or business.

'Then perhaps what you need to do is find something you think is worth running and see if they'll give you a job,' Shirley observed. Margaret was just digesting this casually offered but wise piece of advice when Shirley continued. 'How's the love life?' she asked.

About twenty minutes later the evening ended and Margaret, who didn't fancy the walk at that time, ordered an Uber to take her home with Shirley's diagnosis that she was having a mid-life crisis and needed to get a new man or a new job or preferably both ringing in her ears.

NINETEEN

BEING A BURDEN

A few days later Margaret had just returned from doing the local shopping late one afternoon and was packing things away in the kitchen, thinking about what she'd cook for dinner, when her phone rang.

'Hello, it's Malcolm,' a voice said. Margaret couldn't think of any Malcolms that she knew and her confusion must have transmitted itself through the ether or wherever mobile signals travel. 'Malcolm from the hospital, a friend of your father's, we met at the funeral,' the voice explained.

'Hello,' Margaret replied, recognising who it was, surprised that he knew her mobile number and with no idea why he might be calling.

'What are you doing on 3 April?' he asked. Margaret was again confused and didn't reply immediately. 'Joan's birthday; your mother's birthday,' he continued after a moment. Margaret flushed with shame and felt grateful it was an old-fashioned voice call and not a video call which would undoubtedly have revealed her predicament. She must have produced cards and gifts as a young girl, but she hadn't done so for many years and couldn't have given her mother's birthday – or for that matter her father's – if asked to do so. 'Have you got anything planned?' Malcolm went on. 'If not, Annie and I were wondering if you'd both like to join us for supper. We thought we could go to the Old Boathouse Inn. It was one of your mother's favourites.'

'No,' Margaret replied hesitantly, 'we haven't. That sounds very nice,' and picking up confidence, 'It's very thoughtful of you to suggest it. I'll speak to Dad this evening but I'm sure we'd like to join you. I'll let you know.'

Jonathan Barber had been dreading 3 April and the memories it would evoke. How he'd go into town the weekend before and always struggle to select a card that seemed suitable, never able to find one saying "Happy Birthday" that didn't look tacky or saccharine, always settling for a blank card with an impressionist painting on which he'd write, "For Joan, with much love from Jonathan", hoping that the picture wasn't one he'd given before, at least not recently. How first thing in the morning, when his wife was in the bathroom, he'd pop out to the garden wearing his pyjamas, dressing gown and wellington boots and make a small posy of the various sorts of narcissi and daffodil that flowered late in the long shaded border by the side of the drive, trying to make sure he selected at least some that were heavily scented. He'd give it to her at breakfast, with the dew still on the flowers and the fragrance filling the kitchen.

Margaret's phone rang fifteen minutes before they were due to be picked up. 'Malcolm here. Sorry, we're running a bit late, see you in about half an hour,' was the message.

'It'll be the dog,' her father explained. 'It always is,' before going on to explain that the inevitable hound-induced delays were previously very useful from his perspective because Joan would always have been caught out if they ever had arrived on time. Today he wasn't in need of such assistance because Margaret was ready and had managed to be so without putting him through the torture of being asked for advice about what she should wear. Margaret considered whether blaming the dog was Malcolm's way of covering up the fact that his wife was also constitutionally unable to keep to time, but as they clambered into the car, after the apologies for lateness, which was only about ten minutes, Annie observed that she thought the dog had a sixth sense and was able to tell when they were trying to go out because it always took much longer to do its business in the garden on such occasions and they'd had a heck of job getting it back into the house. If this was a way of covering up her lack of punctuality, then she and her husband were clearly sticking to the same story.

The restaurant was in a village a few miles out in the country. Margaret sat in the back with Annie who explained that her mother had particularly liked the Old Boathouse Inn, although nobody seemed to know why it was called that as it seemed to have been used for storage by a local farmer before being converted. As they left the main road and started winding through narrower lanes Margaret found it increasingly difficult to pay full attention to the conversation, conscious that Malcolm's style was to occupy the centre of the road, even when approaching and driving round blind corners. She consoled herself with the thought that he didn't drive quickly and it was most unlikely that they'd meet anything bigger coming in the opposite direction, but she recognised that this would be of little comfort to anyone on a moped who might be travelling towards them but thankfully wasn't.

There was the crunch of gravel beneath the tyres as they pulled into the car park next to the river. In the dusk, before their eyes were blinded from looking directly at the light coming through the restaurant's windows, it was just possible to see the silhouettes of a few ducks sitting at the water's edge and somewhere overhead was the beating sound of one or two swans that had just taken off, squeaking characteristically as if they needed drops of lubricating oil on their wings.

The worn stone flags of the floor of the restaurant suggested they had witnessed a lot of traffic over many years and those of the timbers that were original looked as though they would have many tales to tell if they could find their voices. On the walls, as seems obligatory in such establishments, were sepia photographs of the village street and building they were now in. One from the twenties or thirties, as judged by a car and a van parked outside, showed what appeared to be some bales of hay and farm machinery through a large open doorway. There was no evidence of any boats.

It was only when they were inside that Margaret was able to see Malcolm and his wife properly. The moustache she'd remembered as his defining characteristic from her first encounter with him at her mother's funeral about a month ago was still his most immediately notable feature, clipped very neatly in contrast to untamed eyebrows and an unruly thin horseshoe of hair that was fighting a losing battle against baldness. He wore a checked shirt, Harris tweed jacket, brown corduroy trousers held up with a belt, and generally seemed to have a very pleasant and easy manner. Annie was a neat woman of middling build and height who, typical of her generation, thought it necessary to get more dressed up than her husband when going out. Over a knee-length dark blue knitted dress she wore a silver necklace with a large butterfly pendant and a tailored jacket along with an evening shoulder bag. Margaret's impression that she was less relaxed than her husband was confirmed when she displayed irritation as their table rocked slightly on the uneven floor, which Malcolm and her father rectified by putting some beer mats under one of its legs which they declared meant they'd earned their gin and tonics.

The waiter, a dapper Italian man of about thirty-five, handed round the menus and advised them about the dishes of the day. Malcolm took a quick glance, recognised two of his favourites, and spoke to Margaret. 'I've been trying to remember when we last met, apart from at the funeral. I think it was when you were home from university and we came round for supper with your parents. You were about to go out for the evening. I'm sure you wouldn't remember,' he said with a friendly smile.

'I must confess that I don't,' Margaret replied, returning his smile, 'but it's certainly plausible.'

'She's been catching up with everything that's gone on since then,' her father interjected. 'We've been talking a lot and I've told her about Joan's illness and the various other trials and tribulations.'

Margaret got the feeling that Annie was poised to say something along the lines of it being a shame that it was necessary for him to have to explain them, but Malcolm – perhaps sensing the same – followed on quickly with, 'And I expect she'll have enjoyed being able to share with you what she's been doing.'

The conversation then moved naturally on to Margaret giving Malcolm and Annie a brief potted account of her career which they listened to attentively, the brief comments they made to encourage her suggesting that Annie had as much knowledge about her business as her father, but Malcolm obviously had quite a sophisticated understanding. She then explained how her father had told her about her mother's illness and – feeling a pang of guilt about concealing her few days' delay in responding to his letter – said she'd come home as soon as she could, but too late to see her. Aware that it was several weeks since the funeral, Malcolm had been surprised when Jonathan – who he'd spoken to on the phone about once a week ever since his retirement – told him that Margaret was going to be staying with him for a while.

'What are your plans now?' he asked amiably.

'I'm not sure,' Margaret replied very directly. 'I saw a friend a week or so ago and she diagnosed me as having a mid-life crisis.'

'Shirley, your nursing friend?' her father chipped in. Margaret confirmed that it was.

Malcolm wondered whether any remedy had been proposed but thought better of it, asking directly: 'What sort of nursing does she do?'

'She works as a matron in an Emergency Department,' Margaret replied, giving the name of the hospital when prompted to do so.

'That'll be a tough gig,' Malcolm continued. 'I worked there for a few years when I was training. I don't know what it's like now, but the reception desk used to be behind toughened glass and metal bars, which says all you need to know.'

Annie and Margaret weren't sure that they did know, leading Malcolm to elaborate his theory that it was a waste of time and money for the government or anyone else to develop complex methods for identifying and quantifying urban deprivation; all you needed to do, he said, was to take a photo of every hospital's ED reception desk. A low counter with staff sitting behind in a normal-looking office was indicative of a genteel area. A range of features making it more difficult to attack the reception staff, but also to see and hear them, appeared progressively with transition to less salubrious parts, with metal grilles, bars and bulletproof glass being the extreme.

'I learned a lot there, including from one of the matrons,' he explained. 'I can't remember her name; a Liverpudlian woman, hard as nails but with a great sense of humour if you got onto her wavelength. "Man in cubicle six, another who's slipped whilst carving a chicken," she would say to indicate that attention was needed for someone who'd been stabbed, many such patients being unwilling to give a plausible account of how they sustained their injuries. But that was many years ago. What did your friend Shirley say about it now?'

'I'm afraid I didn't ask her about the reception desk,' Margaret answered with a smile, 'so I can't tell you what that's like now, and we didn't talk about patients who'd been stabbed. I asked her about frail and demented patients arriving in the ED.'

Immediately the words left her lips she was conscious of her father stopping in the midst of a chew of his whitebait starter, but it was Malcolm who spoke next. 'What did she say?' he asked.

'The same sort of things that Dad has told me,' Margaret replied, before going on to give some examples, after which Malcolm spoke again with an amiable chuckle.

'It seems to me,' he said, 'that your friend Shirley is the sort of nurse we need to clone, ignoring the fact that it would be illegal to do so. They're an endangered species now, proper nurses.'

Jonathan knew exactly what he meant and following the exposition on changes in nursing that she'd had from Shirley, Margaret thought she probably did as well, so it was left to Annie to ask for explanation. Malcolm obliged in a manner that led Margaret to wonder if the pizza place had been bugged. He recalled the first consultant he'd worked for when he qualified as a doctor, a sour surgeon on the verge of retirement, saying after there'd been some minor mistake in implementation of his directions for the management of a surgical wound that he knew it would be a catastrophe when the hospital allowed ward sisters to marry. Sensing that his wife was about to pounce, with Margaret likely not too far behind, he hastened to reassure them that this wasn't his view, but it did emphasise the importance of the job. 'If I was allowed to do one thing to improve the hospital,' he said, 'I'd make it so that apart from the chief nurse and their deputies, no other nurse could earn more than a ward sister.' Margaret knew that Shirley would approve and told him so. 'There's a great quote from one of my heroes, the Liverpool manager, Bill Shankly,' Malcolm continued, 'who said "a football team is like a piano: you need eight men to carry it and three who can play the damn thing." We've forgotten the importance of your friend Shirley and others who do the carrying.'

There was a lull as the starters were cleared away. Annie spoke next. 'I don't pay a lot of attention to medical things in the news,' she said, 'but whenever I do there's often something about some new advance, a new test or a new treatment, but (nodding in the directions of her husband and then Jonathan) whenever I hear you two talking, you're always moaning that things aren't as good as they used to be.'

There was a pause, helpfully occupied by the waiter arriving to top up their glasses and receive a request for another bottle of fizzy water. Her husband spoke first. 'I think that's a fair comment,' he said, with some hesitation in his voice suggesting that he'd considered saying it wasn't but thought better of it. 'In fact I was thinking about that only yesterday when I learned that Robert the Bones had a heart attack earlier this week.'

It was established that Annie had met him, a large extrovert orthopaedic surgeon wearing a red bow tie, at a party last Christmas, and Malcolm and Jonathan agreed he would definitely have made the shortlist of the hospital's consultants most likely to suffer coronary misfortune. 'When I was a medical houseman,' Malcolm continued, 'we used to treat heart attacks by admitting the patient to the coronary care unit and monitoring for R on T ectopics, starting a lignocaine infusion if we saw them. I can even remember the dose.'

Malcolm and Jonathan then went into reminiscence mode, during which Annie and Margaret understood little, excepting that Jonathan's recollection of the dose was different from Malcolm's. A break followed after Malcolm declared, 'It was, of course, completely bloody useless,' and he and Jonathan both hooted with laughter.

Margaret picked up the thread. 'I presume it seemed sensible at the time,' she said. Malcolm and her father confirmed that it did, explaining that patients with heart attacks died when their heart stopped beating properly because the electrical signal telling it how to do so became chaotic and the pumping chamber stopped being able to pump the blood in the right direction. The tutorial continued with a brief description of the electrocardiogram, ECG for short, which is the squiggly tracing of the electrical signal controlling the heartbeat, and how R and T are the names of two of the squiggles, and how if an R landed on top of a T it could precipitate the electrical chaos, and how an infusion of lignocaine – now typically confined to being used as a local anaesthetic, for instance when having a filling or extraction done at the dentist – could reduce the chances of that happening.

'The reason it didn't work, except perhaps by delaying things for a short while,' her father explained in anticipation of the obvious question, 'is that it was treating a symptom and not the cause,' and he went on to recount that it was discovered that the underlying problem was the development of a clot in a coronary artery supplying blood to the heart muscle, and recognition of this led to treatments designed to dissolve the clot and get the blood flowing again.

For a short while it seemed as though musings not of interest to Margaret or his wife about a clot-busting drug called streptokinase were about to take over, but Malcolm recognised the danger and described to them how it was given by injection into a vein with the intention that it travelled round in the bloodstream and dissolved the clot in the coronary artery. Big trials showed that it worked, he said, before going on to say that further improvements in outcomes were obtained when other drugs were given down tubes fed through the arteries so that they were delivered right on top of the clot in the blocked blood vessel, and – coming now to the treatment given earlier in the week to their colleague Robert the Bones – even better results were now had by putting a wire through the clot to guide an inflatable balloon into position to stretch up the channel through the artery and then put a stent in place to keep it open. 'Perhaps,' Malcolm commented, 'he'll now accept that physicians are of some use on some occasions,' leading Jonathan to produce an appreciative chuckle before they both lapsed into silence.

The arrival of food in restaurants stimulates some people to provide a running commentary along the lines of whether what's served is as expected from the description of it on the menu, and which of the diners has made the best choice, ignoring the fact that a verdict on the latter would require knowing what each individual would most like to eat at that very moment and how what was in front of them matched up to this. Annie was such a person and offered the table her thoughts as the main courses arrived, concluding that Margaret was to be congratulated on her choice of fish of the day and the side of vegetables she'd ordered to go with it. She said she found it very difficult to cook broccoli, with the stalks hard if the florets were right or the florets mushy if the stalks were well done. Margaret – noting that the men were not contributing to the discussion – agreed both out of politeness and because she thought Annie's comments on the difficulties were true.

Annie, aware of her husband's silence and suspicious

of the reason for it, turned to him: 'Malcolm, you're being very quiet,' she said inquisitively.

'Sorry,' he replied. 'I was thinking,' and when pursued as to the subject continued, 'No, not about broccoli; about something you said earlier; that we were always moaning about what's wrong with medicine and not talking about the things that have changed for the better, and there have been a lot of them.'

After turning to Margaret and explaining he was a rheumatologist and looked after people with joint problems, he went on to say that when he started in the specialty the clinics were full of people in miserable pain from rheumatoid arthritis whose hands became more and more deformed as they watched, and although there were some drugs that could alter the progress they frequently weren't very effective. All he and his colleagues could do in such cases was to try to relieve the inflammation and the pain with drugs that often caused serious stomach and kidney trouble, with physiotherapy and physical aids to help maintain function. 'You don't see that nowadays, at least you pretty well never should. Biologics, that's drugs made from proteins designed to zero in on various parts of the immune system that are causing the trouble, have changed things completely. They're not perfect by any means, but they genuinely have changed the game and it's been wonderful to be able to use them.'

Jonathan was aware that Malcolm could be irritated by his wife's tendency to volunteer her opinions on matters of taste, culinary or otherwise, to captive audiences, and that this typically stimulated him to withdraw into a sulky silence. Recognising this he felt as though he was colluding by remaining quiet, and he had in fact been engaged in similar cogitation. 'That's right,' he said. 'I was thinking along the same lines. As you know, I used to be a gastroenterologist, and when I started off, peptic ulcers were common and all put down to acidity in the stomach. Patients used to take buckets full of antacids and went to bed at night with glasses of cold milk. Lots of operations were done to cut the main nerve – the vagus nerve – supplying the stomach to cut down the acidity, or to chop out the bit of the stomach responsible for making the acid.'

At this point the medics digressed into recollections of the changing fashions for vagotomy and pyloroplasty, highly selective vagotomy and partial gastrectomy, and how in the absence of any good evidence surgeons would argue about which was best until they were blue in the face. 'Anyway,' Jonathan continued, bringing Annie and Margaret back into the conversation, 'two sorts of drug were invented that were good at stopping the stomach from producing acid, so the operations weren't needed any more and the surgeons had to find other ways to spend their time. But that wasn't the end of it, a couple of Australian doctors then discovered that most cases are caused by a bacterium and antibiotics are the answer, antibiotics along with drugs to cut the acidity. Goodness knows,' he concluded after a brief pause, 'what two doctors sitting at this table in twenty or thirty years' time will be saying about the treatments we give now!'

Margaret found this fascinating. As she listened to Malcolm and her father telling their stories, heading off enthusiastically down rabbit holes from time to time before returning to their main tracks, it was clear that over the courses of their working careers there had been many discoveries leading to significant improvements in treatments. She tried to think of other lines of work where two people in or very near their sixties would be able to look back and give similar accounts. Those with a lifetime in computers and IT could undoubtedly do so, the mobile phone in her pocket that had just buzzed being clear evidence of change and change for the better. One of her friends who worked in the City regularly talked about changes in financial instruments whenever she asked him what he was doing. As far as she could make out these enabled him to get very highly paid for lending or spending increasing amounts of money that the fund he managed didn't really have. She remained to be convinced that this was a good thing, excepting of course for him and others receiving the large salaries and bonuses. Her contemplations were cut short before she could come up with any other examples by Annie's intervention. 'I don't suppose,' she said, 'that in twenty or thirty years' time they'll have discovered a cure for old age,' before going on to add, 'Mind you, I'm not sure that would be a good thing – I don't think I'd want to be a burden.'

Hearing the word "burden" triggered echoes in Margaret's mind of one of the early conversations she'd had with her father when he began to explain the various issues that eventually led to his early retirement. She couldn't remember if, to use a clunky expression that one of her management consultancy bosses was fond of for a time, they'd wrestled to the ground what was meant by the phrase. This seemed a reasonable occasion to explore the matter further. 'I remember,' she said, looking at her father, 'you talking about people in the past saying they didn't want to be a burden, but that they didn't say this anymore.'

'That's right,' he replied. 'It's a phrase from another age.'

Margaret pursued the point. 'But what did they mean by it, and why don't they say it now?'

'They were thinking,' he said, 'about impact on their family, and they don't say it now because families don't expect to care for elderly relatives who can't look after themselves.'

The silence that followed was broken by Malcolm, who'd been quiet for a while; 'Perhaps I could tell a family story,' he said with a glance towards his wife.

'I remember talking with my grandmother when I was about thirteen or fourteen. She was a straight-talking northern woman who looked and sounded like Thora Hird and sometimes spoke as if Alan Bennett had written her scripts – look her up on YouTube if you don't know who I mean. I don't know why we were talking about the subject, but she said she never wanted to be a burden; that being a burden would be a terrible thing.

'I didn't understand and asked her what she meant. She said she never wanted to be dependent on other people, on her family. When my time comes, I'm ready to go, she said.

'This didn't mean much to me at the time; I suppose it wouldn't to most teenage boys, but it started to when I began speaking to patients and families as a medical student and young doctor. Most people seemed more frightened of becoming disabled and dependent than they were of dying, and they often used the phrase "not wanting to be a burden".'

Margaret wasn't sure if she'd heard correctly. 'Less afraid of dying?' she asked.

'Yes, I think so. I'm sure there'll be a literature on it, which I've never read, but at the risk of being proved stupid I'd say this was down to several things. Life was tough for many people and they didn't expect it to be different. Don't get me wrong, I think life's tough for lots of people now, but they're not nearly so likely to accept this as inevitable. Most people had some sort of faith and a belief that after death something good could happen. I don't think many people think this now.'

'And the fear of being a burden?'

'Most people lived with or close to family. They knew that if they became dependent it would be their relatives who had to look after them. Many talked of their experiences of the miseries that they'd seen this cause. They didn't want to impose that burden.

'Now, of course, it's very different. Most of us don't live with or close to our families, and even if we do, most families – white English families I'm talking about, it's sometimes different in other ethnic groups – don't expect the burden of caring to fall on them.'

'Did they used to?'

'They did. There wasn't the option of the state-funded four times daily care package, that's someone – sometimes two people – going into a patient's home to provide care four times a day, or the twenty-four-hour live-in carer. Someone in the family had to do it.'

'Who was that?'

'Whoever the family decided. Often the youngest daughter stayed at home and did the caring. That was their role. I learned after my grandmother died that she, the youngest girl of eleven children, had been expected to do it. But she escaped,' he said creasing with a smile, 'by getting pregnant with my father!'

There was no sight of the ducks or sound from the swans, presumably all settled down for the night, as Margaret guided the party back to the car using the torchlight from her phone. It had been a warm spring day and the evening chill had just begun to make the gravel and the grass border of the car park damp with dew. It could have been a difficult evening but in fact it hadn't. All were grateful that Malcolm had prepared a few good words to toast Joan at an appropriate moment, and although there'd been a lot of talk about medicine – which Joan and Annie never permitted – all had independently found it helpful to have had topics on which conversation flowed easily. The journey home was therefore completed in comfortable silence, each lost in their own thoughts, with the front seat occupants the only ones to catch sight of a fox – completely unconcerned by their presence – that ambled across the road about thirty metres ahead of them, not changing its stride pattern in any discernible way despite a large motor car lunging towards it, eyes preposterously bright in the beam of the headlights and no doubt plotting some act of skulduggery.

Routine thanks for an enjoyable evening were exchanged as Margaret and her father got out of the car, with Malcolm adding to Margaret as they parted, 'I hope you manage to work out what you want to do. Don't be in too much of a hurry. Something will come to mind; it always does.'

'You could do a lot worse,' her father added as they approached the front door and Margaret was rummaging in her pocket for the key, 'than have a chat with Malcolm about it. I'm sure he'd be willing if you wanted to.'

TWENTY

SUPPORT AND ENCOURAGE

Dr Old thought that Margaret might have had second thoughts, but she got in touch about ten days after their meeting for supper. The weather was forecast to be mild the following weekend and he didn't have anything planned for the Sunday. They agreed it would be good to go for a walk. To keep the logistics as simple as possible he met her at the car park she'd used previously, which thankfully had spaces at two in the afternoon so the contingency plan wasn't needed. As he made his way to the rendezvous he realised that he hadn't advised her what sort of walk he was thinking of and an ancient family experience came to mind, very difficult at the time but funny in retrospect and still sometimes alluded to about forty years later, when five people came down to breakfast suitably attired for a day on the fells in moderately bad weather and one wearing a long skirt, white tights and patent leather shoes. He had just hastily plotted a pavement-only option in his mind when he caught sight of her and was relieved to see she was wearing walking shoes that looked as though they'd seen action other than on paved or tarmacked surfaces. She told him she had an anorak in her shoulder bag to frighten off evil spirits, providing further reassurance that plan A would be acceptable.

They wandered from the city centre, not that Cambridge has anything that really looks very like a city centre, past Scudamore's boat yard where an earnest young man wearing a straw boater was trying to entice a group of Japanese tourists into taking a ride on a punt. Across Coe Fen, the Fen Causeway and Lammas Land they meandered through Newnham Croft to the side of the River Cam flowing from Grantchester. The main path wasn't crowded but there were people on it, as there usually are, and so they decided to follow the almost empty but in some places muddy track by the river's edge, the water brown with a tinge of green, moving reluctantly as if unsure which way was downstream.

Margaret opened the conversation about medical matters: 'I had an interesting conversation with my father and a friend of his, a rheumatologist called Malcolm, a few evenings ago. We went out for supper with him and his wife on what would have been my mother's birthday. After learning about the problems my father had it was good to hear them talk about some positive things, how medicine has improved over the years they've been doctors. They said there were examples in just about every specialty.'

Dr Old agreed that there were and was asked about the biggest advance in his, renal medicine, since he started as a doctor. Dialysis and kidney transplants were already available when he qualified, although not as often and not as good as they are now, so he said he couldn't say these. Same for treatments for blood pressure. 'I think I'll give the prize to a thing called epo,' he said. 'Patients with kidney failure get anaemic and there wasn't any good treatment when I started as a doctor. You could give blood transfusions, but afterwards a lot of these patients would make antibodies against them and the blood bank couldn't provide any more. Dying very slowly of anaemia, gradually getting more exhausted and more breathless, is one of the more unpleasant ways to die. I can still remember a couple of young patients – that's younger than I was at the time – and it was truly horrible.

'We knew that the kidney normally made something to tell the bone marrow to make red cells and it didn't do this when it failed, leading to the anaemia, but we didn't know what the something was. The discovery of epo, the hormone that's critical, was the game changer. Within a few years we could inject it into patients and dial up the blood count that we wanted. It was magical; no other word for it; absolutely magical.'

'That's a fantastic story,' Margaret observed. 'Malcolm and my father said similar things. I wonder,' she went on, feeling her way into the conversation, 'if it's the discoveries and improvements in medicine that have driven the changes in expectations that led to the difficulties my father got into when he saw the woman in the Emergency Department and decided that she couldn't be made better and should be allowed to die comfortably.'

Dr Old was taken aback by the acuity of her suggestion and realised he was going to have to concentrate more than he normally did on a Sunday afternoon walk. 'There may be something in that,' he replied. 'I hadn't thought of it as the main driver, but it's certainly part of it. To me the bigger picture are the broad societal changes. People won't accept such things as bad luck or hardship or ill health: they're certainly much less likely to do so than they used to be. There must be someone to blame and there must be a cure. I guess that's where your point comes in. More treatments available. Greater awareness through the media. Everything hyped up by commercial and political drivers making it harder and harder to swim against the tide.'

Margaret broke in. 'Is that what you think my father was doing, swimming against the tide?'

'Yes,' he replied, 'and I don't think he thought a lot about the reasons for the way the water was flowing or took enough account of it. I never had chance to talk to him about it, but I got the impression he just felt intuitively that the reluctance to accept someone was dying and couldn't be cured was wrong, and he couldn't understand how anyone couldn't see that the proper thing to do was to keep them comfortable. In many ways I think he was right, but the tide's running strongly in the other direction.'

They halted by a short section of two-bar fencing close to the river edge, uncertain why this part of the bank had been singled out as worthy of such a construction when most of it hadn't. A couple of men walked past them at considerable pace and talking animatedly. The only fragment they overheard contained the phrase "constitutional crisis" and referred on familiar terms to one of the law lords. Only in Cambridge they agreed, or perhaps Oxford, and smiled to each other, failing in the moment to recognise that others catching snippets of their conversation that afternoon would undoubtedly have concluded they were very serious types.

Margaret asked Dr Old to enlarge on what he'd said about the drivers and he began by talking about the influence of industry. No new test or drug ever becomes available without enormous commercial effort and expense. If you ask most people to guess how much money it costs to bring a drug to market, then if you multiply by twenty or fifty times you might be close to the mark. Without biotech companies and drug companies there would be nothing new, but their primary purpose is to generate wealth for their shareholders. So yes, they make money out of things that are wonderful improvements in care, but they also have an interest in creating diseases and exaggerating benefits by aggressive marketing.

'I don't know how many eighty-year-old men I've seen in clinic, referred because their kidney function is a bit reduced,' he said. 'They have an invented disease called chronic kidney disease stage three, CKD stage 3 for short, which sounds bad. They're on a load of pills for their blood pressure and cholesterol and other things and say they think these are making them feel unwell.

Their wife tells me earnestly that they've put them on a low-fat diet and I glance at the poor man who looks unbearably weary. The wife is under the impression that dialysis – kidney machine treatment – is inevitable in the near future and often seems to expect me to advise even more draconian measures to prevent this.

'I have to be careful in how I explain things lest they think that Dr Old isn't taking matters seriously or is being disparaging about what other doctors or nurses have told them, but I try to get across a few facts, including that 30 per cent of people over the age of seventy-five have CKD stage 3 and their chance of ever needing a kidney machine is less than 2 per cent. I hope to feel a relaxation of tension in the air when I say this, although some patients and their partners remain suspicious and resistant to accepting good news. But if things are going well we get into a discussion of risks and benefits of medications, the importance of having enjoyment in life – including eating food that you like – and I make it clear that it can be an entirely reasonable decision to stop some of the pills, saying which I think are most likely to be causing side effects, which are the most important to continue with, and which are of less certain benefit. As regards diet, if the mood in the room seems to be receptive, I say that I'd be very cross if I was told I could never eat another chip, but it would be a bad thing to eat chips every day.

'This is me swimming against the tide. There are hundreds of trials saying that blood pressure or cholesterol should be treated aggressively and dozens of guidelines saying the same. By all sorts of routes the might of industry ensures that doctors and patients are continually bombarded with them. But what none of the trials or guidelines does or can do is look at the whole picture, the consequences of adding one thing on top of another, on top of another, on top of another. They all focus on their particular thing. There's a literature on the problems caused by taking too many pills, polypharmacy it's called in the jargon, but it's completely swamped because there's no money to be made by stopping pills, only by starting more of them.'

Making an obvious comment that he was talking a lot he checked in with Margaret, who smiled and nodded to indicate she was still interested in the topic. 'Don't get me wrong,' he continued, 'if you've got high blood pressure or heart failure or vascular disease or diabetes or chronic kidney disease then there's good evidence that some drugs can help, but frail elderly patients – and there's a lot of them about – commonly have several if not all of these problems and if you talk to them, which people running drug companies or organising drug trials very rarely do, you hear about the problems they have with their tablets and it's often far from clear that prescribing handfuls of pills does more good than harm, but there's always a reason why you could advise adding another one and many doctors do. It's a question of balance and at the moment I think there's a lack of it: there's a collusion which leads to more and more treatment with less and less benefit in more and more cases.'

'Who's colluding?' Margaret asked.

'The short answer,' Dr Old replied after thinking for a moment, 'is that we all are, the politicians and the voters,' and he went on to explain why he thought this. The demand for healthcare is insatiable and whoever is in power or wants to be in power has to promise good things. Would you vote for a politician who did otherwise? Would you put your cross in the box for someone who said spending on healthcare couldn't be increased any more, or not increased enough to keep up with inflating medical costs, and so their plan was to restrict access to things that are expensive, including any new treatments which are always very expensive? I very much doubt that you would, and I don't know of any politicians who've made that pitch. Avoidance of bitter truths is one of their key skills and the best are truly masters at doing so. 'Optimism is so much more attractive than pessimism,' he said, 'so politicians are always looking for magic answers that are going to take away the problem. It's clear to everybody attached to planet Earth that health and social services aren't able to meet the demands being placed upon them, and finding the money to meet these demands in conventional ways can't be done because it would involve tax rises fatal to prospects of re-election or other widely unpopular interventions that the electorate – that's all of us – would certainly punish, so the answer has to be something else, and the something else has to have fantastic properties.'

'So what are today's snake oils?' Margaret asked. 'The things with fantastic properties?'

'A good question,' Dr Old replied with a smile, 'but I think snake oils is a bit strong! As far as I know they've never been shown to have any beneficial property.' They had now reached the end of the riverside walk and were climbing up the incline of the field, which was steeper than it looked at first sight, towards the main path. The effort of breathing put a temporary stop to conversation, enabling him to put his thoughts in some sort of order as they headed through the kissing gate towards the tearoom they'd agreed as their target at the start of the walk, reckoning that it was just warm enough to sit outside.

'You were going to tell me about the things with fantastic properties,' Margaret prompted.

'Yes,' he replied as they settled themselves on rickety chairs, 'and I'm glad of having had a few minutes to think about it whilst we were trekking up the field and ordering tea. There's lots of things that are over-hyped and lots of pressure to over-hype them. It's obvious why drug companies will exaggerate the benefits of their products, but it's the same for doctors. If you're applying for money to do research it's not going to help if you underplay its possible impact. Same if you're presenting work that you've done. And if a politician in power is desperate for something that will change the game then it's hard to resist the temptation to say that you have such a thing, or at least be slow in correcting them if they decide it's in their interests to make extravagant claims about whatever you're doing. Anyway, to get to the point and answer your question, the thing for which the most implausible claims are being made now is genomic medicine.'

Margaret confirmed that she'd heard of this and read a number of articles about it, which again surprised Dr Old.

'A few years ago my management consultancy firm won a contract with a company involved in DNA sequencing and it's always important to find out something about what the client does before you walk in. Makes it less likely that you'll come over as a complete prat on your first morning, which is hard to recover from,' she said with obvious good sense and directness, 'and recently I looked a few things up after my father told me about some of the treatments my mother was given.'

Dr Old confirmed that oncology was one place where genomics really had made an impact, with tremendous developments in cancer diagnosis and treatment over the last ten years, and more were coming – assuming of course that they could be paid for. Knowing what's driving a particular tumour in a particular patient sometimes means it can be targeted with a particular treatment, and there had been some absolutely spectacular results. 'But the problem,' he said, 'is that genomics isn't the answer to lots of medical problems but there's a pretence that it is,' continuing, 'I was reading some Bernard Shaw the other day, which I'm sure your father would approve of,' leading Margaret to laugh and nod in confirmation, 'and there's a place where he says something along the lines of – let me try to get this right, it's wonderfully written – "wise men used to take care to consult doctors qualified before 1860, who were usually contemptuous of the germ theory. Now we are left in the hands of doctors who, having heard of microbes much as St Thomas Aquinas heard of angels, suddenly concluded that the whole art of healing could be summed up by the formula: find the microbe and kill it". I think there's a pretty close parallel here with genomic medicine. Germs, infectious agents, certainly cause some illnesses – we've just lived through a pandemic! – and understanding this has led to knowledge about how to prevent catching them and how to treat many of them, but no one thinks they cause every ailment. It's the same with genomics. There are a few areas of medicine where it's having a massive impact but in most it won't, although you're not allowed to say this, not allowed to challenge the high-level medical commercial political collusion. I don't know how long it will be before the pyramid selling of genomics as the cure for all ills comes crashing down.'

'I've worked on projects in businesses that are failing; that's a time when management consultants often get called in,' Margaret observed, 'and one thing you often hear is that no one is allowed to challenge the board. They have their view of the world and hand out instructions to the troops, and if anyone tries to say, "I don't think that's right, can we talk about it?" or "no, I think you've got that wrong" or something like that, then they're silenced one way or another. One of my tests of whether an organisation is healthy and likely to do well in the long run is to ask members of staff – when I'm talking with them one-to-one – if they've made a suggestion about how to improve anything to their line manager in the last six months. If they say no it means that whatever they've suggested in the past hasn't been welcomed: they've learned that it's best just to keep their head down and plod on, even if they think the plodding is in the wrong direction.'

Dr Old smiled again. 'I can see that that's an extremely good question to ask,' he said. 'I'm sure I'll be able to find opportunities to use it in the future! Thinking about my hospital and other hospitals I've been involved with, I suspect the answers would discriminate pretty accurately between those bits that are being run well and those that aren't. You can just feel the hopelessness when you talk to staff who've given up on trying to change and improve things, because any attempt they make is squashed and it's made clear to them that their observations aren't welcome. A few battle on against the odds, but most take the line of least resistance and keep their thoughts to themselves, or at least don't share them with their managers. Coming back to the issue with genomics, I've no doubt that the responses to your test question wouldn't indicate a healthy state of affairs and I'm pretty sure things aren't going to go well.'

'What do you think is going to happen?' Margaret asked.

'A good question, and I'm not sure I can give a very good answer,' he replied after a bit of thought. 'What's the saying? – "I can predict anything except the future" – but I'm sure that like everything else it will find its place. It's not my field of expertise but a friend who's in it and who I rate very highly, one of the people who's still trying to battle against the odds, uses me as someone they can let off steam to periodically, and they say a lot of things that seem to make very good sense. They've given me all sorts of detailed examples, some of which I think I understand, but to the point you make, the people running genomics in the country are doing all they can to marginalise the doctors who specialise in seeing patients with genetic problems, who've spent their careers thinking about them, because what they say doesn't suit their agenda.'

He paused to have a sip of tea and take a bite out of his lemon drizzle cake.

'I think I know some of the agenda from my time in the sequencing company,' Margaret said, 'and it was fairly simple: sequence everything and everyone, and of course we're the people that should do it for you!'

'That would certainly fit with what my friend says,' Dr Old replied, 'and that's the beginning of the problems; today's version of find the microbe and kill it. Given the way they're driving things, the amounts of sequencing to be done and data to be stored are colossal and completely overwhelming the system. Tests for what's called whole genome sequencing' – Margaret nodded to confirm that she knew what this was – 'are being requested and they tell me there are no results a year later, but the doctors aren't allowed to organise the tests that they used to. They can't order much, much simpler genetic tests for what they think the patient in front of them might have because that doesn't fit with the big agenda. It's a bit like me, if I want a scan of a patient's kidneys because they've got a kidney problem, being told no – you can't have that – but you can request a scan of the whole body, although there's a very long waiting list and we can't tell you when you'll get a result. And relating to when the whole genome is actually sequenced, the powers that be are also putting a lot of effort into silencing anyone who says anything along the lines of "it's really very difficult to interpret all this information and know what it means; you've got to put it together with detailed knowledge of the patient". These are bad signs: as my mother used to say, "truth will out in the end".'

'What do ordinary doctors – if I'm allowed to be rude and suggest that any doctors are ordinary – think about this?' Margaret asked.

'Most,' Dr Old replied, 'are mystified. They think it's irrelevant to their practice and their patients. After hearing a talk, I asked a group of colleagues at our regular weekly medical meeting if they thought that having whole genome sequencing done on all of the inpatients on their medical wards would be helpful in any way. None said yes. One, a very bright woman who'd spent some time in a molecular laboratory during her training, said she thought that doing a panel of genetic tests to look for things that would predict the patients' responses to drugs would be useful and then went on to make the practical point that unless done for the whole population in advance of them arriving in hospital the test would have to be done quickly at the front door. There certainly wouldn't be much point in sending off anything that took a year for the results to come back! But aside from arguments about whether genomics is being developed and implemented in the best way,' he continued, 'which

I'm not an expert on, is the fact that it's being used as a smokescreen to avoid difficult conversations about the problems that health and social care are facing. Don't worry, the fantasy goes, the genomic cavalry are coming over the hill and all will be well. Patients won't get so ill because diseases will be prevented and healthcare costs will go down. If anyone believes that they'll believe anything!'

The air suddenly felt colder. They hadn't noticed the shadows creeping towards them and now simultaneously saw that the sun had sunk lower in the sky such that they were sitting in the shade. It was going to be a nice sunset. They gathered their bits and pieces, buttoned and zipped up their jackets, and headed back along the main path, walking briskly to warm themselves up and glancing repeatedly at the changing array of reds and yellows gradually diminishing in the sky to their left.

'Isn't that something that you got attacked about in the media after the regulator's case?' Margaret asked after they'd been walking for a couple of minutes, recalling something that her father had said to her.

'What?' Dr Old replied, confused and not sure where they had been in the conversation, leading her to explain.

'That the reason you agreed with my father that the poor woman shouldn't have been treated was because you were a medical manager and wanted to avoid costs for the hospital.'

'Yes, it was over the business of the costs of treatment that some people had a go at me, although this hadn't been part of my thinking at all and I wasn't asked about it during the hearing. But if we didn't already know it, we all learned the lesson that facts aren't necessary to whip up a media storm, although I shouldn't put them all in the same boat; there were some balanced and thoughtful accounts. But it suited some people's purpose to have a medical manager character who was intent on stopping doctors from treating patients to save money to balance budgets, and in the absence of anyone like this, I had to do.'

Margaret saw him looking thoughtful and gazing at the clouds, which were particularly luminous at that moment, before he continued. 'People are generally less trusting than they used to be and some are suspicious of your motivation as a doctor in a way that they never used to be. At the end of last week I had several conversations – alone and together – with an elderly woman, her husband and her son. She's been getting frailer and frailer over the last eighteen months or so and hasn't ever really recovered from a chest infection she had at around Christmas. Along with all her other medical problems she's got kidney failure, but it's not the main thing that's making her unwell and I don't think that putting her on a kidney dialysis machine would make her feel any better. In fact, I know it wouldn't, it would make her worse; the strain of going onto the machine would leave her feeling continually exhausted even more than she is now. I could see in the son's eyes – as I often can – that he was thinking, "you're only taking this line because you don't want to do it, you want to save the money" so I tackle this head on and say, "I'm not saying this because the hospital wants to save money, I'm saying it because I think putting your mother on a kidney machine would cause her misery and not do her good," but it's so much easier not to have the difficult conversations and let the medical interventions continue.'

Margaret thought he sounded very sad as he continued his reflections. 'When I go onto the Intensive Care Unit nowadays,' he said, 'there are always a number of patients where the staff and many of the relatives are thinking, "how did we get into this situation? How did we let this happen? How on earth are we going to stop this and allow the poor person to die with some dignity?" but it's hard, it's really hard, to stop it.'

He looked directly at Margaret. 'This is what got your father into trouble,' he said. 'He tried to stop it. You see patients who you know are going to die soon, whether that's within a few hours – like the woman he saw in the Emergency Department – or within days or a few weeks. It's clear they're slipping away. The destination is not in doubt, I say to the junior doctors working with me, it's the route we need to consider and plan, and we need to take the patient – if they can be involved in the discussion – and the family along with us. It's this bit that your father didn't pay enough attention to, and it's much more difficult to navigate than it used to be.'

'What you say about my father rings true,' Margaret replied with a measured tone. 'He's talked a number of times about finding it difficult to understand why various things happened to him. The court case, the hearing, the disciplinary panel in the hospital.' Dr Old was unaware of the latter.

'The disciplinary panel? I didn't know about that,' he said. 'What happened?'

She recounted what she knew, concluding 'Although the details were different, I think the themes were the same, the not taking people along with you. That's one thing I've learned in the management consultancy business, you can have the best idea in the world, you can be absolutely right about something but – one way or another – you'll land up in a mess if you don't take people with you.'

'Indeed,' Dr Old replied, the word instantly triggering further thoughts of her father in Margaret's mind. 'I've seen that many times in the hospital. Someone's had a genuinely good idea, tried to drive it through without preparing the ground, and it's ended in tears.'

'But a thing that really bugs me, that I can't get out of my mind – I don't know why, but I can't – and I feel very guilty about it because I wasn't there,' Margaret continued, 'is that my mother would have died with people sticking things into her if he hadn't been there to stop it, and from what he says, that often happens, which just seems terrible.'

'Yes, I'm afraid it sometimes is,' Dr Old replied quietly. 'Many doctors are afraid of making the decision to stop going on with tests and treatments; they avoid the difficult conversations I mentioned earlier and plough on until the patient dies anyway, bruised and battered by repeated efforts to do blood tests or put up drips, or some other doctor steps in and grasps the nettle,' before continuing with a sheepish look, 'but what's the management quote, not that I should be quoting management aphorisms at you, "every system is perfectly designed to deliver the results it gets".

'Are you talking about the advanced care planning form, the DNACPR form?' Margaret asked. 'My father is extremely critical of it.'

Dr Old was impressed that she knew of such detail but was beginning to get used to not being surprised. Sometimes a short incisive question can illuminate much more than any amount of exposition, and this did for him.

'It's a product of our times,' he said, 'and I think it encapsulates the problems.' Various associated thoughts that he'd mulled over intermittently since before the hearing started putting themselves into some sort of order, rather as when discovering the answer to one clue on a crossword allows the rapid solving of others. 'But I don't pretend it's easy and I know there are problems and dangers with self-fulfilling prophesies and perceived conflicts of interest and doctors being hung out to dry.'

As they walked along the path, now between fields, Margaret made it clear with nods of encouragement and the occasional few words that she was keen for him to expand on these issues.

'The problem with self-fulfilling prophesies – I talked about them in the hearing – is a real one,' he said. 'If you see a patient and decide they're going to die and so the proper thing to do is keep them comfortable, then when they do die your own prophesy has been fulfilled. If you talk to relatives and explain things well, saying you don't want to cause pain or discomfort doing things that won't lead to restoration of life but may extend the process of dying, then most will understand and agree it wouldn't be right to put them through lots of futile interventions, but more and more now challenge this and try to insist treatment is given. "How do you know?" they say. "Because I've seen this many times" is the essence of your reply. "But if you don't treat, then you can't know what would happen if you did" is the rejoinder. Of course you do know, at least you do if you visit ICUs regularly, but the fact that what you're trying to do is prevent a protracted death is lost on those who are finding it impossible to come to terms with the fact that their nearest and dearest is dying, particularly if they are suspicious of your motivation and in the growing group who assume any suggestion that further active treatments should not be provided can only be due to a desire to save money.

'That's why I thought it was good idea for the hearing panel to suggest the regulator convened a working party to consider producing practical guidance for doctors on the determination of futility, but of course they didn't. I should have known from the start that they wouldn't. Far, far too difficult. Certain to resurrect media interest in doctors' death squads. Much, much easier for them to maintain a detached position, keep well away from the nitty gritty and couch their guidance for doctors only in the most general terms to allow themselves maximum room for manoeuvre. Producing worked case examples, including what they'd expect a doctor to do if confronted with the situation in which your father found himself, would be really useful to doctors up and down the land. Not some high-level document discussing the ethical principles involved, but something practically useful.'

'I can see why doctors would want that,' Margaret replied, 'also why the regulator would be keen to keep their distance! I'm sure those who get appointed to run regulators of all sorts are selected with the intention that they maintain the status quo, avoid controversy, and kick difficult things into the long grass. Anybody who gave the slightest impression that they might do otherwise wouldn't get past the first round of the appointment process.' Dr Old couldn't resist smiling as he'd come to the same conclusion over the years and was just about to say this when Margaret continued, 'But if you were on a working party, what would you say?'

'I won't pretend it's easy,' he began, 'but I think the debate needs to start with recognising that, because of their training and experience, doctors are the people best able to identify that someone is dying and attempts to prevent this will be futile. They may prolong the process of dying, but not do more than this. One of my colleagues has a good turn of phrase. He talks – not of patients slipping away – but of them being on the slipway, with no hope of getting off it and no triumph in making the slipway a long one. When colleagues talk about the age of a patient who's very ill, he sometimes says there's two ways of measuring how old someone is; one is time from the beginning and the other is time to the end. The point he's making is that, whatever the patient's age, the doctor needs to recognise if they're close to the end when deciding how to treat them.'

'Those points were made in the hearing,' Margaret recalled, 'not using the same words but the same points, and my father was criticised for making the decision on his own.'

'Yes, I remember,' Dr Old replied, again impressed by Margaret's knowledge of what had happened and her ability to identify key issues. 'I'm not sure I found the right words, but I tried to say I thought it was perfectly reasonable of him to do what he did and that it would create an impossible situation in people's homes, care homes, nursing homes, Emergency Departments, hospital wards, anywhere you can think of, if a doctor couldn't make a decision to keep someone comfortable without convening a committee meeting.'

Margaret became animated. 'My father has strong views on that point!' she said – which Dr Old could well imagine – 'In fact, he's pretty disparaging about committees making medical decisions in most circumstances.' As she went on to explain his views about multidisciplinary team meetings and his suggested cost improvement plan, Dr Old began to understand more completely why events turned out for him the way they did: "Grit in the oyster can turn into a pearl but more often gets spat out", he thought but didn't say, although he was sure that Margaret would have known what he meant if he had done.

'The demand for MDT meetings to make or ratify decisions,' he continued, 'is driven – same as the advanced care planning forms – by the big picture: lack of trust, a culture of blame and demand for punishment if anything goes wrong. They help protect patients from dishonest, devious or otherwise poorly performing doctors, which is obviously a good thing. They reduce the chances of doctors being subjected to personal attacks, which is also a good thing – it's the MDT, not me, which decided what treatment options you'd be offered, that said you weren't suitable or eligible for some treatment or other. They make slow but defensible decisions of generally average quality. What they decide is determined mostly by the way key participants are interested in and capable of influencing others when decisions are finely balanced. The extrovert's opinion generally prevails over the introvert's and the naturally confident person's over the diffident person's, even if they don't know much about a case, which doesn't stop some from pontificating. But it's hard to argue against what seems like a democratic process until you recognise that making the best medical decision depends on having a great deal of knowledge about the individual patient and their views, and on the many possible outcomes of the various management options. People will readily accept that democracy isn't a good way of solving a tricky maths problem and you're much better off asking one or two good mathematicians. Paraphrasing Winston Churchill, the best argument against MDTs is a five-minute conversation with the average member.'

The images of several of her colleagues and how they habitually behaved in meetings sprang into Margaret's mind and she couldn't help but agree with these observations about how supposedly collective decisions were made, but beneath this her visceral response was to think of her father and understand why he approved of Dr Old, stimulating her to ask him again about his thoughts on patients who were dying and the advanced care planning form, issues inextricably linked to her father's enforced early retirement which – despite her recognition that he was far from perfect – she felt was fundamentally wrong.

'At the risk of repeating myself,' Dr Old began, 'the consumer society struggles with death, which I agree isn't an easy thing to contemplate although it comes to us all. The form reflects the times we live in where the customer is king. It assumes that circumstances allow a rational discussion. It emphasises what the patient wants, which is often very different from what's possible. It's very hard to use when it's needed most. Without having a form in front of me it's difficult to explain.'

Margaret pulled her phone out of her pocket and glanced at him. 'I realise this is a heavy conversation for an afternoon walk,' she said with a plaintive look, 'but I've got a copy. Would you talk me through it? It's important to me.' Dr Old thought she looked particularly attractive glancing up at him, smiled, and indicated that he would.

'It begins,' Margaret continued, 'with a heading that says, "Shared understanding of my health and current condition".'

'And that's the start of the difficulties,' he replied, going on to say he thought this would be an entirely proper place to commence if it could be assumed that the patient had capacity to make decisions about their care and the circumstances allowed considered debate. 'But,' he went on, 'if you're dealing with someone who's cognitively impaired – in simple terms can't think properly – because they've got dementia or are acutely confused because they're ill, or both, then you can't reach any shared understanding about anything. And even if a patient does have capacity, it's pretty well impossible to have a proper discussion if they're very ill, for instance they can't breathe properly.'

He paused for a moment before continuing, 'I'll give you a common example: a patient with a very bad chest, using lots of inhalers and other treatments at home, who gets short of breath getting dressed and undressed, able to walk a few steps around the house using a frame to support him but can't go outside unless taken in a wheelchair. He's been going downhill for many months, with several recent hospital admissions, and he's brought to the Emergency Department again because the carers that attend to get him up in the morning found him looking terrible, unable to speak because he was so breathless, and they called an ambulance. You might well say that a plan for his care in this situation should have already been made and documented, but it hasn't been and it rarely has. You tell me – rhetorical question – how the doctor seeing the poor man in the ED can reach any sort of shared understanding with him?'

Dr Old hesitated whilst moving to one side of the narrow path, now next to some college sports' ground and approaching Newnham, to make way for a group of four or five students, two wearing light blue rugby shirts, who were jogging at a decent pace towards Grantchester, perhaps on a training run. He continued after they had passed. 'I've heard lots of excruciating conversations where well-meaning doctors, desperately wanting to do the right thing, have tried to explain to patients like our friend who can't breathe that they think it wouldn't do any good and would prolong their misery with no hope of real recovery if they took them to ICU and put them on a breathing machine – which is all true – and,' his voice rising in pitch, 'the patient's eyes get wider and wider and they look more and more terrified, and it's truly awful.

'Remind me of the wording of the next bit of the form,' he said after taking a moment to quieten down.

'What matters to me in decisions about my treatment and care in an emergency,' Margaret read quietly from her phone.

'Again,' Dr Old replied, 'what chance is there of being able to discuss this with our dying friend? And what's next?'

'Clinical recommendations for emergency care and treatment,' Margaret read again.

'Ah yes,' Dr Old continued. 'Should you give CPR, cardiopulmonary resuscitation, it asks; give your reasoning, it says – or something very similar – like in maths exams, or at least it used to when I had to take them.' Margaret nodded to confirm that reasons were required. 'And then, after all that, it asks whether the poor man has capacity for involvement in making the plan,' he continued. 'Surely anyone with any common sense, anyone with any practical experience, would recognise that this question should be at the beginning, straight after a question asking if an advanced care planning form has already been completed? And if the patient hasn't already expressed their views and can't engage in proper discussion now, then shouldn't the doctor draw on all the information that is available to them, including of course talking to the next of kin if possible; decide on the level of intervention that is appropriate, seeking advice from colleagues when unsure; decline to do things that would extend the process of dying but not provide realistic prospect of recovery; and assure comfort so far as possible at all times. Isn't that the sort of medicine we'd want for our friends and family, for ourselves at the end of our days? The form should support and encourage this instead of making it difficult, but that would depend on trust.'

They both fell silent in the twilight as they retraced their steps across the park and back into the centre of Cambridge. To their right were the grey silhouettes and shouts of some boys playing football, soon to be driven home by the fact that even they with their young eyes could no longer see the ball.

TWENTY-ONE

AN IMPRESSIVE MAN

Margaret was sitting in the lounge checking through emails on her laptop when she became conscious of the sound of a motor mower close by. She looked out of the window and was surprised to see her father cutting the grass, wearing a pair of jeans and what she took to be an old work shirt with sleeves rolled up to the elbows. She couldn't remember ever having seen him in jeans before, didn't know that he owned any, and it was the first time since she'd been home that he'd taken any interest in the garden, although she knew from comments made to her by others that he was a keen gardener. After writing a few responses she went out to offer moral support and ask him if he would like a cup of tea. She noticed beads of sweat on his forehead, patches of dampness on his shirt under his armpits and in the centre of his chest, and a small cut on a bruised or oily knuckle on his right hand. He made light of this and insisted that an Elastoplast was not required and wouldn't stay on anyway. 'Always a struggle,' he said, 'to get the mower started for the first cut of the year. I had to take the spark plug out and clean it, which is a fiddle, but then it's fine until the winter.'

It was agreed that refreshments should wait until he'd finished the mowing, not least because it was forecast that it might rain, and Margaret watched him complete his paced straight march up and down the length of the lawn a couple of times and then turn down the motor speed and start on the slow, precise arc he'd trodden many times before curving carefully around the edge of the pond. She returned to the house, kept an eye out for progress, and put the kettle on when she saw him heading off towards the garden shed, in front of which she could just see him flip the mower on its side and go down on one knee to reach in and start removing the grass cuttings impacted on the chassis around the rotor blades.

If anything, the weather had improved when they sat down in the side garden in a warm spring sun with their tea and some chocolate Hobnobs, her father's favourites. 'Very therapeutic, the first mow of the season,' he observed, wiping a mixture of oil and grass stains off his hands and onto his trousers before taking a biscuit from the plate. 'Makes the garden look much neater and tidier and gives you a chance to take careful stock of the borders.' He went on to say that a ceanothus and couple of other shrubs had died over the winter and he'd need to get some replacements. 'Not a bad thing,' he said. 'That border was the next I'd planned to overhaul before garden projects got put on the back burner when your mother got ill. I think I'll go for some variegated hollies at the back, they seem to survive pretty well here, with some daphnes and hebes in front of them. Some of the daphnes have a wonderful scent and there's one in the back garden that seems very healthy so hopefully new ones would like it here.'

Margaret was pleased, both by the heat of the sun, back from its wintry travels and feeling good on her cheeks as she leant back on the patio bench, and by what her father was saying. Not the details about the plants. She'd be able, she thought, to recognise the hollies. Daphnes and hebes, however; these were names she vaguely knew belonged to plants of some sort, rather than wild animals for instance, but no more than that. She was cheered deep down by the fact that, as with spring in the garden, life was beginning to move on again for her father. After the winter of her mother's illness and death, since when nothing excepting memories stirred in his imagination, and these not yet capable of stimulating anything other than pain, new ideas and initiatives were beginning to push themselves forward. Shoots beginning to appear from the soil; buds showing evidence of life on trees that had appeared to be dead.

After saying he was going to limit himself to two biscuits so he didn't spoil his appetite for supper, he wiped his lips with the back of his stained and slightly bruised hand, turned towards Margaret and – looking at her directly – said in a kindly way, 'It's been very good having you around for the last month or so, but are you any nearer to knowing what you're going to do?'

'Perhaps a bit,' Margaret replied. 'I think I'm clearer in my mind that I don't want to go back to doing what I've been doing, at least not in the same way. My skills are in managing things and I think I'm reasonably good at doing that. A client's never asked to have me taken off a project, which they sometimes do. I've asked the bosses in the firm for lots of advice over the years and at times they've given me very clear direction as to what they wanted me to do, but they've then always let me get on and do it. They've never felt it necessary to bring anyone else more senior onto a project I've been working on to help move things along because they weren't going well, and there's not many in my position who could say that. I enjoy managing things, producing a sense of order and getting reasonably decently paid for doing so, and I like working with people who are generally pretty lively and driven. But somehow going back to the same doesn't seem attractive.'

'Why's that?' her father asked, conscious he'd been happy working in the same hospital for many years and the prospect of being an itinerant locum – the closest parallel he could think of to his daughter's working life – would have filled him with dread. 'Is it because of the continual moving about, never being able to settle down in a place?'

'That may be part of it,' Margaret replied, 'but in the past I enjoyed that, the feeling of not being bogged down anywhere. If things weren't good on a particular job, the fact you knew you'd be moving on somewhere else when you'd done it was comforting. I think it's more to do with whether what I'm doing is worthwhile.'

'Worthwhile?'

'Yes, whether it really matters. I've been working on a project with a mobile phone company for the last nine months or so, trying to help them improve various aspects of their customer service, make it more attractive for people to buy their phones rather than someone else's, but to be honest it doesn't really matter to me. Of course I want to do as good a job as I can, I always do, but if they don't succeed in improving their market share, I'm not really bothered, and I don't want to go on doing something I'm not really bothered about.'

After forgetting his resolution, reaching for and taking a bite out of a third Hobnob, her father continued. 'I can understand that,' he said, wiping a crumb from his cheek with the back of his hand. 'My medical career didn't end as I would have wanted, and lots of doctors now retire early – earlier than I stopped working – because they're ground down by the system and simply exhausted, but very few have doubts that being a doctor is fundamentally a worthwhile thing to do. The discoveries and changes over the course of a medical lifetime – we talked about some of them when we were out with Malcolm and Annie last week – are intellectually interesting and stimulating, and the business of helping people when they're in need has a timeless value to it and always will do. It's rewarding beyond what you get paid.'

This struck home. 'I think that puts it very well,' Margaret replied. 'Rewarding beyond what you get paid. I think I need to find something like that,' continuing after a short hesitation and with a sly smile to herself that her father didn't notice or didn't enquire about if he did, 'Shirley said something similar, but not quite so eloquently.' She then lapsed into silence pondering the other advice that Shirley had dispensed but didn't think this a suitable topic for discussion with her father.

When she woke from her trance her father was dozing quietly in his chair. Taking care not to disturb him she collected up the mugs and plate and took them back to the kitchen, helping herself to one of the remaining biscuits as she did so. As she munched on this she mulled over what her father had just said, and the more she did so the more she was impressed; impressed that – despite his career ending in the miserable way that it did – he could rise above anger and bitterness and speak of the essential value of it. She must tell him that, she thought, before the conversation was forgotten.

Opportunity arose after supper when they'd completed their habitual tasks. Her father had stacked the dishwasher in his obsessional way – table knives as always in the front right of the cutlery tray, teaspoons front left, etcetera – then hand-washed the wine glasses and the pans and dried the glasses with a tea towel. Margaret had cleared the table and wiped it down, taken the empty wine bottle and various bits of packaging out to the recycling bin, moved some clothes from the washing machine into the tumble dryer, and made their drinks. She began as they were moving into the lounge, drawing the curtains, switching on the lights and settling down in their chairs. 'It's not a very English thing to say, but I was impressed by what you said this afternoon when we were talking after you'd cut the grass.'

Her father was mystified and said so.

'The business of medicine being valuable beyond what you get paid,' she continued. 'It can't be easy to stand back and have that perspective when things in the hospital finished the way they did.'

Her father sipped his coffee before responding. 'I'm sure I would have said different things just after I stopped working, but with time, with what happened to your mother…' His voice tailed off before he continued on a tangential track, 'I always promised myself I wouldn't get bitter. I've seen too many bitter people over the years. Patients who give vivid accounts of the death of a relative, putting this down to a doctor who didn't diagnose something as quickly as they might have done, with such distress in their voices that you think it must have happened last week but discover it was ten years ago, and they bring this up every time you see them. Colleagues who didn't get some job or other and remain unshakably convinced that this was unjust and can only have been for improper reasons, carrying this belief like a festering sore that never heals and inhibits them for evermore. Even if the relative might have lived with a quicker diagnosis, even if the colleague should have got the job, there comes a point where it's best to say shit happens, forget it and move on; and all in all it probably was time for me to move on. Medicine has changed and is changing and I didn't and I couldn't, at least not quickly enough.'

Margaret was intrigued by what he meant but didn't have to ask.

'When I started as a doctor,' he continued, 'if you were treating a patient in their seventies or eighties who was very ill the commonest reaction from relatives was to express surprise that you were bothering with someone so old, even if they were in pretty good health before. Now the attitude is more likely to be that a relative dying must indicate medical negligence. In my last week at work a woman from the hospital chaplaincy service arranged for me to meet the wife of a man in his eighties who'd died on my ward about six months before. He had a bad chest and a bad pneumonia, and when he was admitted I explained to her and her son that he was very seriously ill and may not survive. I used my standard phrases when I spoke to them: "I'd like to be proved wrong, but…", that sort of thing. A week later he wasn't very different. The antibiotics seemed to be just about holding things but he wasn't getting better. He looked more tired and had less fight in him. I knew where things were heading and arranged to meet his wife again. Before I said anything she got in first: "You're not going to give me bad news, Doctor, are you? One of the nurses told me he was doing very well yesterday morning". We agreed not to talk and that I'd speak to her son, saying – because I asked him if he wanted to know the score and he confirmed that he did – that the odds were about eighty-twenty against his father surviving the admission. About a week later the juniors told me he'd deteriorated overnight when I did my routine daily check in on the ward before going off to my morning clinic. His wife and son were sitting at the bedside, curtains drawn around. He was unconscious, breathing erratically and unaware of who was there or what was going on. I spoke to his wife, "I don't think he's in any pain or discomfort," I said. "Will it be long?" she asked. "No, I don't think so, probably sometime today," I replied. "But I haven't had time to say goodbye," she said. He died about an hour later.

'After he died they asked for copies of all the notes of his admission and for bereavement services to arrange a meeting with me. His wife said things I'd heard dozens of times before and expected her to say. It was disgraceful that on one occasion when she'd visited he'd told her that he hadn't slept well overnight because of noise on the ward and wasn't I aware of the importance of patients getting a good night's sleep. It was disgraceful that on another occasion she found he'd spilt milk and cornflakes down his pyjama jacket and he told her that there hadn't been anyone to help him eat his breakfast and wasn't I aware of the importance of patients eating to give them strength to recover. I apologised for the fact that the ward was often noisy at night. In fact, sometimes it's like an Attenborough soundtrack of the night life of a Madagascan forest, except the strange hooting and screeching sounds aren't made by lemurs, but I didn't say that. I did wonder what she thought I should do to other patients who were distressed and crying out, but I didn't ask her. I apologised for the business with the breakfast and the state of the pyjamas, explaining that the nurses and healthcare assistants needed to prioritise and had probably been busy dealing with more urgent needs that morning. I did wonder what she thought they should do if they saw another patient trying to get out of bed and about to fall when they were helping her husband with his cereals, but I didn't ask her.

'She then moved on to other things that were troubling her: but he was only eighty-two, she said; his brother lived to be ninety. I don't know how many times I've heard that sort of comparison, but unless two people die at exactly the same age, one has to die before the other. Did she think her husband's earlier death must indicate medical negligence? Was she concerned others might think it indicated she hadn't taken good care of him over the years? I didn't find out but simply established that the brother hadn't had a bad chest or any other medical problems before being found dead one afternoon in his armchair. Not a bad way to go, I thought, but didn't say.

'Why did the nurse say her husband was doing very well, she asked, and why did a young doctor tell her at one point that he thought he was getting better? I said I expected they were probably trying to be positive and optimistic but think it more likely they either didn't recognise how ill he was or realised that they were dealing with someone for whom the possibility of failure did not exist, and they'd be detained for questioning and get behind with their list of jobs if they said anything else.

'There were a few technical things she didn't understand in the notes and I explained them. She then got round to the fact she hadn't had time to say goodbye. I glanced at her son – who at least had the good grace to avert his gaze and look embarrassed – and said I was sorry, but really, what more could I have said or done, short of taking out a mallet and hitting her between the eyes to impress upon her that things weren't going well.

'At this point the timer I'd set on my phone for forty minutes went off and I said we had to draw things to a close. They hadn't got any other questions, thanked me for talking with them and said it had been very helpful, and I left them with the chaplaincy woman who sent me a lovely email later that day. I'm not sure, she wrote, that looking through 2,000 pages of hospital notes is the best way of grieving, but it seems to be becoming more common.'

Margaret could hear a deep weariness in her father's voice as he told the tale.

'I'm sure it's very wearing having those sorts of conversations,' she said. 'Is that what made you think it was time to move on?'

'Part of it,' her father replied, 'but really everything that's behind the need for having them. I got very frustrated when I saw patients with no hope of recovery being tortured on the wards with needles and tubes of one sort or another, and I wanted to stop it. It just seemed totally wrong. I used to talk with Malcolm about it. He understood and agreed, but he could stand back in a way that I couldn't. He said it was essential to keep the medical and nursing teams onside, and if most in the herd were continuing to trample blindly in the wrong direction, planning or doing all sorts of well-intentioned but futile and hurtful things, you had to wait for the right moment to turn them round. It was a dark art, he said, picking the time to suggest that enough is enough, and comfort is the only thing that matters. Sometimes it took many days or even a few weeks. When I asked if it bothered him that some poor soul was suffering pointlessly all this time, he told me he could only do his best. You can't make everybody see sense right away, he told me, you have to wait until something happens, anything that causes the herd to pause gives an opportunity to change direction, to say the green grass is not over there, it's over here, come with me and I'll show you. He was very good at doing it and I'm sure he still is, but I couldn't sense the moment or bring people along with me the way he can.'

Margaret's first impression of Malcolm at the funeral had been of a man with a squeaky voice and a silly moustache but her estimation of him had risen with every encounter or conversation since: 'An impressive man, your friend Malcolm,' she said. She also felt he'd benefit from some grooming advice but kept this to herself.

TWENTY-TWO

CAST YOUR BREAD

Margaret was sleeping poorly during an unpleasantly muggy night following a humid day that really needed a thunderstorm but didn't get one. She was worried that she hadn't made progress in deciding what she wanted to do with her life, beyond knowing that she definitely needed a change. What would she tell one of her team who was stuck with something and didn't know what to do? Doing nothing clearly wouldn't be an option. Was there anything she could do that might be helpful and wouldn't have a significant downside? As she lay on top of sticky sheets she heard a few rumbles of thunder, the sound of the wind picking up and suddenly the air seemed a bit cooler. She got out of bed and went to the window, separating the curtains a little to peer into the garden and stare at the welcome rain. She waited to see if there would be any lightning but there wasn't. By the time she went back to bed she'd decided to take her father up on his offer of organising for her to talk to Malcolm.

A time was fixed when Annie was away doing grandmotherly duties. Malcolm would come round for tea and Margaret's father would busy himself in the garden. In the event, he decided, no doubt after much consideration rather than on the spur of the moment, that he needed to go to the local garden centre to buy some geraniums for the pots in the garden and new line for his garden strimmer. All recognised the contrivance, but it was helpful, no objections were raised, and he headed off, leaving Margaret and Malcolm alone in the kitchen.

'It's very good of you,' Margaret began, 'to keep in touch with Dad so closely.'

'It's kind of you to say so,' Malcolm replied, 'but it really isn't an effort on my part. Annie says we're like two old soldiers who've been in action together, forever keeping memories of campaigns fresh with nods and winks, and I guess we are. We're old-school doctors.'

'Yes,' Margaret responded, 'Dad says that. He told me he was an old-school doctor who couldn't move on with the times, and you're an old-school doctor who could.'

'We've had many conversations on that theme over the years,' Malcolm said quietly. 'I used to tease him that he was born a hundred years too late, although in fact thirty would probably have been enough. It's a great shame.'

Margaret thought he might be going to stop there, mindful that this wasn't the topic for which their meeting had been arranged, but before she said anything he continued and she was glad he did.

'It really is a great shame. Your father was a remarkable doctor. He knew more medical facts than any of us, and he was incredibly good at sensing when something didn't seem right about a case, when a patient had been labelled with a diagnosis that wasn't correct. I remember him telling me shortly after I first met him that the most important diagnosis for a doctor to make is, "I don't know". At the time I thought this was an odd thing to say, and I've heard him say it to other doctors who've looked at him as though he'd lost his marbles, but I've now seen enough to know he's absolutely right. Keeps the mind open to allow the possibility of the correct diagnosis appearing in it. It's just such a pity that he couldn't learn how to take people along with him, and that's critical in a way that it wasn't when he began as a doctor.'

'I know it's not what we're supposed to be talking about this afternoon,' Margaret replied, 'but why's that? I'm really interested to understand.' Following discussions she'd had with her father and David Old she thought she probably knew but was keen for confirmation.

'Your father said you were trying to work out what happened to him and to your mother, and that was clear when we went to the restaurant on her birthday,' Malcolm replied. 'I imagine there's something in you trying to catch up for the years you missed, the years when you weren't in touch.'

Margaret had been perplexed by why, deep down, she felt such a need to talk over the details of her father's encounters with courts, regulators and disciplinary hearings, including arcane matters such as the details of the advanced care planning form, and the precise circumstances of her mother's death. At times she'd been concerned that she had become mentally unwell and suffering from some form of obsession, and worried that her father or David Old might think so too, but the answer seemed evident when Malcolm put it like this. However emotionally intelligent we are, we always maintain the capacity to miss the obvious, the thing that's hiding in plain sight, and the person who thinks, "no, I'd be most unlikely to do that" is guaranteed to do it often.

As these thoughts tumbled around in her mind, pieces of a jigsaw falling into place, she may have missed something that Malcolm was saying, but when she tuned in again she heard, 'Different times. Much less questioning. If you said something as a doctor, then that was the answer. It was very rare to be challenged, and it was the same for others in authority – police officers, teachers, priests. What you said was almost always accepted, but now it's wise to assume that it won't be. At least that's my working assumption when I start to talk to patients and relatives, and some colleagues, in the sort of situations that got your father into difficulties. I often hope they'll accept a recommendation that comfort should be the priority, but I work my way carefully into the conversations, keeping on the lookout for signals that they aren't ready for this.'

Malcolm paused to take a sip of the builder's brew he'd asked for, glancing at Margaret over the rim of the mug and clearly giving her opportunity to speak.

'But my father says that it's for the doctor to decide about treatment,' she said, 'and' – after a pause in which she debated what to say next – 'I've been speaking with Dr Old, David Old, who was one of the expert witnesses when Dad had his hearing with the regulator, and he says the same.'

Malcolm took a further sip of his tea and fixed his gaze on Margaret for a few seconds, although it felt much longer to her. 'You have been doing your homework,' he said in a measured tone before lapsing into another silence which Margaret broke.

'Do you know him?' she asked.

It was rapidly established that Malcolm did know who he was. They had never worked together but had both been on a medical Royal College committee about general medicine many years previously, when Malcolm had found him a kindred spirit in – to use his words – "struggling unsuccessfully against educational clap trap", and he'd seen an opinion he'd written a couple of years ago on a difficult medicolegal case that he thought was very sensible.

Referring to David Old, Margaret went on, 'He quoted me the saying, "thou shalt not kill, but need'st not strive officiously to keep alive", causing Malcolm to become unexpectedly animated.

'Have you said that to your father?' he asked.

'No, why?' Margaret replied with some surprise. 'Would it cause a problem if I did?'

'No, not really a problem,' Malcolm continued, 'but it might have brought out the pedant in him.' Margaret looked confused. 'You know how he can be a stickler for historical accuracy.' Margaret smiled and nodded. 'Well, I got a lecture when I first used the phrase when we were talking in my office. "Did I know who first said it and what the context was?" Of course I didn't, it just seemed appropriate to what we'd been talking about. "A man called Clough", he told me. I couldn't think of any Cloughs, other than another of my footballing heroes – Brian, the football manager (you know I'm a football addict) – and it seemed unlikely that he'd have offered a view on the subject even though he was very free with his opinions. "Arthur Clough, in 1862", he informed me, "and it was part of an ironic take-off of the Ten Commandments, not a considered argument on the duties of a doctor". When he'd finished we agreed it was a memorable phrase and he even allowed that it was reasonable to use it in the context I had done, which I still regard as something of a triumph. In fact, striving became a standing joke between us and some of the ICU consultants. We gave the name to one of our surgical colleagues who would never give up on a patient under any circumstances. Necessary decisions were timed for when Striving was off duty.'

As Margaret topped up the teapot she felt drawn again towards the murky considerations of decision making as patients approached the end of their lives, such as her mother had done. 'So how can you stop striving officiously if the patient or their relatives say you must do everything possible?' she asked.

'I wish I had a good answer,' Malcolm replied. 'That's the sixty-four-million-dollar question of modern medicine; in fact, an awful lot more money than that would be saved – sixty-four million dollars would be peanuts, less than peanuts, less than the husk of a peanut – if we could move everyone on from the pretence that it's possible to live for ever with striving officiously being the rule.'

'Like my father?' Margaret asked rhetorically.

'Yes, like your father,' Malcolm continued. 'I expect he's told you about the headlines, or you'll have discovered them. Doctor Death, that sort of thing! Completely ludicrous, but not the worst that happens. God help the doctors if they're dealing with a child who's doomed and the family won't accept the inevitable. Have you heard of Charlie Gard?'

Margaret hadn't, leading Malcolm to explain that he was a baby with a rare and fatal genetic disease. The doctors caring for him decided that there was no appreciable chance of improvement, the parents didn't agree, and the hospital applied to the High Court for permission to withdraw treatment and allow him to die. The parents, via social media, raised money by crowdfunding to take him to the United States for an untested experimental treatment. The court wouldn't allow this, authorised the doctors to withdraw active treatments, and Charlie died.

'Put like that it just seems immensely, terribly sad,' Malcolm continued, 'and if it had been just like that it would have been, but it wasn't. Staff at Great Ormond Street received thousands of abusive messages, including death threats. One of my friends, a woman I've known since medical school, was given security advice by the police. Had she got a safe room in her house? Could she vary the way she travelled to and from work? That sort of thing. It made me very angry when she told me. Angry but impotent.'

Margaret had no difficulty in understanding why. 'What do you think should be done?' she asked.

'I really don't know,' Malcolm replied with obvious exasperation. 'I don't know if there needs to be a new law to stop harassment and threats towards people working in healthcare. Whatever laws there are at the moment don't seem to be very effective. But I'm not the right person to ask. You're outside the system. What do you think?'

Margaret wasn't sure. She could see why hospital staff being bombarded with unpleasant messages and threats whilst trying to do their best in very difficult circumstances would probably welcome a law that explicitly said "you can't do this", but what about other groups of workers who sometimes suffered from similar unacceptable behaviour?

'I don't know,' she replied. 'They did change the law about causing death by dangerous driving a few years ago, so I guess someone keeps things under review,' although she didn't know who that someone might be and nor did Malcolm, and neither considered it likely it would be top of the list of priorities of whoever that someone was, but they didn't share the thought. 'But cases like that must be extremely rare,' Margaret continued.

'Yes, thankfully they are,' Malcolm replied, 'but they're the tip of an iceberg, the iceberg of unreasonable expectations which doctors and nurses have to deal with, day in, day out.'

Margaret wasn't sure what he was referring to and asked for clarification.

'They're caught between a rock and a hard place,' Malcolm explained. 'The rock is the promises made by those in government and senior management positions that patients should expect X and Y and Z to be provided, and the hard place is the reality that it's simply not possible to deliver those things with the resources available. All this compounded by the number one rule of government and senior management, which is that all praise must be centralised and all blame decentralised.'

Margaret smiled and made an effort to try to remember the phrase, which she thought she'd find opportunity to use in the future.

'The story from above is that the reason that X and Y and Z aren't being delivered,' he went on, 'is because the troops on the ground, the doctors and nurses, aren't doing what they should be doing. They're inefficient. They've been given policies and protocols to make it as easy as possible for them, but they haven't done what they're supposed to.' He was clearly on a roll and Margaret chose not to intervene, not that she would have found it easy to do so.

'I know I'm speaking to a management consultant and so I won't try to argue that it isn't possible to improve efficiency,' he continued, demonstrating he wasn't so impassioned that he'd forgotten his audience, 'but it's a matter of reasonable expectations.' Continuing after a pause, he said, 'Let me give you an example. Last week, when I was on my ward, one of the staff nurses told me that Sister was upset. I went into her office and she was crying. I asked her why and she showed me a letter that the hospital's complaints department – they call it something else, but that's what it is – had sent to a patient's son. His mother had been admitted in a state of terrible neglect after a neighbour reported that she hadn't been seen and the police broke in and found her on the floor. There weren't any obvious acute medical problems beyond those caused by not having eaten or drunk properly for several days. What she needed was feeding and watering and cleaning up. She improved over a few weeks, but not such that she could return home and it took some time to find a place in a care home for her. Was everything in the hospital done perfectly? Of course it wasn't. But what galled the sister was the bending over backwards to apologise for minor things whilst completely missing the bigger picture. Scoring 99 per cent wasn't good enough. Sorry we did not meet your expectations. We will share your comments with the team for their learning. We have asked the ward sister to emphasise this at every handover meeting. Of course, reading such things is usually water off a duck's back, but sometimes you've had enough and think no, can't we say it as it really was! A not unreasonable summary of the case could have read, thank you for your letter regarding the care that your mother received in our hospital. Due to neglect of her by you and your family, who all live locally, she was admitted in a terrible state due to not having eaten or drunk properly for many days. She was delirious when she arrived, shouting at nursing and medical staff and attempting to scratch or bite anyone who came near to her. With considerable patience and skill she was given first fluids and vitamins, then food, and she gradually improved to a point where she could be discharged to a care home, which the hospital organised along with colleagues in community services. Our staff have asked me to say that, although they do not think the care they provided was perfect in every respect, your frequently aggressive and sometimes obscene outbursts when you attended the ward were not helpful. Yours sincerely.'

'What did you say to the ward sister?' Margaret enquired.

'I pretended to dictate the alternative letter and gave her a hug,' Malcolm replied with a grin before becoming serious again, 'but it all sustains the culture, coming back to what we were talking about, where it's more and more difficult not to strive officiously.'

Margaret knew it wasn't necessary for her to ask him to expand on this, and she didn't need to.

'Many doctors are simply frightened to make decisions to limit care,' he went on. 'They often know they're prolonging individual misery and don't like this, but they shy away from the difficult conversations with patients and their relatives and it's hard to blame them when there's an ever increasing likelihood that complaints and criticisms will follow. Easier to be seen to keep turning the handle, even if you know you're doing it in a lacklustre way and it's not going to do anything useful, until the inevitable happens. Much less stressful.'

Both were quiet and took sips of their tea. Margaret broke the silence. 'I've been thinking a lot about that since Dad told me about the way Mum died,' she said, 'and I've talked about it with him and with David Old, about how the decision that enough is enough and it's time to give up and let someone die should be made. It must be really hard.'

'Yes, it is,' Malcolm replied softly, 'and if any doctor ever says they're finding it easy, I'd say it was time for them to hand in their licence.'

'But they both say it's a decision that should be made by the doctors,' Margaret continued.

'That's right, it is, but the difficulty now is that the culture has changed from one where the doctor's decision was almost always respected to a situation where it's frequently challenged. I can't argue that doctors' decisions should never be challenged, but the consequence is that we are where we are, with lots and lots of futile treatments and protracted deaths. What's the management saying? "Every system is perfectly designed to get the result that it does", and continuing in a deeply disappointed tone, 'I'm not sure what the answer is.'

'Aren't palliative care services supposed to help?' Margaret asked.

'Not this bit of the business,' Malcolm replied. 'They rarely get involved before the decision to move to symptom control and palliation has been made, and that's the difficult bit, once what you're trying to do is agreed the rest is usually pretty straightforward. It's the deciding to stop striving that's the issue, and they don't teach you that at medical school or on postgraduate medical courses or in medical textbooks or online courses, and the Medical Regulator and the law run a mile from providing any practical clarity. Of course it's perfectly understandable why the elephant in the room isn't spoken about. It's much too difficult. If you give a lecture or publish an article or draft a policy, you're expected to give evidence for what you say or write, to reference that treatment A is better than treatments B or C because of the following studies. Evidence-based medicine is what it's called, and it's clearly not reasonable to argue in favour of medicine that isn't based on evidence, but the problem here is that there isn't and never will be any evidence of the sort we generally now rely on. It touches on something really fundamental, the difference between being alive and being human, the difference between life and human life.'

Margaret was engrossed. 'Do doctors ever talk about this?' she asked.

'Very rarely,' Malcolm replied, following after some consideration, 'in fact – now you ask – I'm surprised how little we do. Sometimes there's a short and quiet conversation in a doctor's office or in a small huddle on a ward round away from the bedsides. Sometimes a colleague asks me for my view and I share my thoughts with them, but I'd feel very uncomfortable giving any sort of formal teaching on the subject or setting myself up as any sort of authority. I don't have a PhD in medical ethics or anything like that, not that I've ever heard anyone who has talk in a way I found useful. I'm sure most doctors feel the same way, which is why we don't talk about it much.'

'What do you say when someone does ask you for your thoughts?' Margaret pursued.

'If it seems appropriate and there's time,' Malcolm replied, 'I tell them that the courts accept that keeping patients in a vegetative state alive isn't the right thing to do, also that some other patients in a hopeless situation on ICUs shouldn't be kept alive for ever, but they haven't helped us with the common situations we all face day in and day out. What are the appropriate limits for treating people with profound dementia? If someone is aware only in the sense that they respond immediately to stimuli they find pleasant or unpleasant, but have no understanding of what is happening to them, is it kind to keep doing things to them which they don't understand and cause them pain or discomfort to prolong their existence, even if that's just turning them in bed?

'I say I ask myself a couple of questions,' he continued. 'Is it at all likely that, whatever is done, this patient will be alive in a few weeks' time? Is it at all likely that, whatever is done, this patient is going to be able to have any truly human experience of life ever again? Of course I'm accused of being paternalistic when I say this, but I was involved in a Court of Protection case where the judge talked of someone's life being so impaired that it could reasonably be presumed that no one would want to live it, which seemed a good way of putting things to me. So those are my tests: if I think it's beyond reasonable doubt that someone will die within a few weeks whatever is done, or their life will be so impaired that no one would want to live it, then I think they should be treated to relieve or prevent symptoms. For me it comes down to something pretty simple: do as you would be done by. But you can't act on your own, even though it is the doctor's decision. You have to take people with you, which is increasingly hard to do for the reasons we've talked about, and if you don't you're increasingly likely to get into trouble.'

Margaret's phone pinged. It was a text from her father. He'd counted the pots on the patio but had forgotten to check how many at the front of the house had had bulbs in them and were now empty. She went out to look: four without anything obviously growing in them, she replied. On getting back into the kitchen she found Malcolm had helped himself to another piece of ginger cake, which she'd offered on leaving on her pot-counting mission.

'I guess we ought to talk about what we were supposed to be talking about,' she said with a smile as she sat down and took a slice. 'Dad says doctors in the hospital often speak to you for careers advice. What do you say to them?'

'Not an awful lot to be honest,' Malcolm replied, 'but people do come and talk to me about all sorts of things, including their careers. I think they regard me as a safe person to talk to. I just encourage them to chat about the things they're considering and make observations if any occur to me. If they're young doctors and not sure what sort of medicine they want to do, I often suggest they think of doctors who are people similar to themselves but ten years older. What are they doing and do they seem to enjoy it? If they do, that might be a good fit. Why not go and have a talk with them? I ask similar questions if it's a consultant colleague who feels stuck in a rut and wants to get a bit more variety into their job. What are they thinking of trying to do? What do they think appointment panels for that sort of role are looking for and how do they match up? Who do they know who's doing a role of that sort now and have they spoken to them? What did they say? But,' he said, looking at Margaret, 'how far have you got with your thoughts?'

As she explained her situation there was something about Malcolm's way of listening – very similar to that of Pessimistic Peter – that seemed to make it easy to talk openly and honestly, leading Margaret to think he'd inspire confidence in his patients and also understand why her father and others in the hospital often sought his counsel.

'It seems to me that you've made a lot of progress,' he told her, which made her feel instantly less inadequate. 'If I've heard you right, you're clear you don't want to return to doing the job you have been doing and there aren't any other sorts of job in the firm that you fancy; you want to get into a line of work that you think is fundamentally worthwhile; you're very clear what your skills are; there are networks of people who've left management consultancy firms and are now working in other sectors, but you haven't yet got down to contacting them. Perhaps now's the time to cast your bread on the water and see what happens.'

Malcolm hadn't said anything that surprised her or would count as rocket science, but she felt his summary was very helpful. 'Thanks,' she said quietly as she heard the sound of her father on the gravel of the front drive. 'Thanks very much.'

'Have you,' Malcolm replied hastily, 'told your father about David Old?'

'No,' she replied. 'Do you think I ought to?' But there was no time for him to reply before her father came through the door talking about colours of geraniums.

TWENTY-THREE

AXIOMS

Flat shoes, David had told her. If you want to have a go at punting then you need to bring some flat shoes because it can be slippery: or you can lie back and trail a hand in the water in the languid manner of a Pre-Raphaelite woman on a May Ball poster. Although she'd never been punting she'd seen the advertisements. He'd phrased things well, implying that she had a perfectly free choice, but what did he really want, Margaret wondered. She thought about this as she was getting ready. Did he really want her to take the risk or would he prefer her not to? Would he be disappointed if she didn't? Would she dare to do so? She wasn't sure. So many uncertainties crowding in.

She felt both excited and worried. Nothing was yet decided. She could still return to life as it was. The team at the firm would be unchanged, the day filled with its quick-witted and generally friendly but superficial and inconsequential banter. The evenings, except when something specific was planned, would be lacklustre. She was no longer interested in reading the latest book by the latest management guru. She'd read loads of them over the years but now couldn't think of a single enduring thing that any of them had taught her. Exercise classes were a thing of the past. Watching episodes of *Friends* for the umpteenth time and trying not to drink a lot more cheap wine than was prudent would be the reality.

Margaret shuddered as she went into her bedroom to get ready. Given the worst that could happen was that she'd fall in, she put on a pair of her skinny jeans. They wouldn't become translucent if they got wet, she thought, and she also remembered a very politically incorrect comment made to her by an office lecher when he'd seen her wearing them. 'You should be flattered,' Shirley had said when she'd told her of it, 'you've got an arse and legs to die for.' With the same watery eventuality in mind she selected a black bra and a dark green long-sleeved cotton top. As she absent-mindedly put on a dab of her most expensive perfume she almost giggled aloud; "I'm behaving like a teenager going on a first date", she thought. Keeping options open she put on her ankle boots and stuffed her trainers into her shoulder bag.

David was waiting for her in his usual place. He noted the heels on the boots but made no reference to them as they walked the short distance to Scudamore's. They made general chit chat as they waited in the queue. 'Yes, I have punted before,' he reassured the young woman with short strawberry-coloured hair and a gold ring through her nose who took his credit card as deposit and then led the way to the shed where they collected the cushions and pole. He went to the rack and helped himself to a wooden one, fearful that he might otherwise have been offered a metallic.

'I can always tell,' she said with an approving nod, 'if people have punted before by the way they carry the pole and get onto the punt. It's amazing how many say they have when they haven't.'

Margaret settled herself on the cushions as David slowly reversed the punt from its mooring and then braced himself against the planted pole to stop its backward motion. By slightly altering the angulation of his push he pointed the punt upstream and then replanted the pole a foot or so from its side, extended his arms a similar distance so that the pole was in a parallel plane, and walked his hands one over the other to the end of the pole, flexing at his hips as he did so to keep the pole on the bottom for as long as possible. Margaret was impressed.

'You have done this before,' she said.

'Yes,' he replied. 'I learned when I was a student here many years ago, from a man who very nearly got sent down.' He went on to tell the tale of how this friend, along with two others from Queen's College, had started a business providing punt trips for tourists using college punts. Within a fortnight their near fatal error of not having got the college's permission to use the college's property in this way was discovered. 'All I can remember about him,' David said, 'was that his technique for buttering toast in the morning was the most brutal I've ever seen, and he's the only man I've ever known who can punt wearing a linen jacket and not get the cuffs wet.

He had a special way of flicking his hands when he took them off the pole to get the water off them which I never managed to master.'

Margaret watched carefully as they moved upstream. The rhythmical raising, dropping and pushing against the pole invited quiet contemplation, broken just before a footbridge where a punt had become entangled in the branches of a weeping willow and the occupants were noisily trying to extricate themselves, whilst on the opposite side of the river someone else had contrived to drive their punt into the bank at almost ninety degrees, leading at least one of the passengers to have what might politely be described as a sense of humour failure following spillage of red wine.

'It's always going to spin if you stand in the middle of the back of the punt and just push,' David explained as he navigated between the two. 'You have to trust yourself to lean out and make sure that the angle of the push is along the line of the punt; then it goes in a straight line.' Trust, there was that word again: trust.

Beyond the footbridge they passed between a wood coming down to the water's edge on one side and the garden of an imposing house followed by farmland on the other. To her left Margaret could now glimpse the path on which they'd walked back to Newnham when they'd talked about trust the last time they met. 'Trust, so many things depend on trust,' she muttered to herself under her breath. 'Big things and little things.'

David, engrossed in the mechanics, didn't hear her clearly: 'Sorry, I didn't catch that,' he said.

'Nothing,' Margaret said automatically before providing necessary contradiction. 'I mean I was thinking about what you said about needing to trust to make the punt go where you want it to go.'

'Yes,' David responded, planting the pole and beginning the climbing up it of his extended arms. 'It's like other things that depend on balance. The child that tries to learn to cycle by pedalling slowly because they're frightened of losing control is the one most likely to fall off. The person who doesn't commit to transferring their weight onto the edges of their skis will never be able to control a turn and comes a cropper.'

'But in big things as well as little things,' Margaret continued. 'We talked about trust in doctors the last time we met.'

'We did,' David replied, breaking into a grin that required explanation, 'and it's clear that we're not trusted as much as commercial punt operators.'

What if hiring a punt was a medical intervention? Lively speculation about material risks followed, these being defined as those that in the circumstances of the particular punting expedition – trips on punts are normally called expeditions – a reasonable person in the punter's position would be likely to attach significance to, or the punt hire operator is or should reasonably be aware that the particular punter would likely attach significance to it. Margaret said she had considered the possibility of falling in and getting wet, but what about drowning? The woman with the dyed hair and pierced proboscis hadn't asked them if they could swim. If punt operators were doctors it seemed inevitable that there'd be a consent process and form to be signed, with the punter given written information including the possibility that their clothing may get soaked in red wine; they might fall in, get wet and find it hard to maintain their dignity, which they agreed would be described as sustaining emotional harm; and that death by drowning was a very rare but recognised complication.

Thinking ahead they decided to keep these thoughts to themselves, fearing that saying anything, even obviously in jest, when (assuming no misadventures) they returned their punt, might precipitate a review of hire processes to the detriment of everyone involved. Such, David said, would almost certainly be the approach of those managing the Health Service if a returning punter were to make a complaint following some mishap, any adverse outcome – even if obviously attributable to some individual failure of common sense – being likely to trigger a review of policies and procedures and the production for all staff of a mandatory online training package of excruciatingly poor quality and doubtful efficacy. Punting before or after a May Ball wouldn't have quite the same attraction if a safety video had to be viewed before getting aboard, all participants had to sign a ten-page consent form, buoyancy aids had to be worn, and consumption of alcohol was prohibited because it increased risks.

'But seriously,' David continued, 'if you don't trust you have lots of regulations and requirements for documentation of communications and processes. These may improve poor performance, or at least make it easier to hold those performing poorly to account, but at the expense of bureaucracy and inefficiency and preventing the best. Like many things in life there's a balance to be had. Giving no information, the old-fashioned paternalistic medical approach, is rightly condemned, but giving too much information erodes trust and often leaves patients bewildered. I see this happening more and more; doctors overloading patients with more and more information, some thinking this is actually what they ought to do and all knowing that saying "you can't say I didn't warn you" is a way of protecting themselves. I just don't think it's the best way of practising medicine.'

He sank into silence whilst continuing the rhythm of the punting. Margaret noticed that the pole was falling further before it hit the bottom, also that David was making a vigorous twisting motion before beginning to raise it after the pushing phase. 'It's deep and muddy in this bit of the river,' he said in response to a question she'd considered asking. 'I don't want to get the pole stuck.'

Margaret picked up the thread of the previous conversation. 'I've talked a lot with my father about it, but what do you think's the best way of practising medicine, of being a good doctor?'

'A very good question and one that's very rarely discussed,' David replied, pausing for a moment to complete a lifting of the pole and get the angle of drop right before continuing. It made a clinking sound as it hit the bottom indicating they were now past the muddy stretch. 'There isn't a widely accepted answer and certainly no easy metric, and,' after catching his breath following another lift of the pole and shaking his arms with some irritation as water ran down them and into the cuffs of his pullover, 'as you know better than me, "if you can't measure it you can't manage it". Often quoted and misquoted I know, but if you can't measure what's important then it'll undoubtedly take second place to something you can.'

Margaret's father hadn't given her a clear answer to the good doctor question and she'd thought it best not to push him, but she had no such qualms about pushing David. 'That may be true,' she said quietly but insistently. 'I think it probably is, but it's not an answer to the question.'

He'd met this woman in most unusual circumstances, sitting on a wall and minding his own business when she'd tracked him down. She wasn't a medic, but here she was, reclining gracefully in the bottom of a punt, wanting to explore the most interesting and fundamental things; things that doctors and those running hospitals ought to talk about but rarely do; things that get to the essence of medicine and healthcare, of living and dying. He found his mind wandering and speculating about possible futures until she said something to attract his attention.

'What's a good doctor?' he said thoughtfully, following after some further consideration, 'I can't give you a neat answer. I'm going to give a composite, something that includes the views of patients and the views of other doctors. I think patients are very good at sensing whether a doctor cares about them, and they're obviously the ones to say how well a doctor communicates with them, but they're rarely good at judging how much medicine they know and if the doctor can make good medical decisions, whether with partial knowledge they can pick the wisest path amidst confusion. So, I'll have some measure of patient feedback, but I'd also want to have input from other medics: do they respect their knowledge and judgement; do they ask them for advice?

'But,' he went on, 'it's a struggle to provide the best medicine given that we live in a world where it's difficult and sometimes dangerous for doctors to say plain and simple truths. Maybe this will change, but I don't see any sign of it doing so at the moment.'

Margaret sat up, stroked back some strands of chestnut hair that had fallen over her eyes, and sat cross-legged on the punt cushion. 'My father,' she said animatedly, 'would certainly agree with that. I don't think he recognised the danger. One of my colleagues at work, when talking about any project, always asks us, "Where are the landmines? Where are the things that are going to stop this working?", which often leads to important discussions. I guess a question along those lines would be useful for doctors to think about when they're entering difficult territory.'

'I'm sure that's right,' David replied, 'and I think many doctors do this intuitively and tread very carefully when they know they're getting into sensitive areas, particularly when more care can be provided – more care can always be provided – but would be futile. In fact, thinking about it, I like your colleague's landmine analogy and I wouldn't say I tread carefully: I'd say I get down on my hands and knees to do a fingertip search of what the patient and their family are thinking.'

Margaret smiled: 'That conjures up a lovely image,' she said. 'Dr Old, senior physician, crawling slowly and nervously towards the patient and their family, feeling for explosive devices as he does so. Best with him wearing a frock coat and painted in oils in the style of an old master!'

David laughed warmly and would probably have done so for some time had he not been standing up and holding a punt pole, the effect of gravity calling his attention back to the necessity of concentrating on his balance with a jerk. 'That was close!' he said a few moments later when equilibrium was restored. 'I've only been in the water once when punting and that was when I was rugby-tackled by someone. Best not to go into the details, but they were as I'm sure you imagine. But I like your picture. Perhaps you could arrange for it to be hung in the National Portrait Gallery or failing that, the Royal College of Physicians.'

'What do you do if you start to feel something that might be a landmine but you're not sure?' Margaret asked after a pause.

'Go very slowly. Speak quietly and don't say too much. Find out how much the patient wants to know. Some want to know a lot; some don't want to know anything at all. Give as much information as they want, but never more. Ask them if they'd like me to lay out the options. Ask them if they'd like me to tell them what I think the best thing to do would be.'

'Isn't that paternalistic?'

'Some might call it that, I suppose,' David replied, 'and I know that's so far out of fashion as to be regarded as a crime, but for me paternalism is when a doctor makes decisions for a patient without asking them for their views. The pendulum has swung so far away from this that I'm sorry to say many doctors are now expert in avoiding giving clear advice or recommending a course of action, even when their patient is obviously begging them to do so. They keep giving more and more information and options and asking the poor patient to decide, phrasing things in a way that leaves them without a clue as to which way to go. It makes me wince every time I hear it, and I hear it a lot.

'But when the chips are down, what a patient wants is a doctor they can trust – that magic word again. When given the option, some will say right away "Just tell me what you think would be best" and I tell them. Others will have done hours and hours of online research and be clutching an enormous sheaf of printouts of things they've looked at and talking nineteen to the dozen.'

'I'll bet that's wearisome!' Margaret observed with a chuckle.

'I must admit it certainly can be, particularly if the clinic or ward round is running late,' David replied, 'and I'm sure you wouldn't believe me if I said anything else! You need to make time – perhaps at the end of the clinic or the end of the ward round – to be quiet and listen. Not many people can talk for more than a few minutes in the absence of any verbal response. When they seem to be running out of steam, I ask them if they've decided what the diagnosis is or what the investigation or treatment should be, and if what they suggest is sensible, I say I agree and we move on to do whatever needs to be done. If it isn't, I explain why – using as few words as possible because long explanations lead to longer conversations – and ask them if they'd like me to tell them what I think. I say which bits I'm sure about and which bits I'm not, and I suggest what I think are reasonable options for things to do next.'

'How do you avoid leaving the patient with lots of options and no way of deciding between them, the thing that makes you wince?' Margaret asked.

'If this is happening, I fall back on a couple of things I take as reference points for making medical decisions when there isn't an obvious right answer. They're simple and I explain them to the patient. The first is that if there's a fifty-fifty call to be made, I'm going to recommend the option that's least active; I only want to do things if the odds are that they're going to be helpful. That's a personal preference of mine: many doctors and some patients always go for the option of doing something rather than doing nothing because it makes them feel better. The second is that interventions with high risks should only be undertaken when there's a high chance of big benefits and the patient is clearly willing to accept the risks. I shudder to think how many frail, elderly patients I've seen who, in a marginal situation and when they were clearly vacillating, have one way or another been persuaded to have major surgery from which they've never recovered.'

'Old's axioms, they ought to be called,' Margaret suggested, 'and the managers would approve. Good to avoid spending money unless there's clear evidence of benefit.'

'First a picture in the National Portrait Gallery and now some axioms: this is turning into quite an afternoon! I think I'd settle for being known as a doctor who knew quite a lot of medicine, was good at talking to people, made wise decisions, but above all was kind and sensible.'

David had now turned the punt round and they were heading back downstream towards the boatyard and the city. Margaret noticed the waves in the water made by the bow and smiled inwardly as she saw a duck and its clutch of ducklings bobbing up and down as the ripples passed under them. She thought about her own situation. Following her conversation with Malcolm she'd got a meeting arranged to talk to someone about a possible new job. But what about the second element of Shirley's prescription? In the past she'd met someone who might have been the right person for her, but at the wrong time. Now she felt it was the right time, but what about the person? She took off her ankle boots, rummaged in her shoulder bag and started to put on her trainers.